THE

HANGED

MAN

The Book Guild Ltd

First published in Great Britain in 2020 by
The Book Guild Ltd
9 Priory Business Park
Wistow Road, Kibworth
Leicestershire, LE8 0RX
Freephone: 0800 999 2982
www.bookguild.co.uk
Email: info@bookguild.co.uk
Twitter: @bookguild

This work is entirely fictitious and bears no resemblance to any persons living or dead.

Typeset in 12pt Adobe Jenson Pro

Printed and bound in the UK by TJ International, Padstow, Cornwall

ISBN 978 1913208 752

British Library Cataloguing in Publication Data.
A catalogue record for this book is available from the British Library.

Part One

Part One

Chapter One

Ian

I WAS COOLING OFF in the swimming pool at Castignac when I heard that Ian was missing. Our large house in south-west France had a garden to match and we didn't always know the whereabouts of everyone staying there. Seven of us shared it as a holiday home and liked the choices it offered. As well as the house and garden, there was the ruined farmhouse with its view of the Pyrenees, or the swimming pool.

Heat lay like a spell over the hills and valleys around us on that summer afternoon and time seemed to have slowed down. I had swum several lengths and was floating on my back, squinting up at the sun, when Jenny came over to the pool.

'Tessa, have you seen Ian?'

She was dressed in shorts and a sleeveless top, and her slim figure was outlined against the blue sky. Her thick chestnut hair, often plaited, was loose. The sun was behind her, putting her face in shadow and making it hard to judge her expression, but her tone was mild.

'No,' I said, treading warm water. 'Not since lunchtime, anyway. I bet he's hiding from Graham!'

Graham was a keen decorator. He had been saying that he was going to start on the sitting room and inviting anyone to join him. No-one else felt even slightly like it in that heat. Ian was the last person to do so, especially since an accident with a ladder in the spring that year.

Jenny laughed. 'Of course! Oh, well, maybe he's gone for a walk, although this heat is still a bit punishing. Normally he would say what he was doing, but I fell asleep this afternoon and I suppose he didn't want to wake me.'

It was about five o'clock. Jenny wandered off and she must have asked some of the others about Ian, because by six we all knew that she was looking for him. I had come out of the pool and changed, and the day was a little cooler, but there was still no sign of Ian.

At nearly seven, Stephen opened a bottle of local sparkling wine. We gathered on the terrace in the shade of the wisteria, as we usually did, arriving by instinct from different corners of Castignac. Lily, Graham's wife, was in the kitchen, making a salad for the evening meal and saying she didn't want any help beyond a glass of wine. The rest of us were having a drink together, thinking in a light-hearted way about where Ian might be and teasing Graham for having driven him away with suggestions of decorating.

I glanced across at Jenny. She wasn't laughing anymore. Her pleasant face looked worried and she was on the edge of her seat. That was when I thought of looking in the ruined farmhouse. A large old building, it lay south and slightly west of the house, straggling around a courtyard. Ian liked exploring it and was sometimes to be found sitting on the bench that gave us our best view of the mountains.

I liked the ruin as well and was pleased to have an excuse to go there. As the youngest in the group, I wanted to impress the others. I would be the clever one to guess where Ian was and bring him back to join us for a drink. A quick search wouldn't let my glass of sparkling wine lose its fizz. It was only later that I wished I'd never thought of doing that.

I slipped away from the conversation on the terrace. No-one asked where I was going and I crossed the garden to the ruin, about a hundred metres away. It was quiet except for the cooing of pigeons and the sharp call of jackdaws, although anyone listening hard might have heard the light scampering of lizards into the safety of cracks in stone walls. Plants stood limply in the still air and I breathed in herby scent. Rosemary, thyme and lavender all grew around the garden.

I went through the arched entrance to the courtyard of the ruin, which was basking quietly in the late sun of the day, a golden painter's light that made me think of Cézanne or Van Gogh. A collared dove landed on the roof with a screech and jackdaws squabbled in the chestnut trees that stood around the building like the protective force that they became when the wind rose. Instead of crossing the courtyard straightaway and making for the tower which rose from one side of the building, I headed towards the south side for the bench facing the mountains.

It was darker inside the building, partly because some of the shutters were closed, but daylight filtered through holes in the roof as well as through the windows. The building had a stone base and a wooden frame filled in with a variety of plaster and bricks. Rooms led off from each other around the courtyard.

I called out as I went, but there was no reply. Silence closed around me and I could have been a thousand kilometres away from the chatter on the terrace.

Doors were hanging off their hinges. I passed what must have been a kitchen with a huge, blackened fireplace and then a living room, with the remains of shelves and cupboards hanging askew. I knew little about the ruin and the lives it had sheltered over the centuries. I wished I had urged the previous owner of Castignac, the old farmer Jacques Lordat, to tell us more on meeting him at a party we had held the week before.

I reached the bench to find no Ian and glanced at the mountains. As solid as ever, but infinitely changeable, they were strung along the horizon, above and beyond the nearer green hills, their sharp peaks softened in a bluish summer haze. Even without time to stop, I was, as ever, impressed by their size and other-worldliness. I turned towards the tower, where a wooden staircase rose from ground level to the pigeon loft above.

Entering the space below the tower, my footsteps so soft that I could hardly hear them, I saw something unexpected lying on the ground. It looked like a bundle of clothes but, coming nearer, I realised with a shock that it was Ian, even though his face was turned away from me. Apart from anything else, no other man in the group wore flowered shirts. He was sprawled on the ground near the foot of the staircase. I gasped and stopped a few feet away, scared of going nearer, my legs trembling. Pieces of wood were scattered on the flagstones around him.

I wanted to run, or scream, or faint, anything to get away, but I made myself stay and go right up to him. I couldn't help saying his name, even though something told me that it would be useless. There was no answer and no movement. I said his name again, my voice rising to a scream as any hope of an answer died. I noticed blood. I touched the nearest hand. It was cool, and I drew back, rubbing my fingers on my cotton top.

There wasn't much doubt about what had happened. Ian had ignored all the warnings that Graham and Mark, indeed all of us, had given him about the staircase to the pigeon loft being unsafe. He had climbed it. I glanced up at the steps zigzagging inside their wooden frame, craning my neck and narrowing my eyes to pierce the gloom. The entrance to the pigeon loft, always closed, was now open. The pieces of wood lying on the ground were spindles from the railing at the top.

A gust of wind caused a creak somewhere and the sound propelled me into action. I ran out across the courtyard and onto the path that led to our house. I ran faster and faster, shouting for the others, until I arrived at full tilt on the terrace. Still engrossed in discussion, they looked up in surprise.

'Tessa, what on earth is the matter?' Angela said, as I gasped for breath.

'It's Ian, he's...' I waited until I had recovered enough to speak. 'He's had an accident in the ruined farmhouse. He's not moving and I can't make him answer me.'

I couldn't bring myself to say what I thought, with Jenny looking at me so intently. Instead, I gave way to tears. She jumped up from her seat, her face pale now.

'Show me,' she said, ignoring my tears. She and I ran back together, with the others close behind us. I wanted to stop Jenny seeing her husband lying so still and broken on the ground, but it was too late. She sped across the courtyard of the ruin into the tower and straight to the foot of the staircase. She gave a scream at the sight of Ian and kneeled beside him, touching his face and hands, but not daring to move him. She said his name, over and over again, her voice climbing into a wail.

'I'll call an ambulance.'

The sound of Angela's voice behind me was calming. Angela was a French teacher in a London secondary school.

Like her husband, Stephen, she was in her forties. Her face was framed by masses of golden hair which hung thickly to her shoulders. They looked so different together: he tall and thin, and she short and plump. I admired Angela. She was friendly, good-humoured and a good organiser.

She had left her phone back in the house and she ran to get it. We knew the number to call. Angela had pinned it up on the kitchen noticeboard, drawing it to everyone's attention on our first visit to the house as the new owners. We had never seriously thought we might need it.

Stephen went with Angela, while Graham and Lily stayed. Lily buried her head against Graham's chest and he held her close. Jenny stood up and turned an anguished face towards me. I put my arm around her, but she pulled herself free and kneeled by Ian again. The others clustered round, saying little.

I was trembling, and Mark hugged me. He didn't share the house with us, but he was the nearest I had to a boyfriend. Not much above average height, neat, clean-shaven and with close-cropped hair, he had a capable, genial manner. He was nice-looking without being too handsome. Warm, brown eyes and friendliness made up for any plainness, but he was looking solemn now.

We seemed to wait for a long time, but I worked out afterwards that the ambulance arrived quickly from St Martin des Remparts, guided into the ruin by Stephen. Thanks to the wide entrance into the courtyard, it was able to drive up to the staircase and stop near where Ian was lying. We all stood back to let the ambulance staff come forward with a stretcher.

They checked Ian for signs of life, but there was nothing they could do. He had been dead for some hours. They placed him in a body bag and lifted him onto the stretcher and into the ambulance. Jenny was unable to watch and turned away. Angela, her face strained, spoke to them and then told us that they were taking Ian to the hospital morgue.

'I must go with him,' Jenny said.

'Not on your own. I'll come with you and drive us,' Angela said.

She spoke rapidly to the ambulance staff and they indicated that she should follow them. She and Jenny took one of the cars we had rented for the holiday, following the ambulance as it drove off. I felt some relief at the departure, but there was no escaping the weight of Ian's death.

Stephen advised us all not to touch the pieces of railing lying around but to leave everything as it was. We walked slowly back to the house. A glance at my watch told me that it was just after eight o'clock. Less than an hour had passed since I had come over to look for Ian, but everything had changed. The slow pace of the afternoon was a world away.

On the terrace, our drinks were still waiting, but the sparkling wine was flat. Stephen had opened the bottle with a light heart, but we all looked grim now. No-one liked to touch the drinks, until Stephen gulped his down with a brief apology for needing it. Graham, Mark and I followed him. Only Lily turned away from the wine, sinking onto a chair, her face crumpling. We could barely look at each other. I felt a mixture of incredulity and horror, and knew that Jenny would be feeling so much worse.

White clouds were fluffing up above the mountains, but there was no breeze and it would be light for some time yet. From the terrace, all we could hear was the distant hum of traffic from our nearest town, St Martin des Remparts, and the sound of birds. It was hard to believe that life was carrying on and that pigeons and jackdaws flying around the ruin were oblivious to what had happened inside it.

Stephen, in many ways our leader, spoke first. 'Why on earth did Ian climb a staircase that everyone had warned him was likely to be unsafe?'

'The railing gave way at the top of the staircase. Ian could have leaned on it, thinking that it was as safe as the steps had been,' Mark said, not answering the question.

'There was blood around his head.' I winced at the memory.

'I expect we'll find out the gory details. Let's not talk about them now.'

Stephen sounded reproving or maybe he was just squeamish. None of us knew exactly how Ian had been injured, only that the injuries had been fatal.

We all wanted to say what we had been doing during the afternoon, as if exonerating ourselves from any blame. We spoke in hushed voices, out of respect for Ian, but it was a futile gesture. Nothing could bring him back.

'I was sitting under the date palms, keeping out of the sun. I must have nodded off, because I didn't see Ian. Coming from the house, he would have passed me. I wish I'd seen him,' Mark said.

'I was in the pool when Jenny asked me where Ian was, but before that I was in our bedroom, writing postcards. It was too hot to be outside,' I said. That was when Mark, no writer of postcards when it was so much faster to send a text, had gone to read in the garden.

Our eyes turned towards Lily. Slim and always elegant even in the most casual clothes, Lily had a fragile air which concealed a tough streak. She seemed to have recovered from her shock and now faced us calmly.

'I was in the sitting room, also keeping out of the sun. I bought an English paper this morning and was catching up on the news. Angela was there with me, reading. Stephen was in the dining room at least some of the time,' she said.

'Constituency business,' Stephen said. He was a London MP, never out of touch with his constituency, even on his summer holiday.

Only Graham was left now, and heads turned expectantly towards him. Graham was a large man, as cautious by nature as he was slow-moving. He wasn't great fun to be around, but he was dogged and hard-working and touchingly devoted to Lily.

'I was starting on the sitting room,' he said.

We had been slow to tackle the decorating that had fallen to us after Didier, our builder, had finally finished the work we had asked him to do. Graham had chosen the quiet time after lunch that day to start stripping wallpaper, arguing that the house was built for hot weather and that high ceilings allowed air to circulate and stone walls kept the temperature down, making it easy to work inside in the heat. Despite his invitation to anyone else to join him, the rest of us had put off thoughts of decorating. We wanted a proper holiday now and had been talking vaguely about coming down as a decorating party when the weather was more suitable.

No-one had been in the ruin when Ian went over there. No-one had seen him leave the house; no-one had had the chance to remind him not to climb the staircase or noticed what must have been a desperate attempt to grasp anything as he slipped through the railing and plunged to his death; no-one had heard the cry that he must have wasted on the indifferent building. Since we all knew that the staircase might be dangerous, no-one else had tried to climb it. Sobered even more by what could have happened to me, I mentioned that Mark had ticked me off one day when he had found me on the lower steps.

We laid the table on the terrace on Lily's orders and she served the salad she had made, with some bread and cheese. I looked at it without interest.

'It's good of you to do all that, but I'm not hungry,' I said, feeling as if I would never eat again.

'Even if you don't feel like it, have something. We must eat,' Lily said.

She was right. The simple actions of eating restored some life to us and we began to talk with more animation as we waited for Angela and Jenny to come back from the hospital.

Chapter Two

Finding Castignac

THE SUMMER BEFORE IAN'S death, Stephen, Angela, Jenny, Ian and I were on holiday together in an idyllic part of southern France when we bought a house. This was not something I had meant to do at all. Mark had been with us for a week but had had to return to work, and the remaining five of us had stayed on.

Buying a house had been Stephen's idea. Tall and lanky, with a full head of straight dark hair, always neatly trimmed, he had a lively face with expressive features. At the time, his party was newly in opposition after losing the last general election. Angela, Jenny and I had helped in the election campaign, which was how we all came to be on holiday together. Stephen and Angela had invited us when their adult son and daughter had refused for the first time to go on holiday with them. Stephen had previously been a government minister and was now not only in opposition, but also on the backbenches. He didn't confide in me, but Angela had told me that he had been surprised not to be included in the Shadow Cabinet and had realised that our new, young leader and younger MPs saw him as one of yesterday's men.

Stephen wanted a new challenge as well as somewhere for holidays. He and Angela were keen on a French house, and Ian and Jenny were leaping at the chance. The four of them had children who were about to leave home or had already done so and I sensed they were feeling giddy with a new-found freedom. My situation was quite different. I was in my mid-thirties, some ten years younger than they were and only just managing on my salary, what with a high London rent to pay. Did I want to buy a share in a property? I had to decide quickly because the others were starting house-hunting the next morning.

I was a librarian on a modest salary and barely managed to save anything from my monthly income. What allowed me to consider the idea of a house in France was that my sister Jackie and I, who rented a flat together in London, had recently inherited money from an aunt who had died young. My share was nowhere near enough for a deposit on a London flat and I was beginning to fritter it away. Putting it into property seemed like a sensible idea, but that wasn't what most attracted me.

I loved France, especially the Midi-Pyrénées where we were, and wanted to get to know it better. I would never be able to afford to buy a house there on my own and sharing would make everything easier.

In our room on his last night with us, I asked Mark what he thought about Stephen's idea. In London, he rented a room from a married friend who had a family. I never felt that we were alone enough there or in the small flat I shared with Jackie. I had a vague idea that a house in France might help change the pattern of our relationship.

'I'm hardly ever in England! I couldn't afford it anyway. We haven't all inherited money, you know,' he said.

'But you like being abroad, you have French origins, you like France and sharing would make it much more affordable.'

Mark had a French grandmother, whom he had often visited as a child. Her favourite phrases and her love of the country she had left on marrying an Englishman after the war had given him a love of France and he spoke French well.

'Yes, but I'm English and I can like France from a distance and come here when I have the time. This has been a great holiday, but sorry, Tessa, I don't feel like taking on a house or even part of one right now. It's not long since I extricated myself from one, if you remember. Besides, that's an old married couple sort of thing to do. You're not trying to trap me, by any chance, are you?'

Mark was divorced and he was referring to the house he and his ex-wife had owned and which they had recently sold as part of his divorce settlement. I sighed with irritation because so many roads led straight back to his failed marriage.

I turned away from him and a short silence followed. Was I wasting my time with Mark? Reaching thirty-five a few months previously had given me a jolt. I wasn't middle-aged, but I wasn't getting any younger, to use a favourite expression of my mother's, and I wanted a husband and family one day. Mark was fun and I was in love with him, although I had never been able to say so, but he was beginning to seem a once bitten, twice shy kind of man.

He reached for me with a smile and I turned back to him. It was our last night together on that holiday and there wasn't a moment to be wasted.

The following morning, Monday, Mark left. I told the others I would go house-hunting with them, knowing that I could always back out if I changed my mind. We set off with high hopes, but finding a house wasn't easy. They were all either too expensive, the wrong size, too remote or too dilapidated. Gilles, an estate agent, spent the week with us. He was a pipe-smoking middle-aged man with a settled air, who had nevertheless risen to the challenge of our demand.

Four days later, at the end of the holiday, we gathered in Gilles's office. His pipe was going in and out of his mouth as we rejected this property and that. It was only out of desperation that we began to look at a brochure about a place just outside the town of St Martin des Remparts, where we were staying. It was surrounded by trees and had a large garden.

'Well, it's more than we want to pay, but perhaps the owner will accept an offer. It's worth seeing, at any rate, because it seems to have everything we want,' Stephen said, with one of the engaging smiles for which he was known.

We set off across the bridge over the river and up a steep road, but it was a short journey and in minutes we were there. The house looked down on the town and offered a good view of terracotta roofs surrounding the church spire. Beyond the town stretched green hills and further south, beyond the hills, lay the Pyrenees; layers of jagged lines strung across the horizon, hazy and indistinct, in colours of smoky blue and grey.

The house itself was set on level ground. Its name, Castignac, was engraved, in a circle, on a big stone by the entrance. It made me think of castles, until Gilles explained that it derived from the French for the chestnut trees standing around the garden. Through their leaves, I noticed another building, perhaps some sort of barn, but then my attention was drawn to a sheet of blue water sparkling in the sunlight. It was so hot that I could have jumped into the pool there and then.

'Castignac is a farmhouse, but much of the farmland has been sold off. The farmer installed the swimming pool as a selling point,' Gilles said.

The house was of two storeys in an attractive stone. Open blue shutters, sagging only slightly, were hanging at all the windows, and window boxes were stuffed with red geraniums. I counted five windows, including the central one with a curly iron balcony, on the upper floor and two on either side of the front door. A roof of terracotta tiles ranged from a pale sandstone colour to a firm orange. The front door was flanked by two date palms, a good sign of a warm climate. The overall impression was attractive and welcoming. High on the front façade, I noticed the date of 1860.

The old farmer who owned Castignac was there, stamping around in heavy boots outside the house. He was tall and solid-looking and wore a hat. He didn't come round with us, but when he spoke a few words to Gilles, I noticed his growly voice and strong accent. His name was Jacques Lordat and he lived there alone.

Indoors, a corridor led on either side to a large reception room. A big kitchen and a sizeable laundry room took up the back of the ground floor, with small outhouses beyond. One of them was a dairy, with a white tiled interior. It was pleasantly cool inside. All the floors downstairs were tiled in a warm brown. With its solid old furniture, the house was homely and I found myself liking it. Upstairs were four large bedrooms with wooden floors.

Ugly piping, hanging wires, dampness and a need for decoration suggested work was needed on the house, but I could tell from the shining eyes and animated voices around me that everyone felt as I did. Outside again, I saw a terrace on one side of the house, shaded by a wisteria. I could imagine myself sitting there, talking or reading.

'Look at this.' Ian pointed to a spear of flowers. 'It's a spotted orchid. There are several around.'

Angela came towards us. Her skill in speaking French was proving useful in house-hunting.

'What's that? It's not included,' she said, scrutinising a brochure on the house that she was holding in one hand. She pointed beyond me.

Largely hidden by some of the chestnut trees and standing quite a way from the house was the building that I had glimpsed earlier. It looked as if a jumble of stone and wood was just about holding up an array of terracotta roofs, which were caving in here and there. It was bigger than I had first thought and built around a courtyard, with a central tower.

'It's on the property, so it must be included. I don't know what it is, though. Probably just sheds thrown up for the workforce which built the house we're looking at,' Stephen said carelessly.

'Do you think so?' Ian said. He had left his inspection of the orchid and was standing next to Stephen. 'I don't know much about buildings, but it looks older than that to me. It might have been the original farmhouse here.'

Ian, a slightly built, easy-going man, was devoted to his family. He didn't take any active part in politics, saying he left all that to Jenny. He was a botany lecturer and his reedy voice had been exercised on flowers all week, saying that orchids would be more numerous in the spring and pointing out other plants that were either less common in Britain nowadays or didn't grow there at all. He spoke French well.

'I'm more impressed by Ian's explanation. That building is far more substantial than a shed,' Angela said.

'Castignac is lovely, but it's too expensive,' Jenny said as we collected by the cars at the end of the visit. Her face was shiny with the heat. 'Also, it's big. A smaller place would be better and cheaper.'

Jenny was a businesswoman who owned and managed a dress shop in London. She and a partner made clothes in bright, plain colours from natural fabrics, like cotton, raw silk and linen, dying the material themselves. I loved her clothes and was one of her customers. Her point of view was always worth listening to.

'So, let's think about it,' Stephen said. 'The five of us can't afford it, but what if we had more people? With eight people, say, we could put in an offer a bit below the asking price. All we have to do is invite people to view it. I'll take some pictures to encourage them.'

The old farmer kept his distance, but he was watching us as we left. He must have been hoping for a sale and I wondered what he thought of us, landing like butterflies on the farm that seemed so much a part of him. Did he want to leave it or did he hate the thought?

That evening was the last of the holiday. Ian grilled fish on a barbecue in the garden of our rented house and Jenny made salads. We sat over a long meal, talking about Castignac. Stephen made a suggestion.

'Listen, people. We have some friends called Graham and Lily.' He was topping up everyone's glass as he spoke. 'We've known them for years, although we haven't seen them much lately. Graham likes old buildings and Lily is something to do with antiques. They love France and come here regularly for holidays. They're looking for a holiday home here and I don't think they've found anything yet. Shall I ask them to join in with us? Of course, you'd want to meet them and approve them, but if that works, we'd only need, say, one other person.'

Angela followed up. 'Gilles told me that Castignac has been on the market for about two years and no-one's been to see it for a while. That means it's hard to sell and my guess is we've got time to find more people, if we get a move on.'

'I wonder why it's been on the market so long,' Jenny said.

'I don't know. Gilles didn't say, but maybe because it's big, or outside the town, or because things don't move fast here. After all, we're in rural France. It's not London!' Angela said.

We agreed that Stephen could approach Graham and Lily about Castignac. He made the call there and then, turning on all his charm.

'Graham is interested and will talk to Lily. I'll send him the pictures. I'm pretty confident that old Graham won't let me down,' he said, coming off the phone.

Before we left the next morning, Angela rang Gilles. I could almost hear his delight at the other end and imagine the dance of the pipe from hand to mouth and back again as Gilles took in the news that he might be selling a property that had been on his books for far too long.

Back at home after the holiday in France, I told Jackie about our discovery of Castignac and showed her the pictures on my phone. Using my inheritance, I could afford a share in the house. I was nursing a hope that Mark might be persuaded to join us, now that we had found Castignac. I did have one concern.

'If he says no again, I'll see even less of him than usual,' I said.

'Not necessarily. He could still go there for holidays with you and an engineer could be useful,' practical Jackie said.

'Yes, and Mark has all sorts of skills beyond engineering. He knows a lot about property maintenance and Castignac certainly needs some attention.'

Angela rang me the next day.

'We've invited Graham and Lily round on Saturday to talk about Castignac. I do hope you're free to meet them. Ian and

Jenny are coming. Oh, and Stephen suggested that if you want to bring anyone to join the group, Tessa, then now's the time.'

'I'll ask Mark,' I said. 'He's away at the moment, but he loves France and might be interested now that we've got somewhere.'

Coming off the phone, I sent Mark a text, describing the house and our visit and explaining Stephen's plans for affording it. I had an answer almost straightaway.

> Great about the house, but it's still no from me. Life still upside down. Amman noisy and westernised, but countryside of bare hills and villages beautiful. Thanks for holiday, better than sweating it out here or shivering on some English beach. Keep in touch. Mark xx

I was beginning to wonder whether Mark would ever feel that his life was the right way up. I was so cross at the dismissal that I hit the reply button straightaway.

> Hi Mark. If you want to see me in future, you may have to come to France. Tessa x

I had set him a challenge. Why shouldn't I seem as unavailable as he was? It was my first decisive move towards him. His reply surprised me.

> Already looking forward to a holiday there – maybe after Christmas? Might get a few days off. Will be in touch. Missing you. Mark xx

My heart rose. It was enough for me that he should come on holiday to Castignac, if ever we managed to buy it, but I still wondered if I'd jeopardised things between us by joining in with Stephen's plan. Stephen was persuasive, but what he wanted might not have been right for me. On the other hand, I was going to be a girlfriend with a holiday home in a beautiful part of France. What more could he ask for? Maybe I'd increased my chances with Mark.

'Would you like to share the house in France with us, Jackie?' I said at home. Because of our inheritance, I knew she could afford it.

Her reply was unhesitating. 'Oh, so you're turning to me now Mark's refused you? No, I want to buy somewhere to live in London one day.'

'You won't have enough for a deposit,' I said.

'I might. Anyway, that's what I want to do. But you can invite me to have holidays with you!'

She was laughing because she would have all the fun of holidays in France with none of the responsibility of managing the house there. I suspected that she might be thinking of living with her boyfriend, Phil. I didn't entirely like the thought. With Mark still keeping his distance, I would be even more on my own.

I found out a little about Graham and Lily before meeting them.

'Graham works for a housing association and he's keen on DIY. He's an old friend of Stephen's. Lily works in the antique trade. They have a daughter, who is a student somewhere,' Angela told me over the phone. 'Graham is serious and shy, but Lily is quite different. She's glamorous, friendly and warm.'

The mention of glamour nudged me into scrubbing up for meeting Graham and Lily. I imagined her to be as tall and elegant as her name suggested and I didn't want to look like a garden weed beside her.

In my bedroom, getting ready for the occasion, I looked in the mirror at my face with its snub nose and at my straight mid-brown hair. I riffled through my wardrobe, despairing at work clothes and casual stuff. There wasn't much party gear, but I dug out a flimsy dress, a lacy cardigan and heeled sandals, which together looked all right. I put on makeup and sprayed on French *eau de toilette* that I had bought on the recent holiday. Its fresh, light scent reminded me of summer in France.

Arriving at Stephen and Angela's house, I sensed anticipation.

'Look, I've been to a bookshop in South Kensington, that part of London that is forever French, and bought a French wildflower book with a good section on orchids. Remember that?' Ian showed me a picture of the orchid he had found in the garden of Castignac.

'And I'm introducing a new line of raw silk clothes, like some I saw in France,' Jenny said.

Angela came over. 'I've made a French meal for us, my last fling at proper cooking before term begins.'

Stephen peppered his conversation with French words and poured French wine for everyone. I took to Lily at once. Angela was right to say that she was glamorous, but it wasn't in a distant or icy way. She was slim and pretty and her manner was friendly. Graham was a big man, not bad-looking, but he had a sombre manner and he wasn't someone who cracked a joke to put people at their ease.

During the meal, we talked generally about France and then about our house-hunting week. Graham asked a lot of questions about the state of the house. We did our best to answer them, but we were struggling. In the end, Stephen told him to wait for the surveyor's report which was on the way. By the end of the evening we had thoroughly aired the subject of sharing the house. Ian had even worked in a reference to wild orchids.

Chapter Three

The Group

G RAHAM AND LILY DIDN'T waste time making their decision about Castignac. Within a couple of weeks, they had gone to see the house and accepted our invitation to join the group. They loved the house and garden and the view of the town and the mountains. Graham was full of plans for renovation. On top of their own share of the cost, Stephen and Angela offered to contribute an eighth share until we could find someone to take it, and so we were ready to buy the house.

With the help of a French-speaking solicitor, Angela steered us through the purchase of Castignac. Once we had put in an offer, we waited like stretched elastic, wanting the house more and more as the days passed. Finally the news came through that Jacques Lordat had accepted our offer. It was an exciting moment. Angela flew to St Martin des Remparts to sign the final contract and rang me on her way home.

'We've done it! I met old Jacques with the notary and we signed the papers. There was a small glass of cognac for everyone.'

I was walking along a London street in the rain when she called, but Angela's words brought visions of red geraniums and open shutters, wooden beams, warm stone and sunshine. I could feel my spirits rising.

'Afterwards, I went to see Castignac! It looks just as nice in the autumn, even though the chestnut trees are almost bare. I met Marianne there and we went over the house together. It's warm at this time of year and she says the good weather normally lasts until late October,' Angela said.

Marianne was a local woman who had worked for Jacques Lordat as a housekeeper. Angela had employed her to work for us for a few hours a week, doing anything necessary.

We loved Castignac from our first visit and we liked to think of it as a piece of heaven. The house was bigger than any home I had ever had. My life in London was cramped, with small rooms and offices, and at Castignac, in the house and garden, there was so much space. Shopping always meant a car journey, but I preferred the countryside. It was the complete opposite of being in London, at the mercy of the noise and pollution from cars and planes.

Jacques Lordat had left us some furniture: a plain, long table, an enormous kitchen dresser and an old wardrobe, all perhaps too big for his new home in the town. We had ordered beds and kitchen stuff before moving in.

The old wardrobe was in my bedroom. During our first holiday at Castignac, as I was unpacking, I opened the door with some difficulty. The wardrobe was dark inside and smelled musty. A few wooden coat hangers dangled from a railing. I hung my clothes, thinking they looked awkward there, as if they could never belong. Still, it was at least a piece of furniture, more than the others had in their bedrooms.

Underneath the hanging space was a big drawer. I pulled it open and started to fill it with the rest of my clothes. I noticed a book lying at the back and picked it up. It was a small photo album. I flicked through pages of black and white photos, small and fuzzy, slowing down to look more carefully as I felt drawn in to what was obviously Castignac's past life. There were several photos of a fair-haired boy, sometimes on his own, sometimes with a dark-haired girl and a woman who could have been his mother. Several pictures of a couple with two girls, probably their daughters, appealed to me because everyone was smiling, but towards the back of the album was a picture of Castignac with a grim-looking old couple standing in front of it. The man was wearing a shirt and trousers and carrying a pitchfork. The woman, in a calf-length skirt, held her hands clasped tightly in front of her. The last picture was of a tombstone, with an inscription that I couldn't make out.

I brought the photo album downstairs the next morning and showed it to Angela. We leafed through it together.

'My guess is that there's nothing here more recent than the 1960s, so it's about fifty years old,' I said.

'I don't know who any of these other people are, but that could be Jacques Lordat as a boy,' Angela said, as we looked at the pictures of the blond boy. I had only seen the old farmer once, on our first visit to the house the previous summer, but Angela had met him over the sale of the house and her guess made sense.

The surveyor's report had told us that the house was solid and well constructed, and the roof wasn't leaking, but pointed out problems with plumbing, electricity and a poor state of decoration. The house was like a strong man, still muscular, but down on his luck and reduced to rags, with unkempt hair and holes in his shoes.

Marianne was in her early forties, bright-eyed and brisk, with tightly curled hair. She and her husband, Didier, had two teenage sons. She spoke no English and those of us with little French were relieved that she was patient with our halting efforts.

Her husband, Didier, came to Castignac, at our request, one day during our first holiday there, to see about some repairs. He ran a small building company and he looked the part, with a stocky frame. A cigarette dangling from the corner of his mouth, threatening to fall, but never doing so, was mesmerising. His manner was friendly and charming, but his French was rapid and incomprehensible to most of us. Even Angela and Ian, the best French speakers, struggled with it.

We gave Didier a list of work to do on the house. It was nothing grand; we merely wanted to improve the central heating and utilities and install an extra bathroom. We didn't have much money for repairs so we decided to do the decorating ourselves, after he had finished.

Meanwhile, Lily was full of ideas for Castignac. She bought old sheets at rock-bottom prices in the market. They would once have been an essential part of a bride's trousseau and would make good dust sheets. They were all of fine cotton, in excellent condition and embroidered with the initials of former owners. None was marked with the initials JL, but perhaps Jacques Lordat had taken all his sheets to his new home.

Lily found old mirrors dumped in the outbuildings behind the house. After mending and painting their frames, she hung them over the fireplaces downstairs, adding a touch of elegance. She found old pots and filled them with displays of flowers and greenery from the garden.

We discovered that we had a gardener. Marianne hadn't thought to tell us about him, but Ian saw a dark-haired young man in the garden one day, cutting down the wisteria that grew over the terrace. His name was Bertrand and he told Ian that he came along a few times a year to tidy up the garden. He had worked for Jacques Lordat and was simply carrying on with his job. When asked about him, Marianne said he would send us his bill each time and we would pay him directly.

'There's no doubt who's in charge here and it's not us,' I said.

'You're right, Tessa,' Angela said, 'I sometimes have the feeling that we've just borrowed this house for a while and that it'll one day go back to its real job as a French farmhouse. But we want to be accepted locally and I don't think it would go down well to start by sacking our gardener. Besides, he's doing a good job.'

One morning, during a short spring break at Castignac, I wandered near the ruined farmhouse. I watched as tiny lizards emerged from the stones of a wall. They were exquisite, standing still like jewelled brooches, eyes unblinking, their green or brown skin intricately patterned. No matter how they liked to bask in the sunlight, they never relaxed their vigilance and were always poised to flee. At the slightest sound or movement, they would jerk into life and scamper away, to hide in the stonework or under a plant.

Then I saw Ian on his knees.

'Look, I've found an orchid. At least I think that's what it is. You have to get down here. It's not dramatic until you look closely. See?'

He pointed to some small plants which at first sight looked nondescript, but when I kneeled on the damp grass to peer closely, I was surprised.

'Lots of little men are dangling from a stem and the face of each one is hidden by a hood,' I said.

Ian brought his phone out of a pocket and within a few seconds identified the plant. 'It's called the man orchid in English. Let's see what the French think... Hey, they call it *l'homme pendu* – the hanged man.'

'Much more dramatic!'

Marianne was at the house that day and Ian dragged her into the garden to inspect the orchid. I followed.

'I've seen it before. It's odd that it grows near the ruin. A man hanged himself there years ago,' she said, peering down at the small clump of flowers.

'Are you joking or is this a story you've heard from Jacques?' Ian asked.

'No, it's true. Everybody will tell you,' Marianne said.

Marianne didn't seem to know any details, but we were curious and conversation later turned to the farming family who had lived at Castignac. I wondered aloud what their lives had been like.

'They were farmers,' Stephen said. 'They grew things and... I don't know... looked after animals.'

'Yes, but who were they? We know a bit about Jacques Lordat, but what about his family?' I said.

We were sitting around the long table that the old farmer had left. His family might have owned it for generations, judging by the many marks on its surface. Angela called it a *monastère* and we had adopted her name for it.

'I've no idea and to be honest, I don't care,' Stephen said. 'I've come here for a holiday, not to study the history of rural France.'

'Gilles said that none of Jacques Lordat's children wants to take over the farm. That's why he sold his house,' Angela said.

Mark and I were in the garden the next morning, trying to help Jenny decide whether a bush near the house had survived the winter, when a loud cry rang out from inside. A crash followed, then silence. The three of us looked at each other with almost comical amazement.

'It's Ian, in the dining room.' Jenny spoke with a sharp intake of breath.

We sped to the dining room to find Ian on the floor, trying to extricate himself from the rungs of a fallen ladder. Everyone gathered around him.

'What's going on?' Stephen grabbed a chair from its place by the table and helped Ian onto it.

'Oh, Ian, are you all right?' Jenny said, gentle fingers exploring his face.

'I'm fine.' His voice was shaky.

'You need a cup of sweet tea. I'll be right back.' Angela disappeared towards the kitchen.

'The ladder slipped and fell, and gravity forced me down with it,' Ian said. 'It was all right at first. It felt quite firm and I made a good start.' He pointed to where he had stripped paper away from the wall.

'There's water all over the floor. That's why the ladder slipped,' Mark said.

'Graham is keen on renovations so I'm trying to do my bit. I was soaking the wallpaper to get it off more easily,' Ian said.

'Don't blame me. I didn't mean you to risk your life,' Graham said. 'You shouldn't be using an extension ladder without someone standing at the foot to stop it slipping. Anyway, there's no point in doing any decorating until Didier has finished his work. Why did you just plunge in?'

Angela appeared with a mug of tea, saving Ian from a reply. 'Drink this. I've put plenty of sugar in it,' she said.

Jenny drove Ian to the hospital. He wasn't badly hurt but was covered in purple bruises for some days.

When Angela asked Gilles why the ruin hadn't been mentioned in his agency's brochure about Castignac, he simply said that Jacques Lordat hadn't thought it necessary.

Everyone had explored the ruin. Lily liked to sit on an old bench she had found there and look at the view of the town below, with the mountains beyond. Mark liked to wander around it with his engineer's eye. Stephen barely ever glanced in its direction, although he had given up his first notion that it was no more than a shack erected for the convenience of builders. Cautious Graham regarded it as dangerous. Jenny found its ruinous state melancholy and Angela said we had enough to do for our house, without wasting time on a ruin that had been abandoned a hundred and fifty years before and that we hadn't intended to buy.

Leaning out of my bedroom window, I could see the uneven line of the roof and the tower of the pigeon loft through the chestnut trees before the leaves came out. I tried to imagine the lives of its occupants, the farmers and their families whose lives had been comfortable enough for someone in 1860 to build a new farmhouse.

Of all of us, Ian was the most attracted by the ruin. One evening, he showed us an intricate old key he had found hidden behind a loose brick there. It must have long outlived any chest of valuables that it had locked hundreds of years before. With it had been a leather purse, which he had opened with high hopes of finding mediaeval coins, only to find it empty.

'Someone beat you to it,' Stephen said with a laugh.

'Yes, too bad, but don't you think the ruin's got a great atmosphere? You can imagine people in a dairy or a kitchen or sitting by a log fire after a day in the fields.'

'Sounds too much like hard manual work to me.' Stephen gave an exaggerated shudder.

'Let's renovate the old farmhouse,' Ian said, his eyes lighting up. 'We could all move to France and run courses there. It's big enough to provide bedrooms and workshops. I'd like to see an artists' studio, a pottery, a greenhouse where I would teach people about the local flora, a big kitchen where we would run cookery classes and space for woodworking, especially as the building provides good examples of traditional methods.'

But Ian was a dreamer, not a man of action, and we all knew he was making conversation and wouldn't put his light-hearted suggestion into action.

Mark was different. When he first came to Castignac, he was curious about the ruin. We explored it one afternoon and he ran a hand along a section of the wooden frame filled with bricks and mortar.

'It's the original farmhouse. It would have been for the animals and for storing food as well as the family's living quarters. The tower is a pigeon loft, a *pigeonnier*. What a shame that it's been abandoned, because it's a fine building. And look at these massive beams.'

He pointed to some of the wooden uprights and the ceiling beams. The building was solid and enormous, with a number of extensions, which made it look so ramshackle.

'The roof is a disaster, but the walls still look pretty sound. The French have so much space in their big country that they don't need to demolish a building when they grow out of it. They can simply build the new one nearby,' he said.

Pigeons were flying in and out of the pigeon loft, jackdaws were chattering on the roof of the ruin, and collared doves were taking off and landing, always with their querulous shriek. Ian had identified the smaller birds for us, and I could see little redstarts flashing orange feathers as they flew and martins nesting under the eaves. The ruin was home to bird and insect life and to small animals, even if people had abandoned it.

Under the tower in the middle of the building, we noticed a wooden staircase. It was set against one wall and zigzagged upwards in four short flights within a frame of uprights, topped by a railing, until it arrived at the pigeon loft. We could see a loft entrance in the ceiling, but it was closed. The staircase looked home-made, but the steps appeared solid enough.

I put a tentative foot on the lowest step and then the one above. Mark was gazing out of the windows in the tower, wandering from one to another, so I was above his head at the top of the first flight before he noticed what I was doing. He strode towards me.

'Come down! Are you mad? You've no idea when the staircase was last used. It's probably unsafe and you could have a terrible accident.'

'Would you care?' I asked, one foot poised over the next step up.

'No, of course not. I'd laugh and walk away.'

He strode off and I climbed down, even though the staircase looked safe enough to me. Mark had disappeared. Left alone, I made my way to the south side of the courtyard and then beyond it into small outbuildings. The roofing was more intact there and glass glinted in some of the windows.

An old bench faced an open doorway, giving a framed view of green hills with the mountains beyond. St Martin des Remparts lay below and I could see the church spire, which always seemed to beckon me. It was the first outline to emerge from the haze when we were driving towards the town and seemed to accompany me when I was shopping or out walking. When the mountains glittered in the sun, the spire rose in front of them.

Near at hand, a small herd of velvety-looking brown cows was grazing. The bench was inviting and I sat down. The mountains took me beyond my tiny life. Their ragged, snowy shapes were entrancing and my eyes traced peaks and dips alike. I was glad not to be climbing them and I had no intention of going all the way up the staircase to the pigeon loft. I had no head for heights, and it was the beauty and the distance of the mountains that held me.

Footsteps sounded behind me and Mark appeared. He looked relieved.

'Oh, there you are. I didn't mean it, you know. Did you think I meant it?' he asked, sitting next to me on the bench and taking my hand.

I dragged my eyes away from the view, puzzled. 'Meant what?'

'That I would laugh and walk away if you fell down the stairs! I didn't like seeing you halfway up what could be a rotten structure, but you might have gone off in disgust at what I said.'

'No, you were joking and quite right to tick me off. Look at this view!'

Instead, Mark continued to look at me. He turned my face towards him and kissed me gently at first, then more urgently. Only when we released each other, breathless, did he look at the mountains. Then he pointed towards a gaunt ruin in the middle distance.

'Look, there's a castle.'

The local tourist office was keen to advertise the Cathar castles perched on impossibly steep mountain crags to the south of us, but the local castle wasn't one of them. Like our ruin, it was there, but never mentioned.

I was interested in the history around us, but it was Castignac that aroused my curiosity most of all. Houses seemed to sell quickly in the prosperous town of St Martin des Remparts, but we hadn't asked Gilles why Castignac had been slow to sell because we had reached desperation point by the time we found it. Supposing something had happened there that meant people avoided it? Could the hanging that Marianne had mentioned be the reason? Was that why the ruin hadn't been mentioned in the estate agent's details? Presented as a folly, it might have been a selling point. And who were the people in the photograph album I had found?

At first, I couldn't think of where to start asking questions. I would have to learn French before I could tackle Jacques Lordat or Marianne or indeed most people in a place where few spoke English. One day, I noticed a museum in the town. It was closed at the time, but it looked promising and I decided to pay it a visit when I had a moment.

Chapter Four

Mark

Until I met Mark, a year or so before Stephen had suggested buying a house in France, I hadn't had a boyfriend for a long time, longer than I cared to say. It hadn't always been like that. In my teens and twenties, boyfriends had come and gone. I had lived with one of them for several years and had even assumed we would get married one day, but it didn't work out. We had slowly become bored with each other and eventually we began to admit it. One day, he accepted a job offer in Birmingham and when he asked me to move there with him, I could tell from the leaden tone of his voice that he didn't want me to say yes. Nor did I want to go. It was over, but I needed to say no more than that I didn't want to leave London. We split up amicably enough. He left and Jackie, who was fortunately looking for somewhere to lay her head at the time, came to live with me.

At first, I was simply relieved and I enjoyed the freedom of going out with different groups of friends. It took months to want another regular boyfriend, but then I began to notice that it wasn't quite as easy to meet attractive, single men as it had been. The nice ones were married or fixed up and the only ones available weren't my type. I had grown up assuming I would get married, if only because my parents always gave the impression they had been made for each other, but I was finding out that it wasn't easy and began to think that I'd missed out.

At the suggestion of a friend, who boasted of her success with it, I tried internet dating, after my thirtieth birthday had jolted me into action. In the course of a series of dates with men who weren't right for me, I didn't meet anyone I wanted to see a second time. I was beginning to resign myself to a single life, secretly resentful that, by then, Jackie had a regular boyfriend. Phil was an English teacher, who was also a poet. He had one published volume to his credit and a growing reputation on the performance circuit.

By the age of thirty-four, I had given up hoping to meet anyone through work, other activities or friends. One day, I went to a party given by the internet-dating friend. Nothing ever came from meeting people at parties, but Jackie was going out with Phil that night and I didn't want to spend a Saturday evening watching television on my own. It was all right to be alone on any other night of the week, but never on a Saturday. That was a sure sign of failure in my world.

My friend played hostess well, introducing me to several people whose names I promptly forgot. As the party began to succeed and people relaxed, I found myself talking to a man just because he was standing next to me. He was about my age, with a solid, reassuring look and a friendly manner. Like me, he didn't seem to know many people there.

'How do you know Joanne?' I said as an opener, referring to the friend giving the party.

He laughed. 'I don't really. I live next door and I think she invited me to stop me complaining about the noise,' he said.

We were in Earlsfield, not far from Wandsworth in London, where Jackie and I lived.

'A smart move on her part,' I said, straining to hear him against the music.

'It's just chance I'm here, because I'm not in England much. I rent a room from the people who live next door, but I spend most of my time in the Middle East,' he said, raising his voice against the music.

'That's dangerous, isn't it?'

'Yes and no.'

He talked about the Middle Eastern countries where he worked as a civil engineer, with a kind of confidence that took war in its stride, while making sure to keep away from it. It was a point in his favour that he didn't at all give the impression that my life as a librarian in London must be dull but listened to my stories of how we were trying to attract people into the library and laughed, not in an unkindly way, at my descriptions.

When we were interrupted and he began talking to other people, I watched him covertly. He seemed good-humoured and laughed easily. Later, when someone turned the music up and conversation became impossible, most people began dancing. He came over to me and we danced together for a long time. It was so much easier than trying to talk and he was fun to dance with, amusing in a way that didn't require words. I enjoyed that party more than any I had been to for ages.

At the end of the evening, it seemed natural to exchange names and phone numbers. His name was Mark. After two days' waiting and hoping on my part, he called me. It was just as well he did, because I wasn't bold enough to make the first move, despite urgings from Jackie. The day after, we met in his local, around the corner from where he lived. It was an ordinary pub, with no music. At least he wasn't trying to impress me and we could hear each other. We talked for about an hour, non-stop, about all sorts of things, before he suggested a walk.

It was a fine summer evening for strolling by the nearby River Wandle. Mark knew the history of the river and the mills which once drew water from it for cloth-making, flour grinding and other trades. We could hear traffic in the distance, but it was peaceful there, with the old industry silenced and a jungle of weeds edging the path. We walked to the mouth of the river and then along the Thames until I was almost home. I could have asked him in for a drink, especially as I knew Jackie would be out late, but although I was attracted to him and felt at ease in his company, I didn't want to rush things. He didn't seem to expect to be invited in and instead gave me a quick kiss on the cheek and left. Immediately I began to wonder if I'd missed a chance, but I needn't have worried, because he rang the next day and invited me to see a film with him and that led to more dates.

One night, walking along the bank of the Thames with no-one nearby, he took my hand and then kissed me. It was neither too soon nor too late. My head was swimming and I felt breathless as we drew apart. Later, he invited me back to his room and I was so relaxed with him by then that it felt right to make love, like a natural progression from a conversation which had become increasingly intimate.

When we talked afterwards, he asked me if I had ever been married.

'No, I lived with someone once for five years, but it ended three or four years ago. We ran out of steam. And you?'

'I was married, but we're divorced now. I found out she was having an affair.'

'Oh, not good.'

'That was the end for me, but I'll get over it.'

He didn't say that he was getting over it, only that he would. It was still affecting him. Would he go back to her? My heart sank. A married man wasn't what I wanted. And why hadn't he told me before? It was some weeks since the party where we had met and we'd seen each other several times since then. I waited for the story, but when he spoke again, he'd changed the subject.

'Tessa, it's great being with you, but I won't be around much longer. I'm working in London at the moment, but I'm waiting to hear about a job in Lebanon and I could be gone for months,' he said.

I knew that, because he had said so before, but it meant more now.

'Oh, well, let me know when you're back in London,' I said, trying not to sound disappointed.

He was nonchalant. 'I'll be back from time to time. Anyway, I haven't gone yet. Come here.'

He pulled me into his arms again. Over the next few weeks, we met as often as we could. I could feel myself falling in love with Mark, despite the circumstances telling me not to. The tell-tale signs were there – forgetfulness of what I was doing because my mind was on him, fantasies about him when I should have been working, that sense of things opening up, a feeling of flying rather than just plodding along. It all revealed itself in a great deal of laughter and a sense of closeness, but I had no idea of how he was feeling except that he liked me.

He certainly didn't want to talk about his marriage. I didn't particularly want to talk about it either, but I couldn't help feeling some curiosity. Was his wife simply unfaithful by nature or had he neglected her by working long hours or being away from home for months at a time? I had to rely on gleaning scraps of information that he let drop about himself because he clammed up if I asked too many questions. He was a great talker on all kinds of subjects – his work, the economy or politics, for example – but he didn't want to talk much about himself. When I challenged him, jokingly, about it, he simply said he wasn't interested in himself. I had to accept that. Given the number of people I had met who were interested in little other than themselves, it was a refreshing change.

Only a few weeks after I met Mark, he had gone. He promised to keep in touch with me, saying he wanted to see me again but with no plan for when that might be. I had been hoping that, once he met me, he would change his mind about working abroad and find work in England, although I didn't say so. I didn't know much about civil engineering, but it seemed to be one of those fields where there were jobs. At least he wasn't a history lecturer, like one friend of mine who was often out of work because jobs were so few and so hard to get in her field. But no, he continued with his plans to work for a company whose main interests were abroad, and I had to watch him go and return to my single life.

'Mark enjoys travelling and working in different countries, but I can't help wondering whether he's escaping from something,' I said to Jackie one day.

Sharing a flat with me meant that she had to put up with my frustrations over Mark, but she didn't mind. She was pleased that at last I had someone, because she was so infuriatingly happy with Phil.

'You mean he's escaping from you!' She gave a squeal of laughter, but I was being serious.

'No, not me, because he was waiting to go abroad when I met him, remember? He's escaping the unhappy marriage. He won't talk about it and the only way he's dealing with it is to flee the country.'

'I'm not sure that'll help. He can't leave his bad feelings behind him.'

Mark had few relatives. His parents were both only children, so he had no aunts and uncles or cousins. His only relatives were his mother, as his father was dead, and a sister. His mother lived in London, and the sister and her family lived in the north of England. By the sound of it, his mother was a capable, healthy woman who had learned to live with the loss of her husband. She may have been coping better than her son, who was living with the breakdown of his marriage.

By the time Stephen suggested buying a house in France, I had known Mark for almost a year, more off than on. He returned to England every few months for meetings with his employer and it was only then that I saw him. In between, we sent emails and texts or we phoned, more frequently just after he'd left or just before he returned, with a gap in the middle which allowed me to fret about whether or not we had a relationship.

When we were together, I was excited about him and willing to make a go of things. I told myself that he would change his mind about working abroad as we got to know each other, but so far, I'd been wrong about that.

'I don't expect you to stay at home all the time when I'm away,' he said one day when I was in his room. The family he rented from were friends of his and relaxed about whether or not I stayed there. 'You don't want to miss out on any excitement.'

'I won't, and the same applies to you,' I said, playing along with the fiction that we were both free agents.

The truth was that I didn't want to see other men in his absence and hated the thought of any women he might meet when he was abroad. I only wanted Mark. I knew that I would miss him, but he didn't respond when I said so, except with some anodyne comment like it's nice to be missed, so I held back on my feelings, hoping that time would make the difference, that I would grow on him. Jackie thought I should show more initiative and set out what I wanted, but I was cautious as well as proud.

Jackie was a potter, supporting herself through various teaching jobs at adult education colleges. I envied her creative talent, and I liked her colourful and imaginative pots. I would turn up at her stall at pottery shows in London and elsewhere, to help out or simply to wander around and examine the display. Not long after I met Mark, Jackie and I had inherited the sum of money each that had enabled me to buy a share in Castignac. My mother's older sister, Aunt Jessie, had died young, after a long battle with multiple sclerosis. She had always said she wasn't going to leave any money to her generation, because they didn't need it. It was the younger generation who needed money. I couldn't have agreed with her more, although, by the time of her death, Jackie and I had set up home together. Our flat wasn't part of the new millennium developments with a river view in Wandsworth, but in a 1930s block tucked in amongst Victorian houses on a side street behind them. I liked old buildings.

The absence of Mark might have been one reason why I buried myself in the general election when it came along. Jackie certainly thought so. I had joined the political party already and I began helping with the campaign by doing some leafletting here and there. Then I was drawn into canvassing. Many party members didn't like canvassing, but I enjoyed it. I liked meeting people and hearing their views about Stephen, as our local candidate, or about the party and the country generally. That was how I got to know Stephen and Angela, and then Jenny. During the campaign, we were out canvassing every night. Once or twice those of us who were regular helpers were invited to Stephen and Angela's for a late meal after canvassing finished. Those meals gave me a chance to get to know Angela and Jenny better.

Mark happened to come back to England for a spell at head office in London during the general election campaign. I was burning to see him, and he rang me as soon as he landed.

'I'm longing to see you. Can we meet in the pub about six o'clock tonight?' he said. His local had become the place where we met before deciding what to do next.

His eagerness was gratifying, but I was torn. The election campaign was in its last week and all hands were needed. I couldn't drop out at the last minute and let people down.

'I'd love to, but I promised to go canvassing straight after work. Can we meet after that?' I said.

For once, I would be the one who was hard to see. He took it in his stride and I couldn't help hoping that he might prefer that I had a life and wasn't simply waiting for him all the time.

A week after the campaign was over and we had lost the election, Angela suggested the holiday in France. She had rented a cottage in anticipation of a family holiday with their two children, both now students, but late in the day neither of them had wanted to come and so she was inviting friends instead. Mark had gone back to Jordan, where he was working, by then, but I accepted Angela's invitation because I had no other plans. I sent Mark a text, inviting him to join us for the fortnight and thinking he would no doubt refuse because he wouldn't be able to get away. I was joyous when he replied saying he would come for a week.

Chapter Five

The Party

ARRIVING AT CASTIGNAC FOR our first summer holiday there, we exclaimed over the advance in the year since our last visit. We had missed the gradual change from one season to another, the replacement of the paler shades of early spring by the stronger colours of mid-summer. The bright yellow of rows of tall sunflowers or the green of tobacco plants or sweetcorn waiting to be harvested stretched into the distance. We loved the brilliant orange of the trumpet flowers hanging over garden walls, the blue, pink and white of hibiscus, and the pink and white of oleander.

Marianne had filled all the window boxes with red geraniums from the market in St Martin des Remparts. The vibrant display reminded us of our first visit and it seemed incredible that a year had elapsed since then.

Graham, Lily, Stephen and Angela were sitting on the terrace over an early evening drink on the day that Ian and

Jenny and I arrived. We had driven from England and had picked Mark up at Carcassonne Airport. Jenny and Ian were both trying to avoid flying, as I was, so Jenny had put me on their car insurance and I had helped with the driving. Stephen and Angela had been at the house for some days, with visitors who had now left.

'You'll never guess what's happened!' Angela said. 'Didier and his men have finally done the work. They've re-wired and re-plumbed the house, putting in the new boiler and dealing with the woodworm!'

Didier and his men had been delaying the work for us all year and this news called for an immediate tour. I ran around examining the changes, as if I couldn't believe Angela until I had seen them for myself. Mark was at my side, as interested as the rest of us. The work had been done to a high standard and even Graham was satisfied.

'Let's celebrate. I don't mean just on our own,' Stephen said that evening. 'Let's have a party for the people we know. After all, Marianne says people in St Martin des Remparts are curious about us. They'll be able to see us at home and it'll give us a chance to thank those people who've helped us.'

We were sitting on the terrace. The wisteria was largely past flowering by then, but leaves were clustered thickly over our heads, sheltering us from the glare of the sun. Hornets buzzed, fortunately staying high.

'A great idea!' Angela said. 'We're always wondering what people here think of a houseful of Brits. And a party will at least show friendliness.'

I liked the idea, but Graham wasn't so sure.

'Why not wait until we've done the decorating? The men have ruined the wallpaper all over the house and the place looks a mess.'

'Oh, yes, and have the party in ten years' time!' Jenny said, laughing. 'It'll be all right, Graham. We can be on the terrace and people will admire the garden.'

Bertrand had kept an eye on the garden in our absence. Old hydrangeas and straggling roses were out, as well as plants we had added. The terrace, with much of the colour in view, was a perfect place for a summer party.

Graham gave in and even joined in listing guests. We mentioned Didier and Marianne, Didier's assistant Philippe, our gardener, Bertrand, estate agent Gilles and the notary who had dealt with the purchase of Castignac. We added the owner of the local hardware shop, a great source of advice; a woman from our favourite bakery; the people who ran a café we visited often; a family who owned a restaurant we liked and the friendly couple from a nearby wine shop.

'Let's invite Jacques Lordat. I want to find out more about Castignac. He's not far away and Gilles will have his address. I often see him in the town square,' I said.

'I don't know about that. What if he hates what we've done to his old home?' Angela said.

'We haven't ripped out any walls or concreted over the garden. Besides, it would be odd to leave him out.'

Angela pursed her lips. 'He's not like Didier. He's not friendly. I would say he likes his own company.'

'So, he can refuse to come, but I'd still like to invite him, and it would give us a chance to find out more about Castignac,' I said, determined not to lose the opportunity.

Ian backed me up and Angela gave in. We agreed on a date for the party, wrote out invitations on cards that Lily found in the newsagent's in St Martin des Remparts and took them round to people. Although it was August, nearly everyone was at home or available. Our guests seemed not to go away every summer and welcomed the invitation.

Jackie and her boyfriend Phil came to see the house and spend a few days with us, and I picked them up from the airport. Jackie was impressed with the house, garden and pool, and I began to wonder whether she would take the last share after all. Stephen and Angela were still waiting for someone to buy it.

By six in the evening of the day of the party, everything was ready, with the table on the terrace at the side of the house set out with drinks and snacks. We wondered if anyone was coming, but, within half an hour, all the guests had arrived, even Jacques Lordat.

Gilles was there, gesticulating with his pipe and basking in the successful sale of Castignac. I hovered, wishing I could understand him. Judging by the bursts of laughter around him, he was entertaining.

The notary spoke no English, but he had a limp-wristed charm. He seemed to know who everyone was, but he had a distant manner and didn't look at me when I was introduced to him. I suspected I would need to be an important resident of the town to merit attention. Didier, like Gilles, was clearly well-known and I watched him shaking hands all round. It wasn't just good business practice but genuine enjoyment of people.

Our French guests were polite but curious to see what we had done to the house. They also wanted some idea of how unrelated *rosbifs* lived together, because such sharing was unknown to them. Angela was laughing as she told me that she had overheard Marianne assuring one small group that we were all quite normal and counting us off one by one on her fingers with a name and a brief description.

Angela was everywhere, introducing and translating, with help from Mark and Ian. There was a continual buzz of conversation. Every now and then a small group would peel off to look around the house and then return. Children played in the garden. We had put up a big notice saying *Danger – Interdit* at the entrance to the ruin, to avoid any accidents. It might have been the sort of place that children would love to explore, but we needn't have bothered, because no-one paid it the slightest attention.

The house seemed to have woken up with the renovations and now with the party. It was spacious and handsome, I thought, trying to see it through the eyes of our guests. Marianne had waxed its wooden floors to a shine; its walls would soon be freshly papered; its shutters were flung open to greet the party and its garden was thriving.

Jacques Lordat didn't join one of the tours around the house, telling Angela that he had seen it often enough. I wondered how he felt about his house being occupied by strangers. Either he wasn't interested in what we'd done or preferred not to know.

'Please ask him about the ruined farmhouse, how old it is, who lived there and when it was abandoned,' I said to Angela at one point. I had the photo album with me and handed it to Jacques, who took it from me with an exclamation. He hadn't realised that he had left it behind. Through Angela, I asked him about the ruin.

He seemed surprised that anyone would be interested in it, but he replied at some length.

'It's about five hundred years old. The old farmhouse was abandoned in the middle of the nineteenth century when the family was doing well and could afford to build a new house. From then on, it was used just for the animals, for cows and pigs in winter, and hens. It's worthless and will gradually fall down and disappear. Some of the stone was used anyway in the building of our house.'

'I've just remembered that Mark ticked me off when I started to climb the staircase there. Is it safe? Can we go up and see the view from the pigeon loft?' I said, through Angela.

'The staircase is safe, as far as I know, but it's some years since I've been up there, so I can't be sure what it's like now,' Jacques said.

'Do you remember what Marianne said about someone committing suicide there? Ask him about that,' I said, and Angela did so.

Jacques didn't reply at first. He seemed to be weighing up what to say and he looked uncomfortable.

'It's true, but you would have to visit the capital of our department, to look at birth, death and marriage certificates, if you want to find out more about my forebears, *madame*,' he said with an air of finality.

I was left with the feeling that he was fobbing me off and wondered what he didn't want to talk about. The photo album was tucked firmly under his arm and I didn't like to ask him about the pictures. I didn't know him well enough and he might have found it intrusive.

'*Merci*,' I said. My single word of French unleashed a reply which Angela translated.

'I couldn't be a farmer anymore. It's because of my hip, although I've kept out of the hospital. I've got my pension. I go shopping in the market. I sit on one of the benches in the square on fine days watching busy people scurry past or playing *boules*. I miss the old place, though, and it's nice to come back. The pool made the difference. I'm sure that it sold the house for me. A house in the country is harder to sell than a town or village house, and foreigners like a pool.'

It wasn't just the pool, at least not for me. I loved the whole of Castignac for the generous house and nearby town, for the views, for the countryside and wildflowers. I wanted to say that to Jacques for myself, but someone was claiming Angela's attention. If only I could have talked to him directly and asked him all the questions about his farm that were bubbling up in my mind. It was pathetic that I didn't speak French. I wasn't going to rely so heavily on Angela in future and decided to start lessons in the autumn.

Stephen behaved like a politician, making sure he talked to everyone, however briefly, and glad-handing freely. He managed to appear fluent in French and to give the impression of understanding when he hardly knew the language.

I hung around Mark and tried to understand his conversations or chatted to the other members of our group. Jackie and Phil were enjoying themselves. Jackie, whose command of French was as poor as mine, was relying on Dutch courage and her glass was often empty.

As the party buzzed on, in the warm evening air, Ian became involved in a long conversation with Jacques. From the way Jacques gesticulated towards the old ruin, I guessed that Ian was drawing him out about his family history, just as Angela and I had done.

The guests began to drift away in the middle of the evening. To our right, in the west, the sun was preparing to set in a great spread of pink, orange and red sky so dramatic that I half-expected to hear a heavenly chorus. As the light faded, the party hosts were left on the terrace on our own. I told the others what I had gleaned from Jacques, but it wasn't much more than we already knew, and I was disappointed that Ian didn't add anything.

'People were curious about us, weren't they?' Jenny said, watching the last of the guests drive off. 'They all came and they seemed to enjoy themselves.'

'I wonder if Jacques was pleased that we haven't gutted Castignac and that we've kept its character,' I said, wanting the old man to like us and our improvements.

'I don't know. He didn't seem interested,' Jenny said.

'It's no good. People here will never accept us, however hard we try. We'll always be foreigners,' Lily said.

'Yes, Jacques used the word "foreigner". Well, we are traditional enemies, but it would be easier if our French were better,' I said.

'It's more than language, though,' Jenny said. 'We don't live here.'

'Even if we did, we'd still always be foreign. Anyway, I don't feel any need to be accepted as a local,' Stephen said. 'At least we got away with breaking through social barriers. My impression was that our guests don't necessarily mix.'

Slipping into bed that night, I thought again about the suicide. Did it explain why Castignac had been on the market for so long? Then Mark reached for me and the thought was banished by his touch.

The August heat continued until everything was so hot, dry and dusty that I longed for rain. It would have been refreshing and maybe things would have turned out differently. After most hot days came a long, warm evening when we gathered on the terrace, at one end of which we had installed a big garden table. We talked for hours and there was plenty to keep us entertained if conversation lapsed.

Starlings roosted in great numbers in the trees in the garden. They sang loudly and stopped suddenly, quite late in the evening, leaving cicadas to add background music to our conversation. Even one cicada could fill the night air with sound. We watched the sun set over the town and saw the twilight creep in. As the birds fell silent, we followed the haywire flight of the bats which lived in the ruined farmhouse, as they fluttered across the evening sky, never clearer than a blur. One by one, lights came on in the town.

In the countryside around us, the moon rose and the stars lit the darkening sky.

After the party, Ian wanted to climb the staircase in the ruin and see the pigeon loft. He seemed excited about it.

'It'll give us the best view of the countryside and the mountains,' he said one evening.

'Wait until we've checked it out. Didier can tell us if it's safe,' Graham said.

'Oh, damn the great god health and safety!' Ian said. 'Honestly, nothing in life would ever get done if we followed that stuff all the time. You're too cautious!'

'Graham is right. You don't know that it's safe,' Mark said.

Mark and Graham, backed by the rest of us, both advised Ian to keep away from the staircase, especially as Jacques had said he hadn't been up there for years and so couldn't vouch for it. Graham referred to woodworm, death watch beetle or termites.

'Ask Didier to look at it,' Stephen said to Angela. 'I don't mean construct another project. Just ask his advice on it.'

'Marianne is coming in tomorrow, because I want to talk cobwebs, so I'll ask her then. Didier might be able to pop in over the next few days,' Angela said.

Marianne promised to pass on our message about inspecting the staircase to Didier. We waited patiently enough, but he didn't turn up. He was too busy, as he and his men spent the summer holidays on repairs to schools. After a couple of days of silence, Ian began to agitate for Angela to ask Marianne to prompt Didier. She did, but there was no response. A week passed after the party, with no word from Didier.

There was a storm one night. Clouds built up to the south, starting as innocent cotton wool balls and becoming thicker and darker. In no time, they had pursued and banished the sun and the temperature had dropped. With the wind rising, we ran around the house securing the shutters. A rash of fat raindrops splashed onto the garden and then stopped, as if teasing the thirsty earth.

Sheets of lightning began to flash and jagged forks stabbed earthwards, as we all occupied the sitting room like a theatre audience waiting for a play to start. Thunder rolled heavily around the sky and rain began to fall in earnest. The storm raged for an hour before it retreated and the sky began to lighten. We ate indoors that evening, under the wooden ceiling beams and chandelier in the dining room.

The sounds of St Martin des Remparts were muted by distance and reached us at Castignac only when unusually loud, like church bells, an angry horn or even the sudden bray of a donkey. With the wind in a certain direction, we could hear a murmur of traffic, but it was a soft sound, like the sea on a calm day, and we were barely aware of it.

Walking into the town, I noticed that chunks of stone were missing from the walls of some of the houses that we passed. The town was built around a square, with a large covered market in the middle, a wooden colonnade all round and a church off to one side. It was neither wealthy nor poor and created a comfortable, only slightly crumbly impression. It was a *bastide*, one of hundreds of planned mediaeval towns in southern France, as it declared on many signs.

The old houses of the town, with their wider upper floors, seemed to lean towards each other in the sun, their painted walls bright. Phone lines looped above the roofs, where thin aerials stood next to fat chimneys and squabbling jackdaws landed with doves.

I liked being able to stand on the crossroads created by the grid street plan of the town and see the green of the countryside in four directions. Hills rose in the distance and the street leading to the bridge seemed to gather pace and leap across the river that bordered the town, free of its burden of houses at last. Some of the streets running north allowed for a view of Castignac, its windowpanes glinting if the sun was out.

'Castignac could easily defend itself from invasion,' Mark said one morning when we were looking up at the house from the centre of the town.

'Were you a soldier in a previous life? I've only been thinking of how you can see Castignac from here and of the great view of the town from our house,' I said.

It was a good moment to visit the museum. Mark didn't share my wish to explore Castignac's past and agreed to wait for me in a café. I promised not to be too long.

The museum was on one side of the main square and occupied a building attached to the church. I went in. A youngish, long-haired man, with a pale, indoor face, whom I took for the museum curator, was standing behind a counter. No-one else was there.

'Are you British?' the young man said as I bought my ticket.

I nodded. No-one ever took my brown hair and pink complexion for French, even before I spoke.

'You are interested in our town?'

I was relieved that he was speaking English.

'Yes. I'd like to know its history.'

'Good. I hope you enjoy our display. Ask me if you have any questions.'

Wandering around the big room which housed the museum, I saw rusty agricultural machinery, faded clothing and old photographs, artefacts like combs and knife handles carved from cattle horn, and jewellery made of jet. I was impressed by how rooted the lives of the local community had been and no doubt still were, in comparison to our London lives. Yet there was something missing. I went up to the curator.

'There's nothing about the two world wars,' I said.

'Some of the items cover that time, but you must visit our war memorial at the end of its avenue of plane trees. It lists the names of many men who lost their lives,' he said.

I had been there. The avenue of plane trees was striking, but the lists of people who had died didn't say more than the name and date of death.

'But what happened here, say, during the last war? Was it occupied by Nazis?'

He said it was, but he was vague about events and mentioned the war memorial again.

'Do you know anything about the old farmhouse at Castignac?' I said.

He pointed to a photograph hanging on the wall behind me, one I had missed in my tour of the exhibits. I recognised it as a larger version of one I had seen in Jacques's album, the black and white photograph of Castignac, with an old couple standing in front of the house. This time there was a caption beneath the photo, which the curator hardly needed to translate for me: *Jean-Louis and Danielle Lordat, outside their farmhouse at Castignac in 1940.*

I was immediately fascinated and felt I had to know as much as possible about these people in whose house I now spent my holidays and whose lives had been clearly so different from my own. They were too old to have been Jacques's parents, but perhaps they were his grandparents. I was disappointed when I quizzed the curator and found he didn't know anything more about the Lordats.

Part Two

Chapter One

Jean-Louis

As a boy, Jean-Louis had explored Castignac in all seasons, becoming acquainted with every animal there, every corner of a field, every nook and cranny of a building, and every possible tree. He had never wished to live in St Martin des Remparts, with its houses and patches of garden jammed together. When he looked down on the town lying in the valley below him with its church spire and listened to the low hum of its life, he felt the freedom of the space that surrounded him.

On one side of the parting of the waters, rivers ran to the Mediterranean and on the other side to the Atlantic. Not far away, in the hotter, drier climate of the Mediterranean side, farming meant vineyards and olive groves, but Castignac was just on the Atlantic side, where the wetter, cooler climate was suited to its wheat, lentils, corn for animal fodder and winter vegetables. A small herd of some twenty dairy cows, and hens, pigs and goats made up the animal stock. The cows spent the warmer months in grassy fields and the winters in a cattle shed living on hay stored there.

The work was hard and winters could be cold, but he loved the strength of wind, sun and rain; the green of grass and trees; the yellow of wheat waiting to be harvested; the endless blue of a clear sky; the mass of clouds billowing up over the mountains; the sound of birdsong; the lowing of cattle; the smell of the earth; and even of the dung heap. He and his family never questioned their lot in life.

Jean-Louis had grown up knowing that he would one day be the farmer like his father and grandfather and countless others before him. As a boy he had begged to learn how to do everything on the farm. He had wanted to plough the fields and plant and harvest the wheat, mow the hayfields, milk cows and goats, feed pigs and chickens, and dig up vegetables. His growing figure had been by his father's side until the day, at the age of six, he had been banished.

'Jean-Louis, you're going to school. The town has opened a school for boys and girls, and I've put your name down. I'll take you every morning until you can go on your own and you'll stay there until I collect you in the afternoon.'

His mother was smiling and sounded pleased. Jean-Louis didn't know what she was talking about, but he soon found out. One morning, his mother drove him to the school in the cart and left him there. He had to sit on a bench in a classroom full of other children, be confined to a desk, and recite verbs and times tables. Except for breaks, when he exploded into the playground like a shot from his father's hunting rifle, he hated it. The parcel of bread and cheese and an apple which his mother gave him every morning was nowhere near enough to persuade him to like school.

At break time one morning a week later, he couldn't stand it any longer. Dashing into the playground, he was out of the school gate in seconds. The cries of the teacher pursued him, but he ignored her. He knew the way back home and he sped up the hill, knees pumping. At Castignac, he found his father preparing to go to town with some tools that needed repairing. The cart was ready, with a horse between the shafts.

'Wait here,' his father said and went off, calling his mother.

She left the hens she was feeding, slapped Jean-Louis hard and sat him in the back of the cart with the tools.

On the way to school for the second time that day, words floated back to him over his father's shoulder.

'Your mother and I never went to school and you're the first child in the family to go. You're lucky to have a place and you should be proud. Learn to read and write and do your sums, my boy. I need your help with paperwork coming my way these days.'

Jean-Louis went back to the classroom. The following day, he noticed a shiny new lock on the school gate. There was no escape. He had to stay at school.

The arrival of twins Henri and Paul, when he was nine, had made him the eldest of three brothers. Two baby girls had died in the meantime and his parents had always said that if they must lose children, it was better that the boys had survived to carry on the farm because girls would only marry and leave home.

His grandfather had been the head of the family when Jean-Louis was a boy. He had been a gnarled old man who spoke Occitan and whose deep voice and strong accent had sounded like the bellowing of the farm oxen.

'I was the one who built the new farmhouse. It was my life's dream to move the family out of the old farmhouse, with its stench of animals. Four hundred years of living under the same roof as the animals ended with building the new house. See the date of 1860 on the front, just under the roof? You were the first child to be born here, twenty years later, my boy,' he had said many times.

'We could afford it. All the sacks of wheat and vegetables, churns of milk, rounds of cheese and butter and joints of ham we produced were turned into handsome stone. We were never one of the leading families hereabouts, but the new house shows we're worth something,' he had gone on to say.

The main invention of his grandfather's lifetime, the railway, had brought the stone and other materials like wood, iron, roof tiles and plaster to St Martin des Remparts for the construction of the new house. Men had laboured for a year, digging foundations, building, and plastering and painting the house.

It shone down on St Martin des Remparts like a beacon in the hills when the glass in the windows caught the sun. Looking up at the shining glass from the town square made Jean-Louis feel proud. Even the pigeon loft of the old farmhouse wasn't visible from the town.

For a while after the family had moved out, the old farmhouse had continued to house the animals, until his father had built a big wooden and tin cattle shed and a pigsty. After that, the old farmhouse was only used for storage, except by the pigeons who lived in the loft.

Jean-Louis, with the benefit of his education, didn't know how his grandfather could have said four hundred years with such confidence. The figure must have been handed down through the generations, growing all the time. The old family Bible, with its record of births and deaths on the blank pages at the end, didn't go back so far. The first entry was dated 1784, less than a hundred years before his own birth in 1880.

Henri and Paul were too young to be Jean-Louis's close companions and they made their own world as they grew up. It largely excluded their older brother whom they treated more like a father figure or an uncle, while the presence of much younger brothers made Jean-Louis feel more like a father to them.

Jean-Louis's best friend throughout his boyhood was Joseph from a nearby farm, who was his age. Joseph had a younger sister called Danielle and they had all known each other from infancy. All year round, the three of them met in the small wood that divided their farms at one point, playing in a stream that ran through it, catching frogs and minnows, building dens or climbing trees, higher and higher, until they could see for miles around. Danielle insisted on coming along, when she could escape her mother's firm grasp. Even though she was a girl, the boys accepted her company.

One summer afternoon, when the harvest was in, Jean-Louis met Danielle by chance in the wood.

'Where's Joseph?' he said.

'He's in bed with a bad cold.'

Jean-Louis had a farm dog with him and they threw sticks for the dog to chase until they tired of that and sat down together.

'I've come out on my own to escape from Mother,' Danielle explained. She complained about all the work her mother made her do. There was no time when she wasn't working. Jean-Louis was aware of that, because Danielle often said so.

'You'll be in trouble when you go back then,' he said.

She nodded and he felt sorry for her.

'I'll come back with you and say you were helping me with something,' he said.

'All right, but what can it be? She's bound to ask.'

'Securing that fence down there, to stop our pigs going onto your land and trampling on those beetroot that you haven't lifted from the ground yet,' Jean-Louis said, pointing with the stick and ready to lie to save Danielle from trouble.

She smiled then and he wanted to kiss her, this girl he had played with for most of his childhood, yet never been alone with before, even though he was seventeen now and she was fifteen. Instead he stood up and they walked back to her farmhouse together where he explained to her mother how helpful she had been with the fence.

After that, there was a feeling of conspiracy between them and they contrived to meet alone until it was understood that they were walking out together.

At eighteen, Jean-Louis and Joseph were called up to do military service. Jean-Louis had never left Castignac before and didn't want to go, but, as with school, there was no choice. His father, who had fought in the Franco-Prussian War in 1870, said gruffly that the army would make a man of him. He said goodbye to his family and to Danielle, and he and Joseph were sent to a training camp near Toulouse and then stationed in different parts of south-west France. In three years, they never saw any active service.

It was all a waste of time. He knew how to shoot already because his father had taught him. He loved going on boar hunts with his father and grandfather and their neighbours. Even if they didn't catch a boar, which was often the case, they shot birds, rabbits or hares, so they always came home with something. A gathering of families at one or another of the nearby farms would follow, with tables of food and plenty of wine. He didn't want to march or do all the other exercises he was put through in the army. The country needed to defend itself if there was a war, but this was peacetime and the farm needed him far more than the army.

Away from Danielle, he missed her badly and her letters showed that she missed him. His love for her was as permanent as his love of the land and he wanted to marry her on his return from the army. He was twenty-one by then. She was still only eighteen and her parents wouldn't agree to her marrying before she reached adulthood at twenty-one. Jean-Louis said it was because they wanted as much work out of her as they could get before they let her go, but he had no choice. He had to wait. The wedding took place in 1905 when Jean-Louis was twenty-five and Danielle just twenty-two.

They were married in the church that they attended every Sunday in St Martin des Remparts. It was a warm autumn day and a wedding party followed at Castignac. A fiddler and his group played and sang, while everyone, including his old grandparents, danced. There was cider to drink as well as wine, because the apple crop had been particularly good that year and Jean-Louis's father killed a pig for the celebration. The *monastère* in the dining room, which his grandfather said was as old as the ruined farmhouse, was brought outside and piled with farm food.

Danielle moved to Castignac on her wedding day, bringing her trousseau which included new cotton sheets with their embroidered initials intertwined. They were a present from her parents. Jean-Louis was pleased with the sheets, but less sure about Danielle's parents. They had made sure to extract a promise from their daughter that she would return to help out on their farm from time to time. Jean-Louis put his foot down and said Danielle was needed at her new home and should only go back for visits, not to work.

Everything went well until the day that Jean-Louis needed to visit the agricultural merchant in St Martin des Remparts to buy some new tools. He and his father rose at dawn to do the milking as usual. After breakfast, Jean-Louis saddled one of the four farm horses and set off down the hill to the town. The path was narrow and sloping for most of the way, but it joined the wider road into the town. Jean-Louis was on the wider road when he heard an unfamiliar sound behind him, growing louder.

In seconds, one of the new-fangled petrol cars had roared up and overtaken him with the loud blast of a horn. Jean-Louis had seen few cars in his life and his horse was quite unused to them. With a neigh to match the blast of the car horn, the horse reared, bolted and, despite his frantic efforts to cling on, threw Jean-Louis to the ground. Landing hard, he banged his head and hurt his knee.

A young man, a stranger he had just overtaken on the road, ran to catch up with him. The car disappeared into the distance.

'Are you all right?'

Jean-Louis felt dazed and took his time standing up. 'I've bashed my knee. But where's the horse?'

'Oh, I can see him just ahead. He's grazing as if he'd never thrown you. I'll catch him in a minute. Look, let me help you into this house here.'

Jean-Louis wasn't feeling well enough to protest and he accepted the offer of an arm to lean on as they limped towards a nearby house on the edge of the town. The woman of the house bathed a cut on Jean-Louis's head, bandaged his knee, gave him a bowl of milky coffee and insisted he rest for a while.

'Those new machines are the devil,' the woman said.

'It's the driver who's the devil. I wish I'd caught him, but he was gone,' Jean-Louis said.

He was still feeling shaken, but, rather than being angry with the driver, he was impressed by the speed and power of the car. He would like to drive one, back and forth between Castignac and St Martin des Remparts and elsewhere, to Pamiers or Toulouse.

The young man went out to secure the horse and when he had done so, Jean-Louis thanked him for his help.

'Can you ride?' he said.

'Yes, we have a horse at home.'

'Could you ride my horse back to Castignac and ask for help? I need a cart to take me home.'

'Give me a few minutes to tell the shop where I work that I'll be late,' the young man said, and Jean-Louis nodded.

When the young man returned, there was no need to tell him the whereabouts of Castignac. Everyone knew that. In less than an hour, Henri, one of the twins, arrived with the horse now attached to a cart and Jean-Louis was settled in and driven home, thanking the woman for her care. He limped into the house on Henri's arm and Danielle made him comfortable on a sofa.

Henri was sent off to fetch the doctor. Jean-Louis had a bad headache and Danielle was more worried about his head injury than his knee. The doctor examined Jean-Louis's head and knee and recommended rest, promising to come back in a couple of days.

His parents managed the farm without him, his grandparents now being too old to do much. The twins, almost young men, were well able to help. The headache went, the cut on his head healed and the knee was less painful. Within two weeks, Jean-Louis insisted that he could return to work. He couldn't help a slight limp, but he wouldn't let it slow him down. Only Danielle noticed at first that his mood was different after the accident. There were times when he was down and he was never again as light-hearted as she remembered Jean-Louis to have been. It was as if the accident had diminished him slightly.

Jean-Louis was thirty-four when war broke out. He didn't want to be called up to serve because the farm was resting on his shoulders now. The only help came from the twins, both hard workers in the Lordat way. His grandparents had died not long after his accident and his father had followed suddenly the previous year. He and Danielle lived with Jean-Louis's mother. Nine years of marriage had brought them no children, but they were still hopeful of a family.

When the army and the town hall set up a recruiting desk in St Martin des Remparts in the late summer of 1915, men of certain ages were summoned to join up. Jean-Louis went down there in person to argue his case against being conscripted.

'I can't leave Castignac. The farm work must continue,' he told the recruiting sergeant.

'All right. You're exempt from military service. The army knows that the country has to be fed. But there are three Lordat men at Castignac. If you're Jean-Louis, where are the other two?' the recruiting sergeant said, tapping a list in his hand. He was a portly man who looked unfit and Jean-Louis felt mildly scornful of him. He wouldn't be much good on the battlefield, although a few days behind the plough would soon sort him out.

'They're the twins, my brothers.'

'How old are they?'

'Twenty-six. They live on the farm with me.'

'Send them down to see me.'

'But they're needed on the farm.'

'Don't you know there's a war on? Send them down. And how many horses have you got?' The recruiting sergeant was beginning to sound impatient.

'Four farm horses.'

'We'll take two and leave you two. That's fair, especially as you'll get compensation. Make sure those lads are here this afternoon or I'll be after them,' the recruiting sergeant said, refusing to listen to any more argument.

Jean-Louis was almost as resentful about losing his horses as about losing his brothers to the war. He wasn't surprised, because he had heard rumours of horses being requisitioned, but they were vital to the farm. How could he manage with only two? He went home and told the twins they must go down to the square and sign up. The twins had done military service already, but their eyes lit up at the news. War was an adventure to them after the drudgery of farm work and they would be going to the other side of France for the first time.

Jean-Louis knew that he would have to manage somehow. His mother didn't do much these days, but Danielle was a capable woman. She wore her hair in a bun now and had a sterner manner than the girl he had met years before. For planting and harvesting, he would get help from other farmers or in St Martin des Remparts. He would have to pay people to work for him on a casual basis.

The same recruiting sergeant was on his doorstep a few days later. Danielle had to call Jean-Louis in from a field where he was clearing ditches.

She was panting from running as she came up to him. 'There's a man from the army to see you. He says a trainload of army recruits is on the way from the west and they want to billet some of them here. I didn't like to say yes without asking you, but he wants an answer straightaway.'

Jean-Louis put down his shovel and strode to the farmyard where the recruiting sergeant was waiting, holding the reins of a horse.

'Good morning. We can help, but how many men do you want to billet here and for how long?' he said.

'About twenty, for three or four days. They're on their way to the front, and your two lads and the spare horses will go with them,' was the answer.

The horses weren't spare. They were badly needed on the farm, but Jean-Louis knew the argument was over.

'All right. They can sleep in the old ruin for a few nights. The roof has a few holes in, but they'll be all right, as long as it doesn't rain heavily. We have a couple of spare mattresses, but you'll need to supply more and enough blankets,' Jean-Louis said.

It was agreed that a cartload of mattresses and bedding would arrive in two days' time to be laid out in the ruin. The men would wash at the pump and Danielle would cook up some of her big stews, the kind that she made for occasions, for which the army would pay. The trainload of men was due to arrive in St Martin des Remparts in exactly a week's time, and Jean-Louis and Danielle would be ready for them. At least he wasn't being conscripted. That had been his fear on hearing who was on the doorstep.

Chapter Two

Hébrard

HÉBRARD MONTVAL HAD GROWN up on his parents' farm outside Orthez in the Basses-Pyrénées, where small fields produced crops and cows grazed. He was destined to follow in his parents' footsteps and spend his life on the farm, with the help of his younger brother. There had never been any question of doing anything else, but Hébrard was content with his life. He loved his family and the work on the farm.

War had come as a surprise in August 1914. All able-bodied Frenchmen had to do three years' military service, but, until the start of war, no-one had expected to see action. It was over a generation since the Germans had invaded France. At first, the young men in Orthez hadn't taken much notice of what was happening, but the following year brought them right into the thick of war.

Hébrard was twenty by then. Late on a June afternoon, wheat and corn were rustling in a light summer breeze in the fields. Mountains were just visible in the distance. He had been working on the farm from dawn, tending to the animals and weeding the crops, when he saw his friend Eugène running up to the main gate. Eugène often came to visit, but never at a run these days. Something had happened.

'Have you seen the notice? We've been called up.'

Eugène, out of breath, had started speaking before he even reached Hébrard.

They had been friends since the beginning of their school days. Eugène was slightly built and Hébrard, taller and stronger, had protected him in the playground from the rougher boys. During school holidays, they had roamed around Orthez or played on the farm together, with Eugène helping out with harvesting. He had no brothers and always said that Hébrard was his brother, a feeling that was mutual.

'No, I haven't seen anything. What's going on?'

'There's a notice outside the town hall. We report for training in a week's time.'

'You and me?' Hébrard was astounded and horrified.

'No, not just us. There's a list of everyone about our age. It only went up this afternoon. That's why I came out to tell you. I happened to be passing the town hall just afterwards and a crowd was already collecting.'

Eugène worked for his father, a vintner with a shop and a warehouse in the centre of Orthez. He had been there since leaving school at fourteen and was training to take over the business one day.

An unpleasant feeling grew in the pit of Hébrard's stomach at the news. The papers were full of the war, but he hadn't expected it to draw him in. It was far away, in northern France, much further than he had ever been. The Western Front might almost have been in another country for all it meant to him.

'They want horses too,' Eugène said, and Hébrard looked across to where his favourite horse stood, his head over the stable door. Like him, the horse belonged on the farm, not on a battlefield somewhere.

'I don't want to be a soldier,' Hébrard said to his parents that night, after Eugène had gone.

'We'll miss you on the farm, lad, but you've got to go if you're on the list,' was all his father said. His mother agreed. His parents didn't ask him why he didn't want to go to the front. They were more interested in working out which of their horses they could keep. The two horses on the farm worked hard and neither could easily be spared, but it sounded as if at least one would have to go to war, as well as Hébrard.

A brief spell of training was all that was offered to the conscripted men. Hébrard, Eugène and the other young men of the town spent the next few weeks in the local barracks doing exercises, marching, learning how to obey orders at the double and how to fire a gun. They were warned in no uncertain terms that anyone caught deserting would be shot. Hébrard's family began to manage without him.

Despite his small size, Eugène joined in with the spirit of the training and seemed to look forward to action. Hébrard remained reluctant. He hadn't bothered much with newspapers before, but now he began to read one when he could and he didn't like what he learned. He might have looked as if he would make a good soldier, with his strong build, but he felt none of the anticipation and excitement that the other young men demonstrated, even if much of it was bravado. The feeling in the pit of his stomach that had come with the call-up seemed to be permanently lodged there, like a hard lump.

He tried talking to his parents again, but they cut him off. He had been ordered to go and so he must. They believed in getting on with life and never wasted time on discussing things beyond their control. Hébrard's younger brother, Philippe, was still at school but might have to leave early to work on the farm now that Hébrard was off to war.

Hébrard tried explaining his dread of the war to Eugène. 'It's madness. You haven't been reading the papers like me. Soldiers at the front are being slaughtered like animals. They're stuck in trenches in the ground, surrounded by barbed wire, with shells exploding all the time and there's mud everywhere. They have to go over the top when the order comes and they stand no chance.'

'You're afraid, mate, even though you're such a big lump. Well, we'll have to stick together,' Eugène said.

Hébrard looked down at his friend. 'Of course I'm afraid. Aren't you?'

'A bit, of course, but… I'm not a coward.'

'I'm not a coward either. I just don't want to be blown up.'

Eugène shrugged his shoulders. 'Nor do I, but what can we do about it?'

'I don't know yet. My parents don't understand. They just think I've got to get on with it. Anyway, I can't hide at home because the authorities will come looking for me and I don't want to get my parents into trouble. But there's nowhere else I can go.'

In early October, the order came to assemble at the railway station for the journey to the front. Hébrard joined the others on the chosen morning. In the weeks since first hearing of the call-up, he had grown determined to avoid it. He would run away when the chance came and he took an extra change of clothing with him to make it easier to escape detection. He had thought that far, but he had no idea of when and where to run and what he would do afterwards. He couldn't imagine becoming a tramp, like the old man sometimes seen in Orthez, homeless and begging.

His parents came to the station to see him off. Eugène's parents were there too. The station was crowded with soldiers and their families milling around. The soldiers were cheerful, even raucous, but Hébrard noticed tense faces amongst the families in the crowd.

The train was panting in the station and the soldiers climbed on. They were going across France in an easterly direction first, before travelling north to the battlefields. It was a long journey from Orthez and Hébrard felt the dread mounting as the train puffed its way eastwards. He had said goodbye to his family not knowing when, if ever, he would return. He had never before been further than Pau, the first place they had passed through, but the train had gone on to Tarbes, Montréjeau, Saint-Girons and Foix, before turning north to Pamiers. They had stayed within sight of the mountains most of the way and he could still see them now in the distance. In the early evening, they had almost reached the town of St Martin des Remparts, where they were to wait for a train which would take them further east and then turn north.

Hébrard had grown up seeing mountains on the horizon and was reassured by their presence as he neared the end of the first stage of the journey to the Western Front. The Pyrenees had framed his life, varying with the seasons. He had never crossed them into Spain. He had never wanted to, but he needed them to be within sight.

He and his infantry company were on a special troop train and had picked up other groups of soldiers on the way. Despite the chatter and nervous laughter around them, Hébrard had fallen asleep as the afternoon had drawn on. After a while, Eugène, seated next to him, gave him a nudge.

'I think we're nearly there!'

Hébrard's eyes were closed, but he was awake now. He grunted and Eugène nudged him again.

'Come on, sleepyhead, we're in St Martin des Remparts. Remember they said we'd be here for a couple of days?'

The train, panting heavily, had drawn into a small station, with a single platform and modest station house. It was late in the afternoon. Through the clouds of smoke from the engine, the men could see soldiers awaiting them. Curious civilians were peering into windows and young girls were waving and smiling.

'Everybody out!'

The sergeant who had accompanied them on the journey was striding through the train, shouting his order. The soldiers tumbled onto the platform and formed neat lines in response to another bark from him.

'No barracks here, so you'll be billeted with families.' Another sergeant awaited them, waving a list in his hand. Hébrard listened to instructions, hoping that he would be billeted with Eugène.

'Right, the next lot are on the farm at Castignac. I want twenty of you.'

The sergeant from their regiment motioned a group of the men forward and Eugène went with them, pulling Hébrard along with him. Shouldering their backpacks, led by the sergeant, the group of twenty men began to march in formation. Hébrard glimpsed a large church with a steeple and a market square off to one side of their route as they pressed on. In a few minutes, they had passed through the town. Leaving it behind, they crossed a stone bridge raised high above a river. The last part of the journey was uphill and he was out of breath as they arrived before an imposing farmhouse of two storeys, built of yellow stone.

It was still warm enough in October for geraniums to be flowering at all the windows. The farmhouse was grander than his own home. He was beginning to expect a comfortable bed for the night when the sergeant, who had gone into the house, emerged with the farmer and ordered them to move on.

'Of course, it'll be outbuildings for the likes of us,' Hébrard muttered to Eugène as they marched off again.

'What do you expect? You're not an officer!'

They didn't have to go far. About a hundred metres beyond the farmhouse, they arrived at a ruin, a big pile of a place, built around a courtyard, with a pigeon loft on one side. The farmer led them through a doorway into a large room. It was still light and Hébrard could see a blackened fireplace, with empty shelves hanging askew on either side. The ruin had been made ready for them, after a fashion. Old mattresses and cushions, each with a folded blanket, were laid out on the floor. The farmer explained that there were more in adjacent rooms.

'Here you are, men,' the sergeant said, as the farmer left them to it. 'You've got the real farmhouse, not the posh new one. There's a pump for washing in the yard. There's a latrine outside or feel free to water the fields.'

He smirked at his attempt at a joke, but the soldiers, newly conscripted and barely out of their training, were unimpressed and stared blankly at him.

'Make yourselves at home. You're to go to the kitchen at the back of the house at seven o'clock for a meal. Take your plates, cups and irons! They might give you some candles, but don't burn yourselves to death tonight. I'll be back at sunrise to make sure you're up.'

The sergeant disappeared and the soldiers set about bagging mattresses. There were just about enough, if some were shared.

'He'll have something cushy lined up, leaving the floor for us,' Hébrard said to Eugène.

It was getting dark by the time they stumbled over to the kitchen at the back of the main house, where they formed a queue. One by one they went in, holding out the army issue tin plate they had received before departure that morning. A skinny woman, who smiled at them in a brisk way that told them not to linger, served each soldier with a ladleful of stew from an enormous pot. Hunks of bread accompanied the meal. Hébrard noticed a baby playing on the floor.

In the fading evening light, the men sat around outside the kitchen where they could, squatting on piles of wood or sitting on the ground by the wall, eating the stew, mopping up the remains with their bread and holding out their tin cups when the skinny woman came out with a large jug of red wine. The wine was her gift to wish them well, and they raised their cups to her. They finished the meal with apples from a basket she offered to them.

They washed their plates, mugs and cutlery under the pump, which, after some effort on their part, gushed with clear water. One of the soldiers, Robert, who was also from Orthez and had been to school with Hébrard and Eugène, was a bit of a clown and started splashing everyone. Others joined in and soon everyone was flicking water around.

Later, they sat on their mattresses talking while the candles the woman had given them lasted. Lying on his mattress in the dark, after the last candle had guttered and gone out, Hébrard felt comforted by the quiet. Apart from the sounds of animals, he was used to silence and dark at night on the farm at home. He pictured his parents and his younger brother going to bed and wished he were there with them. He had never been away from home before. For the first time in his life, he missed his family. Nevertheless, with a pillow made out of his backpack, he slept well that night, fortified by the food and wine. He woke only once or twice on the hoot of an owl, even though the straw mattress was too thin to protect him from the hardness of the flagstone floor beneath it.

The sergeant appeared early and bellowed to get them out of bed. Hungry again, the men queued at the kitchen door and were passed more hunks of bread. Spooning jam from a large bowl onto the bread, they ate, drinking milky coffee which the skinny woman poured from a large jug into their tin cups.

On a pleasant autumn day, war seemed a long way off. The sergeant put them through exercises and marches of the kind they had experienced during their training, and the morning passed quickly. Lunch was more stew, then apples and cheese, washed down with red wine.

The farmer came to talk to them, introducing himself and saying he hoped they were comfortable enough in their makeshift quarters.

'From what I've heard, this is better accommodation than you'll be getting at the front,' he said.

He wasn't tall, but strongly built and, from his weather-beaten look, used to an outdoor life. When he asked where the soldiers were from, Hébrard spoke up.

'Most of us are from Orthez, in the Basses-Pyrénées.'

'You've come a long way,' Jean-Louis said. 'What were you doing before the army?'

The young men answered that they had been shop assistants, clerks or labourers.

'I'm from a farm, a bit like yours. My parents have to manage without me,' Hébrard said.

'Oh, so you're a farmer's lad, are you? It'll be the same here. My two brothers are going with you and two of our horses. We're going to be shorthanded.'

Hearing those words, a plan began to form in Hébrard's mind. As Jean-Louis moved on, the sergeant arrived to tell them that they could go into St Martin des Remparts for the afternoon.

'I want no complaints about your behaviour. And you're to be back by seven o'clock sharp if you want anything to eat tonight!'

The men strolled down to the town after their lunch, scattering into small groups. Hébrard and Eugène stuck together.

'I didn't want to come. I'm not going on the next train,' Hébrard said, once he and Eugène were out of earshot of the others.

'You must. You know the penalty if you don't. They'll shoot you for a deserter without thinking twice about it. Don't you remember they told us that?' Eugène said.

Hébrard shrugged. 'What's the difference? We'll be shot in the trenches if we go there.'

Eugène looked at him closely. 'Like I said before, I feel nervous too. Dad's always said that I'll get married and have a family and that one day I'll inherit the business. I want to travel, see a bit of the world, have some excitement, but I never thought it would be like this,' he said.

'I don't want any excitement. I just wanted to stay on the farm,' Hébrard said.

'Yes, but we haven't got any choice. The Germans should be sent packing. That's our job. It would be shameful to be a deserter.'

Eugène spoke sharply, as if regretting his earlier sympathetic tone, but nothing that he could say would change Hébrard's mind.

The town of St Martin des Remparts was different from Orthez, although of a similar size. Both places had a river and a wide stone bridge and narrow residential streets, but Hébrard and Eugène had never seen anything like the picturesque wooden colonnade which ran all the way around the central square of St Martin des Remparts, providing shelter from the sun and rain. Behind the colonnade were shops and bars. On one side of the square stood the church they had glimpsed the night before, with its soaring spire, easily visible from their billet at Castignac.

The other men, led by the clownish Robert, were busy chatting to the girls who had gathered round them. After sharing a bottle of cider, which they bought from a bar, Eugène and Hébrard looked around the main square. With little money in their pockets, they couldn't afford to spend more, so they wandered into the church. It was bigger than the church in Orthez and all the walls inside were painted in bright colours. Hébrard thought of his parents, who were regular churchgoers. He had been brought up as a good Catholic, but he wasn't sure what he thought about religion these days. What kind of God allowed wars?

Leaving the town alongside a canal and passing a mill, they followed a footpath to the river that they had crossed the previous day on the way to the farm and again on the way into the town. They walked alongside the river to the enormous stone bridge which now reared above them. Sandy banks edged the water. It was shallow in places and they heard the sound of the river rushing over stones. A large white bird, which Hébrard identified as an egret, flapped slowly past. They took a path up to the bridge, crossed the river and walked back up to the farm, talking about their lives at home. Hébrard didn't mention the train journey again. He was trying to block it from his mind. As long as they were in St Martin des Remparts, they were safe.

The next morning brought the same routine: an early breakfast, with exercising and marching afterwards, and the reward of free time in the afternoon.

'I want to go up to that pigeon loft and see the mountains. It should be a good view and it's a last chance, because we'll lose them when we travel north the day after tomorrow,' Eugène said after lunch. The sergeant had told them that morning that they were travelling in two days' time.

'Are you coming up with me?' he asked.

'All right,' Hébrard said.

He had spoken little that day and his face was pale and set. He was busy thinking about what to do.

Chapter Three

Hébrard

Eugène and Hébrard invited the other soldiers to join their visit to the pigeon loft, but no-one else was interested. They were all going back into the town that afternoon. Local girls had clustered round them on the previous day and they wanted to meet them again while they could.

The two friends mounted the wooden staircase that clung to the wall of the ruin. A hinged door at the top opened with some effort and fell with a clatter to one side. It was dark inside the loft except where pigeonholes, appearing in a pattern around the walls, let in light. Inching their way across a boarded floor, they struggled with rusty fastenings and flung protesting shutters back against the outside of the walls.

Light flooded in. They were facing the mountains on a clear autumn day. It was too late in the year for any snow and the mountains were merely some shades darker than the pale blue sky, but they looked more impressive from this height. Hébrard and Eugène gazed at them for a long time, not speaking. Dark green hills were ranged below and beneath them were the rooftops of the town.

'It reminds me of home,' Hébrard said. 'We're not so far away yet.' He felt safe with the mountains in sight.

'We will be soon,' Eugène said.

Hébrard looked at his friend, gauging his reaction to what he wanted to say.

'Remember what the farmer said yesterday? Both his younger brothers are going to the front with us. He's going to be short of labour.'

'So is your father. So is mine, especially as I'm the only son,' Eugène said.

'I could work here and no-one would know. When the war's over, I'd go back home,' Hébrard said.

'Are you quite mad? They'd find you here,' Eugène said. 'Stop talking like this, Hébrard. You can't stay here. You must come with us. It won't seem so bad once we get stuck into it.'

Hébrard was aware of his friend's alarm, not only at the possibility of his desertion, but at being abandoned by his protector. He sighed. Things were different now.

'How do you know? I've told you, it's going to be hell,' he said. The lump that he had first felt on hearing of the call-up now felt bigger than ever.

They turned away from the window, with pigeons fluttering and cooing around them. Crossing the loft, Hébrard opened shutters on the other side, from where he could see the new farmhouse, its roof below them. He looked at fields of stubble where the harvest had been taken in and the small herd of cows that the farmer owned.

The floor was covered in pigeon droppings which crunched under their boots. Eugène brought out the knife that he carried in his pocket. It had a wooden handle where the blade nested and he flicked it open now.

Slowly and carefully, Eugène Vigneron began to carve his name in the plaster. Hébrard watched, noticing how his friend held his tongue between his teeth as he concentrated. Hébrard liked being in the pigeon loft, away from the other soldiers. It was peaceful and the war, brought closer on their journey, seemed further away. Time seemed to stop while Eugène was carving. Some of his letters were uneven and straggled, but he didn't abandon the cursive writing that they had been taught at school. He added his date of birth and his town, Orthez. He paused for a moment to inspect his handiwork and then added *soldat*. The word "soldier" described Eugène best now.

Hébrard glanced out of the window facing the farmhouse. He liked seeing the warm, yellow stone, tiled roof and red geraniums of what the farmer and his family called the new house. It wasn't that new in 1915, because he had seen the date of 1860 high on its front wall, but it seemed solid and reassuring when they were threatened with war, the last home they would know before the trenches.

He knew without being told why Eugène was leaving his name and details. If he were to die, there would be some record, even if no-one knew it was there. Plaster was almost as good as stone, and the bare plaster was asking to be marked.

It was even quieter in the pigeon loft than down below, apart from the soft cooing of pigeons and the flutter of wings. Eugène carved in silence and Hébrard watched him patiently. Away from the other soldiers, they could almost forget why they were here.

'Not bad,' Hébrard said, when he had finished. 'Let me have a go.'

Eugène passed him the knife and Hébrard carved his name. His letters were even and perfectly formed: Hébrard Montval.

'You're quite an artist. Your signature is better than mine,' Eugène said.

Hébrard handed back the knife.

'Aren't you going to add anything?' Eugène said.

'No. My name's enough and you've put Orthez. I don't want to say I'm a soldier.'

It rained hard the following day and the men were cooped up in the farmhouse with little to do. The sergeant put them through indoor exercises in the ruin, but an air of boredom persisted. Hébrard told the others how he and Eugène had carved their names with a knife on the bare plaster wall of the pigeon loft.

'Let's go!' Antoine said. He was one of several local lads who had joined them. Others, including Robert, echoed his shout and picked up their knives.

Hébrard and Eugène watched as over twenty men climbed the wooden staircase and disappeared into the loft. They followed, to see what would happen. Just as they had, the men opened the shutters and gazed at the mountains.

'I wish we could go that way, to Spain,' one of them said, and the others agreed.

They examined Hébrard's and Eugène's signatures. One by one, they took knives from their pockets and began to carve their names or initials, standing in a row around the four walls of the loft, intent on their work. It was something to do and a rare opportunity to make their mark unseen and not be reprimanded for it. Afterwards, Hébrard examined names, initials, dates, names of girlfriends and places, even an attempt at a gun.

Jumping up and stretching out his arms, Robert tried to catch the pigeons, but he was no match for them. They fluttered lazily out of reach or out of the loft. There was nothing else to do and soon the clatter of boots was heard on the staircase as the men left. Hébrard shut the door carefully behind him, and he and Eugène followed the others down.

It was their last full day at Castignac. They were going north on the train early the following morning and Hébrard had decided that he must make his move beforehand. Otherwise, he would be caught up in the war and any chance of escape would be lost. Yet he hesitated. Going to war now seemed to be the easy thing to do. He would simply be following the crowd. Not going meant taking action, separating himself from everyone else, even if it was the cowardly thing to do.

He could imagine staying here at Castignac, working on the farm, but first he must get away before the soldiers left. He would return when they had gone. He would be taking an enormous risk because, as Eugène had said, he might well be found and shot, but he was sure he would be giving himself a better chance of staying alive than if he went to the front. He was sorry not to confide in Eugène, but his friend would only try and make him stay with the regiment. He was on his own now and he was no longer Eugène's protector.

He had to be up early in order to make his getaway at dawn, so he hardly slept on that last night at the billet. Eventually, he guessed from a change in the darkness that dawn was approaching, and he rose from the thin mattress on the ground. He had slept in his underwear, wrapped in the blanket, and his uniform was neatly folded at the end of the mattress. It was still too dark to see properly.

Trying not to wake Eugène, who was sleeping soundly next to him, he slipped on a pair of moleskin trousers and a cotton shirt and wool jacket that he had brought with him in his pack. Fortunately, the weather was still warm. He crouched down to put on his boots and tied the laces. The boots were army issue, but he had no other shoes with him. He had a few coins and had saved a hunk of bread from the meal on the previous evening, stuffing it with an apple into his jacket pocket. He had nothing else apart from what he stood up in. He left his army issue pack on the bed.

He was ready to go. He moved slowly and quietly away from the bed, wishing he had slept near the open door, where a faint lightness beckoned. He began to creep towards the light, edging around any obstacle. Halfway across the rows of sleeping men, he trod on something soft. There was a yelp and he held his breath, expecting someone to grab him and everyone to wake and realise what he was doing, but whoever it was merely turned over and went back to sleep. None of the others stirred.

Hébrard reached the doorway at last and slipped into the courtyard. There was enough light now for him to make out the shape of the building with its sagging roof. Dawn was coming, the sun would be up soon and he needed to be on his way. He set off in the opposite direction from the town, looking for a path he had seen in the daylight and that he hoped led north to other farms and villages. He stumbled around in the fields beyond the farmyard until he came across the path. Taking a deep breath, he began to stride away. No-one called after him, but he was pursued by the sudden, harsh bray of a donkey, like mocking laughter. He was risking his life by deserting, yet he felt safer now. The lump was still there, but it was shrinking now.

Hébrard traipsed through the countryside for days, telling the time by the sun. Feeling hunted, although no-one was obviously chasing him, he kept on the move, eating what he could find in the way of vegetables and fruit. Apples and pears were plentiful, and he resorted to pulling up such root vegetables as he found still in the fields. Once he was chased away by an irate farmer. Dogs, guarding farmhouses and cottages, barked angrily and were a constant nuisance. At night, if he was lucky, he found an empty barn to sleep in, otherwise he was out in the open, in autumn nights that were chilly but not cold. He was exhausted by the time darkness came, because he was constantly on the move and so he slept well.

He swam in rivers to keep clean and appeared briefly in markets where he was able to steal food like bread and even one day a fruit tart, without being noticed. He could almost hear his parents telling him not to steal, but he needed to, once he had spent his few coins on bread in a village bakery. He drank from village drinking fountains and streams, and people were kind without being too curious when thirst drove him to ask for water. He was glad that October was a mild month, because he didn't have a winter coat, only his jacket, which was beginning to seem too light. He was hungry much of the time, but at least he didn't have to face the winter cold or the trenches. He wondered where Eugène was and whether he had been surprised to find him gone.

He missed his family and the farm at home. Would his parents hear that he had deserted? They would worry about him, but he couldn't try to go back there. It would get them into trouble. Better for them to say to the authorities with a clear conscience that they had no idea where he was. He would write to them when he could.

In the meantime, he was quite alone, far from home and not even amongst strangers. He didn't like it much, but at least he wasn't going to war. His plan was to stay away from Castignac for several days, longer than it would take for the soldiers to leave and anyone who was looking for him to give up. Then he would go back and plead with the farmer to take him on. After losing his two brothers to the army, the farmer would need help.

He counted the days by remembering where he had slept each night, calculating at one point that he had passed four nights on the road, then five, then seven. Deciding to return to Castignac after a vagabond week, he realised that he was lost. Signposts had ceased to point to St Martin des Remparts and instead gave directions for farms and villages he had never heard of. In the end, feeling stupid, he was reduced to asking someone the way, explaining that he had taken a wrong path. Fortunately the farmer he asked knew the area well and was able to tell him where to go.

Hébrard found Castignac at last. Approaching the house, he remembered arriving with Eugène and the other soldiers, but all was quiet now. They had gone a week ago. He stood for a moment before announcing himself. There was no choice but to see the farmer if he didn't want to die in a ditch somewhere. He only hoped that the farmer wouldn't arrest him and turn him over to the army. He couldn't go back to his own home as he had no money for a journey and didn't want to imperil his parents. He went round to the kitchen at the back of the house, looking for the farmer's wife.

She was there, with the baby. She seemed a bit taken aback, but not afraid, at the sudden appearance of a strange man. He was aware that he must look unkempt, but he had managed a swim in the river that morning, so at least he was clean and didn't smell.

'Are you the one they were looking for the other day?' the farmer's wife said when he had explained himself. 'The army came up here asking for someone, but the name escapes me. Anyway, so many soldiers were staying here last week that I couldn't tell one from another.'

'It was probably me they were after. I'm here to see the farmer because I'm looking for work,' Hébrard said. There was no point in pretending anything, and her manner wasn't hostile.

'Oh, you'll have to wait outside, or you can go and find the farmer, if you like. He's out there in one of the fields. If you're any good, he could do with some help now his brothers have gone.'

At least she didn't seem inclined to tell the authorities that the deserter had turned up. She pointed out of the window. Hébrard could see someone in the distance, but his eyes were drawn back to the food on the kitchen table. He hadn't eaten that day and it was already mid-morning. She noticed his glance and took pity on him, handing him a good slice of meat pie from the larder. He thanked her and was already starting to wolf it down as he left.

He trudged off into the fields. There were plenty of jobs to be done on a farm in the early autumn. It was a mild, almost summery day, and his hopes rose as he approached the farmer, who was mending a fence. It made it easier that they had spoken the week before, when Hébrard had told him about the farm near Orthez where he had grown up. He could hope to be remembered.

'I'm one of the soldiers who was billeted here last week. Remember I spoke to you? I'm looking for farm work. If I can stay here, I'll work for my keep and nothing more.'

The farmer downed his tools and looked closely at Hébrard.

'I remember you. You're a farmer's boy, aren't you? The army were looking for someone the other day when they came up here. I didn't know who, but I hadn't seen anyone.'

The farmer looked about ten years older than Hébrard. He had a hard face, and Hébrard guessed he wasn't easy-going but would be unafraid.

'I'm Hébrard Montval from Orthez. I couldn't go with them,' he said.

He didn't try to explain why he had deserted and the farmer didn't ask.

'Jean-Louis Lordat. I need help with the farm now that my brothers have gone off to the front. There'll soon be winter planting to do. I can handle the cows on my own, but milking and seeing they're fed takes time from other necessary jobs.'

'I can see to the cows and the other animals. I can plough as well. I was used to that at home. Our farm is like yours.'

Hébrard had had a good look around the farm in the days he had stayed there and he knew what it produced.

'I can't let Castignac be neglected. It's our livelihood. No-one will see an extra hand, in the normal course of things. Only my wife is here with me now that my brothers have gone and she can be trusted to hold her tongue.'

Hébrard was desperate. 'I'll stay here all the time. No-one'll see me.'

'All right,' Jean-Louis said slowly. 'I'll give you a try as you're a farmer's lad. There's a cottage you can have, but keep out of the way of strangers and stay out of the town. The authorities need to understand that farms have to keep going. I don't expect the army will be back looking for you again and I'm not going to turn you in. If they find out you're here, I hope they'll have the sense to keep quiet about it. Now you can help me with this fence and then I'll tell Danielle to lay an extra place for lunch.'

With a sense of relief, Hébrard took the saw held out to him. He worked hard on the fence that day, sawing and sharpening posts, banging them into the ground and securing barbed wire between them. During the days following, he gladly took on any work that Jean-Louis gave him. Apart from mending fences and clearing ditches, there were the animals to see to and the preparation of the ground for winter crops by burning stubble and later spreading manure and fertiliser.

Chapter Four

Hébrard

Hébrard and Jean-Louis started work at dawn every morning by milking the cows and filling churns with the creamy liquid. What the farm didn't need for its own use and for the weekly market stall that Danielle had made her own was sold to a local dairy.

The farm was doing well, except for a shortage of labour. Hébrard was pleased to see modern machinery: a harrow for preparing the ground, a plough, a sower for casting seed and a reaper for cutting the crops. The two remaining horses shared the work of pulling the machines. As days passed, he began to think that he had fallen on his feet.

Hébrard ate with the Lordats, who included Jean-Louis's mother. The family attended church on Sundays and after that Jean-Louis went back to work. Hébrard lay low on Sunday mornings, planting and tending a vegetable garden around the cottage and doing odd jobs.

He had only the clothes he stood up in and dared not go into the town to buy more, so he wore castoffs that had belonged to Jean-Louis, which Danielle produced from the ragbag for him. She even found him an old coat when winter came. Jean-Louis wouldn't let Hébrard work just for his keep and paid him a small wage, saying he couldn't afford more.

The orchard at Castignac produced a good crop the year that Hébrard arrived and he helped to pick late apples. Using an old cider press, he made cider under Danielle's instruction, loading the fruit and turning the handle to press the juice out of the apples, then siphoning it into wooden barrels to ferment before transferring it to bottles.

The cider sold well at Danielle's market stall, alongside her ham and sausage, cheese and butter, jams and pickles, as well as pies and cakes when she had time to make them. She also took live hens to the market in a small cage she kept for the purpose. Her stall was an important source of income for the farm. Hébrard gave her the produce from his vegetable patch, both for the stall or to use in cooking.

Hébrard rarely saw anyone apart from Jean-Louis and Danielle, and felt as if he were in hiding, but at least he was alive and free. No-one had a telephone, so he wrote to his family in his careful handwriting, telling them where he was and asking them to reply to M. Lordat, as his own name on the envelope would give him away. His family would have been worried by any reports that he had deserted and he could trust them not to betray him.

His parents didn't read or write, but his brother had been to school and he wrote back, addressing the envelope as directed. Jean-Louis brought the letter back from the post office in St Martin des Remparts.

10ᵗʰ December 1915

Dear Hébrard,

We've been waiting all this time to hear from you. Mother says why didn't you go to the front like Eugène and the other lads? She saw his mother the other day and heard about how proud she is of him.

Don't come back here yet, because the army's been snooping around. We told them we don't know where you are.

Nothing much has changed here, but we have more to do without your help.

Your brother, Philippe

It was the first letter Hébrard had ever received and he read it carefully several times. He replied, not trying to explain himself, simply telling them about his life now. They would understand that, even if they didn't know why he had deserted.

In the late autumn, Jean-Louis and Hébrard planted winter vegetables: potatoes, carrots, onions and beetroots. Hébrard dared not try to go home for Christmas, so he stayed at Castignac. In January, there was ploughing to do, before planting wheat, maize and lentils. Jean-Louis and Hébrard took turns in ploughing with the carthorses. It was heavy work.

The two meadows were full of wildflowers in the spring, including hedge bedstraw, yarrow, yellow rattle, clover, stitchwort, speedwell, chalk milkwort, gentians, poppies and orchids. Hébrard knew them all. Wildflowers grew among the crops as well, and he spent much of his time hoeing and weeding. Jean-Louis and Hébrard cut the meadows in early June and left the grass to wither before stacking it and then storing it in the barn, for winter fodder for the animals.

The ripened wheat and maize were golden in the fields and the lentils were ready by July. Long summer days were spent harvesting. Everyone came to help, including Danielle, who left little Jacquot with her mother. Her brother Joseph and the rest of her family came from the neighbouring farm, in exchange for the Lordats' help with their harvest. The reaper cut the crops and they were left to dry. The lentils went to the local market and the wheat was later threshed to release the grain, which Jean-Louis sold to a flour mill. The wheat straw and maize became winter fodder.

Hébrard understood the rhythm of the farming year and worked hard, conscious that the absence of the twins risked lower yields at Castignac now. He couldn't make up for the loss of two men, but his family farm near Orthez would also be suffering from the war, now that he had left. Farms all over the country were in the same position.

Little Jacquot was walking by then and getting into everything he shouldn't, but one morning he was ill with a temperature. He was so hot and distressed that day and during the night that the following morning Jean-Louis saddled a horse and rode into the town to fetch the doctor. He was back fairly soon, saying the doctor was busy but would come later. When he did arrive, with his pony and trap, the doctor diagnosed scarlet fever. There were other cases in the town.

Jacquot required constant nursing and Danielle hardly left his bedside, while Jean-Louis's mother did the cooking for everyone.

'How is Jacquot?' Hébrard asked every morning as he arrived for breakfast and again at lunchtime, but he never seemed to be any better.

One morning brought the news that everyone had been dreading. Jacquot had died during the night. It was a terrible blow and gloom settled over Castignac, but neither Jean-Louis nor Danielle gave into their grief. Farm work didn't allow them to falter.

A sad little funeral followed and Jacquot was buried in the churchyard in St Martin des Remparts. At home, Danielle whisked his baby things out of sight and his name was scarcely mentioned after that.

Jean-Louis would pass Hébrard a newspaper from time to time. Nothing he read or heard about the war persuaded him that he had made a mistake in deserting. Men continued to die in great numbers in the trenches. He was glad to be so far away from the front. In lonely moments, when he missed his family and his home, at least he felt safe.

That year, 1916, after the Battle of Verdun, a man on a bicycle arrived at Castignac, out of breath from the steep climb. He handed over a telegram for Jean-Louis's mother and sped off down the hill. It told her of the death of Henri at Verdun from an exploding shell. After his twin Paul died in the Battle of Passchendaele, the following year, a similar telegram arrived at Castignac. Jean-Louis and his mother didn't say much and carried on working in the usual way.

Hébrard noticed Jean-Louis had become more taciturn since the loss of his son and that he could be short-tempered. Clearing ditches one day, Hébrard broke the handle of a fork. Jean-Louis uttered a stream of harsh words.

'It was my fault. I was trying to get a root out of the bank. I wonder if he wishes me gone and the twins back here,' Hébrard said to Danielle when she noticed the fork awaiting repair.

'He's lucky to have you. We couldn't manage on our own,' Danielle said briskly.

Whether or not they knew of his presence on the farm, the authorities never pursued Hébrard. When the war ended, over three years after his arrival at Castignac, Jean-Louis poured a measure of cognac for everyone and Castignac celebrated the victory. Hébrard raised his glass to peace along with the others, but he felt an extra relief. He didn't know if he might still be caught and shot, but he felt he was no longer a deserter. He even wondered whether Eugène might one day come and see him, perhaps on his way back from the front. Eugène had known what he was going to do.

He was at last free to go back home because it was unlikely that the army would be pursuing him now. The question was whether he wanted to. He liked Castignac and his work there. Jean-Louis was not much given to talking, but Hébrard got along well with him on the whole and liked Danielle.

'I hope you're not going back to Orthez now the war is over,' she said to him one day, in her direct way. 'Jean-Louis says the farm has never been so well-run and we'd like you to stay.'

They were in the kitchen having breakfast.

'I don't know how I would have managed without the twins, if you hadn't turned up,' Jean-Louis said, sawing off a hunk of bread and spreading it with butter and jam.

'I like it here, but it's a long time since I've seen my family,' Hébrard said.

'No need to decide now. Think it over,' Jean-Louis said, and Hébrard nodded.

Then something happened which made the decision for him. A letter arrived from his brother a week later. Seeing the December date on the postmark, Hébrard was surprised because he normally wrote only after New Year.

20ᵗʰ December 1918

Dear Hébrard,
I'm sorry to write with bad news. Eugène was killed in the war and you will want to know. His mother said he

survived until almost the end but was caught by a sniper's bullet trying to rescue an injured soldier. He died at once. There is to be a memorial to the war dead in Orthez, and his name will be inscribed. He has no brothers to take over the business, which is a problem. Mother says that his parents are proud of him.

When are you coming home? You're needed here.

Your brother, Philippe

He was stung by the last sentence about Eugène. Would his parents have preferred him to die like his friend and be commemorated on the war memorial in Orthez? Although the end of the war had brought him relief, the news of Eugène's death caused his desertion to prey on his mind again. He would never forget his friend.

If he hadn't deserted, would he have fought by Eugène's side? Could he have saved him in some way, just as he had at school, so that they would both now be alive and could have gone back to Orthez together on the train, arriving in triumph to pick up the threads of their old lives? That was nonsense. He knew no returning soldiers to talk to about the war, but the newspapers that made their way to Castignac from time to time told him that it was more likely that they would both have been killed.

He remembered Eugène trying to persuade him to carry on, to go on the train to the north. His friend had been more frightened than he had admitted to. He himself had deserted out of fear, even though at the time he had said it was about staying alive and had made it seem like the sensible thing to do. Eugène had wanted Hébrard's company on the journey and at the front because they were friends and would be in it together. Eugène hadn't been independent enough to stay away from the war and Hébrard had let him down.

The news of Eugène's death showed Hébrard that his new life was no longer a stopgap, but a permanent change. He couldn't go back to Orthez, where not only would Eugène's name always be on the war memorial, but the names of other boys as well, and he would be known as a deserter. He would let his brother inherit the family farm. It was a sacrifice he would have to make out of shame for what he had done.

He was leading a different life now, not the one he had been born to, even if he was still on a farm. He was a man, twenty-three years old, not a boy anymore. He wouldn't run away again.

Hébrard kept his feelings to himself. Jean-Louis was a decent farmer, but his conversation was mainly about the farm. Danielle was more sympathetic, but Hébrard didn't tell her about Eugène. She was expecting another baby in a few months' time and Jacquot was never mentioned these days. Jean-Louis was pleased and hoping for a son to carry on the farm in his name. The Lordats had taken Hébrard in and that was enough. He wouldn't bother them with his troubles.

Hébrard remained at Castignac, feeling safe enough after the war to walk into St Martin des Remparts on a cold January evening in 1919. It was his first visit since the afternoon he had spent with Eugène four years previously. He wandered around the central square. The shops were closed, but he had money in his pocket and looked in shop windows, thinking he needed to buy some clothes soon. Jean-Louis's cast-offs were wearing thin and he had saved his pay.

It was dark in the square and few people were about. Finishing his tour, he noticed a small bar with lights on and hovered outside, wondering if he would be recognised as a deserter and denounced if he went in. But it looked homely and he decided to risk it. It was time to stop hiding.

The bar inside was dimly lit. He almost came straight out again because the few people there looked up at his entrance and he felt he was intruding. It was like stepping into someone's private home. As he hesitated at the door, the barman held out a hand in a welcoming gesture, beckoning him to come in. Hébrard noticed that he had only one arm. The other sleeve of his shirt was empty and tucked into his waist. That empty sleeve and the welcoming gesture made him decide to stay for a glass of red wine.

Hébrard took his glass and joined a table of two men when one of them indicated he could sit at a spare seat there. They were about his age.

'We haven't seen you here before,' one of them said.

'No. I work at Castignac. I don't get down here often.'

'Oh, Jean-Louis' place. We know him,' the other man said. 'He must need help after losing the twins in the war.'

'That's right. I've only got one pair of hands, but I do what I can,' Hébrard said.

'You're not from round here.'

The first man was scrutinising him and Hébrard felt uncomfortable under his gaze. It wasn't friendly, merely curious.

'I grew up on a farm near Orthez,' he said.

He didn't have an explanation ready and hoped they wouldn't pester him with questions.

'I'm Raymond and he's Pierre, my brother,' the first man said, gesturing towards the barman.

'I'm Guy and Pierre is my brother too,' the second man said, smiling.

'Oh, I see. You're all brothers,' Hébrard said, introducing himself. They were playing with him, but they seemed harmless.

'Seven boys in the family means seven brothers,' Raymond said.

Guy ran a building company and Raymond, who was younger, worked for him. They were having a drink together after work. With their curiosity satisfied, Hébrard felt he had passed a test, but knew that he must tread carefully. Working for Jean-Louis would go a long way towards guaranteeing him acceptance in the town, but some people would be disparaging of deserters. The war might be over, but it wasn't forgotten.

Pierre had lost his left arm in the war, but he didn't make much of it. Hébrard was impressed by his dexterity in serving drinks and liked his welcoming manner. When he came into the town again on the following Saturday, to buy clothes at one of the shops on the square, he stopped at the bar for a cup of coffee.

That winter, as days were short, he formed the habit of visiting the bar once a week after work. His cottage was bare and comfortless, and he hadn't troubled to make it into a home of any kind. He sometimes made a log fire on cold evenings, but he didn't cook there and had to rely on oil lamps or candles for lighting. The visits to the bar made a welcome change.

He talked to Guy and Raymond but found Pierre friendlier. He was the youngest of the seven brothers. Two had died in the war and their names were going to be on the town memorial. Guy's small building company employed Raymond and the other two brothers.

'Why didn't you follow your brothers into the building trade?' Hébrard said in the course of getting to know Pierre, surprised he should have taken a different path.

'It wasn't necessary, with so many of them! They take up all the work that's going and I'm free to do what I like. I found a job as the barman here at the age of fourteen and never looked back. It was just as well, because I wouldn't have been able to do any building work like this, but I came back to the bar with no trouble,' Pierre said, tapping his empty sleeve. He maintained that a barman with one hand was almost as good as one with two hands.

Pierre knew all about the goings on in St Martin des Remparts from his customers and had many friends and acquaintances. He told Hébrard stories about who was powerful, whom to avoid and who was decent and honest.

He was curious about Hébrard. 'Are you going back to Orthez?' he said one day.

'No. I've been at Castignac for several years now. I'm settled there.'

'But why did you leave your family farm to come here and work for someone else?'

Hébrard had been dreading this question. No-one but the Lordats knew his story, but now he was coming down to the town and getting to know people, it was only to be expected that someone would ask more about him.

He looked at Pierre's friendly face and decided to take a risk. In a few words, he told him the truth about how he came to work at Castignac. Knowing that two of his brothers had died in the war and Pierre himself had been wounded, he was nervous, but he didn't want to lie or evade the truth as he had done on first meeting Guy and Raymond.

Pierre heard him out and nodded as he finished. 'It must have taken courage to disobey orders and risk your life.'

Hébrard felt a mixture of relief and surprise at Pierre's words. He had never thought of deserting as courageous and afterwards he felt less ashamed. Yet he was still careful. He wouldn't make the mistake of assuming that all Pierre's brothers would feel the same way.

Guy, the eldest, whom he met in the bar from time to time, was all right, but he wasn't drawn to Raymond. He knew from Pierre that Raymond had been close to the brothers killed in the war and felt bitter about the deaths. Raymond himself had been invalided home with a broken leg in 1916 and had managed not to return to the front, but he was scathing about any man who hadn't fought in the war, for whatever reason. He made dismissive comments about the men at Castignac and Pierre warned Hébrard to keep a distance from him.

Chapter Five

Hébrard

ON HIS NEXT VISIT to the bar, Hébrard was surprised to see a lively, dark-haired young woman talking to Pierre. Women stayed at home and only occasionally accompanied a male relative for a drink. He wondered if Pierre, who was single, had a girlfriend.

'Meet my sister, Nicolette,' Pierre said, introducing her.

Hébrard was shy with women, but greeted her politely, shaking her hand.

'I didn't know you had a sister,' he said. Pierre had only ever mentioned his brothers.

'Oh, yes, my big sister. She's older than me and she's spoiled because she's the only girl,' Pierre said, placing Hébrard's usual glass of red wine in front of him.

'*She* can speak for herself,' Nicolette said. 'Don't mind my little brother, *monsieur*. He's spoiled because he's the youngest, the baby of the family!'

Listening to their banter, Hébrard found himself missing his family and friends in Orthez. He began to talk about his parents, and brother and their farm.

Nicolette was slim and tall for a woman, with curly hair and olive skin. Her eyes were shining as she listened to Hébrard.

'I've hardly been anywhere, but you've been all across France! But is life different in Orthez from here?'

Hébrard had to admit that it wasn't so different. Both Orthez and St Martin des Remparts were market towns surrounded by villages and farms.

When Pierre turned away to serve another customer and became caught up in conversation, Hébrard and Nicolette carried on talking. She told him about her life in St Martin des Remparts. She had been to school there and now she worked in one of several local bakeries, making bread and pastries, starting work even earlier than Hébrard, before dawn every morning.

Hébrard finished his drink, but instead of leaving as was his practice, he bought another, including one for Nicolette.

'The market benefits from Danielle's stall every week. I buy things there for my mother and I'm sure you contribute to it,' she said.

That was true enough. Hébrard looked after the cows, goats and pigs from which came the cheese and ham that Danielle sold at the market. Under Nicolette's interested gaze, he told her about his work on the farm.

When Nicolette had to go, because of her early start, she mentioned that she would come to the bar for a drink on the same evening the following week. Hébrard, seeing this to be an invitation, nodded and said he would probably be there.

The following week, Hébrard found himself telling Nicolette how he came to be at Castignac. Even more with Nicolette than with Pierre, he didn't want to tell a lie or evade the truth.

As she plied him with questions, he talked in much greater detail than he had given Pierre about the train journey from Orthez, his discussions with Eugène, his escape from Castignac and his return there to plead with Jean-Louis to take him on. He hadn't talked to anyone at such length for years, perhaps never, but once he started, the words came tumbling out. He stopped after telling her about Eugène's death, wondering if he had said too much, and he waited for her condemnation.

Nicolette didn't flinch. 'Oh, the war. It was all we heard about, but people had to eat and it was important to keep a farm like Castignac going.'

She hadn't commented on his desertion and Hébrard relaxed, feeling that he had overcome a hurdle. He smiled at Nicolette, but with strangers, he kept quiet and hoped that they would think, if they thought about him at all, that he hadn't been called up because he was an essential farm worker.

Over the next few months, he got to know Nicolette, meeting her at the bar on the same night every week. It soon reached the point where he would say, 'See you next week,' as they parted and he could rely on her being there.

Hébrard's life in recent years had starved him of the company of women, except for Danielle. Nicolette didn't push him away and they began a quiet courtship in the bar, until they wanted more privacy. They would take a turn around the central square of the town, arm in arm, past the bakery where Nicolette worked, before Hébrard saw her to the door of her home nearby and climbed the hill back to Castignac. They moved easily to holding hands. They were used to kissing on the cheek when they met, but one evening in the dark under the colonnades of St Martin des Remparts, Hébrard dared to do more and was rewarded by a warm response from Nicolette.

It wasn't long before Hébrard admitted to himself that Nicolette was the woman for him and he felt a new joy and a passion for her, which ballooned when she agreed to marry him. He wished he could carry her off to Castignac straightaway, but things had to be done properly.

First of all, he talked to the Lordats, because he needed their permission for Nicolette to come and live in the cottage at Castignac. They knew that he was walking out with her. Danielle already knew and liked Nicolette and she wasn't surprised to hear about the wedding. She was glad because she needed help in the dairy and with the animals, especially now that their baby, Brigitte, was walking, and Nicolette had already indicated her willingness. Jean-Louis was pleased because it was less likely that a married Hébrard would think of returning home. He readily agreed that the young couple could live at the farm cottage.

Hébrard spent his spare time renovating the cottage to make it fit for his bride. He whitewashed the walls inside and out. Jean-Louis was having electric lighting installed at Castignac and a supply for the cottage was added. There was a coal-fired range in the cottage kitchen, a sink and a copper for laundry. There was an outside privy and Danielle gave Hébrard a spare zinc bath.

Hébrard and Nicolette were married in the church in St Martin des Remparts, in 1921, a year after they met. Nicolette came to live at Castignac with Hébrard. Adding to her knowledge of baking, she learned to make butter and cheese, cure hams and make pies for sale in the market. She and Danielle worked hard together during the day when the men were out in the fields. Jean-Louis increased Hébrard's weekly wage to take account of Nicolette's work for Castignac.

As part of modernising the farm, Jean-Louis bought a truck with a petrol engine. It was his answer to the car which had impressed him by its speed while causing his accident with the horse before the war. The truck was useful for taking supplies to the market every week and bringing back purchases for the farm. Hébrard learned to drive and it began to replace the farm cart.

One morning, Jean-Louis disappeared on foot to St Martin des Remparts. Hébrard noticed he hadn't taken one of the horses but didn't get round to asking Danielle why not. He was surprised and delighted later that morning when he saw a tractor appearing with Jean-Louis at the wheel.

'Henri had one for sale and he agreed to give me a lesson or two,' Jean-Louis said, referring to the agricultural merchant in the town, as he climbed out of the seat.

The tractor didn't entirely replace the horses, because petrol was expensive, but the soil was light enough for it to do most of the ploughing and Hébrard was quick to learn to drive it.

Hébrard and Nicolette had two daughters, Marie and Jeanne. When Nicolette began to serve on Danielle's weekly market stall, she left her little girls in the care of her mother while she sold the produce which she had helped to make at Castignac.

One summer morning, when his two girls were still small, a letter arrived for Hébrard from his brother. He knew before opening it that it contained bad news because, like the letter about Eugène's death, it had arrived at the wrong time of year.

17ᵗʰ June 1926

Dear Hébrard,

Father is ill and not expected to last. His lungs are bad and he can scarcely breathe. Mother is asking you to come home.

In haste as I must get out to the fields.

Your brother, Philippe

Hébrard knew that he must do what he had been putting off for years and go back to visit his family. Only complaining slightly that it was a bad time for him to go away, Jean-Louis gave him leave. Hébrard and Nicolette scraped together the money for the train fare. At the last minute, Danielle gave him a package of cheese and bacon as a gift for his family in Orthez.

Reaching the station at St Martin des Remparts, he was reminded of the only other time he had been there. He hadn't travelled by train since his journey during the war over ten years previously. On the train for much of a day, he felt he was going away from home, not towards it, and he was certain that Castignac was where he belonged now. He thought of Eugène's life cut short and wished there was something he could do to rid himself of the discomfort he still felt about deserting. These days, it wasn't about the war as a whole, but a kind of betrayal of his friend.

From the station in Orthez, he walked to the farm. He didn't see anyone he knew, but he was in no doubt about the way. His mother was in the kitchen when he arrived and he was shocked to see an old woman turn towards him. He had been thinking of her as unchanging. Exclaiming over how he had filled out, she gave him a firm hug and took him straight upstairs to where his father was lying in bed. They spoke only briefly, because his father was struggling for breath.

Even though the family greeted him almost as if he had never been away, Hébrard found changes. His brother, Philippe, who had been too young to be called up during the war, was taller and stronger, and now ran the farm with his wife. Hébrard had been invited to the wedding but had not been able to go because it had coincided with the birth of his elder daughter, Marie. His mother was preoccupied with the care of their father, and Philippe and his wife were running the farm.

Hébrard was aware that a question hung over his place on the farm at Orthez. He had decided to make his position clear from the start. On the evening of his arrival, in the garden outside the farmhouse, he looked at the familiar view, the fields stretching towards hills and beyond to the mountains. It was the view he had grown up with and had expected to accompany him through life. It was similar to the view from Castignac, but, with no town in sight, it now seemed incomplete.

Later, he spoke to his mother and Philippe.

'I'm only visiting. I'm giving up my claim to the farm. Nicolette wouldn't want to leave her family and I'm settled there now.'

It wasn't the whole truth, but he didn't want to talk about his desertion from the army, which was bigger in his mind now that he had returned to Orthez.

'I thought you might say that,' Philippe said. 'When you married there and then wrote to say you have a family now, it seemed likely that you would stay.'

'I should have said something about the farm before.'

'It's all right. I haven't been worrying about it. Of course, I'll pay you in time for taking your share.'

Inheritance laws meant that the brothers would share the farm on the death of their parents and so it was only fair that Philippe would buy Hébrard out. Hébrard was relieved that he hadn't had to mention money.

Not having seen his father for so long, Hébrard was surprised at how upset he was when he died only a few days later. It didn't change his feelings about the farm, but he wanted to be sure that his mother would be all right. She would remain there and help Philippe and his wife with the chores.

'You will go and see Eugène's parents, won't you? I said you would when I met his mother in town this morning,' his mother said, the day after his father's funeral.

She was busy sorting through his father's things, deciding what to keep and what to throw or give away. She had given Hébrard some of the clothes, trousers, shirts and a coat. They fitted well and he was glad of the gift. Bringing up a young family on his wage was a struggle, even though Nicolette, who had also taken over the cottage garden to grow vegetables, helped by selling her produce and baked goods in the market every week.

Hébrard nodded. He didn't want to visit Eugène's parents, but it was the least he could do. He set out that afternoon, on foot, refusing Philippe's offer of a horse. He had always walked into the town as a boy and a young man, and he wanted to do the same now.

Approaching the centre of Orthez, he came across his old school and stood for a few moments looking through iron gates, remembering teachers and boys he had known. Nearby was the town hall with its flags, looking unchanged, but next to it was something new, in a prominent position, a structure in white stone, with a neat gravel area in front and flowers laid at its base.

Hébrard stopped to look at the war memorial. Dozens of names, in alphabetical order, were inscribed. Some of them were new to him, but he was dismayed to see how many of them were familiar. They were boys he had known and their brothers. Several of them had travelled with him on the train to the Western Front. He read through the names steadily until he came to the last one, the name he least wanted to see there, that of Eugène Vigneron.

His own name might have been inscribed if he hadn't deserted when he did. He believed that he had done the right thing and yet because of that act of desertion, he was certain that he could never return to live in Orthez. Because he had grown up there, he would be known to everyone as the deserter, far more than in St Martin des Remparts. He had never thought at the time that deserting from the army would make him an outcast in the town of his childhood. How lucky he was to have found a different life and yet it had been forced on him; he would always be something of an outsider in St Martin des Remparts. But for the war, he would never have chosen to leave his family and the world he knew so well.

A tapping sound behind him broke into his thoughts.

'So you managed to keep yourself alive, Hébrard.'

Hébrard turned round to see a man of his age standing behind him. The voice was familiar at least, but the man had lost a leg and was using a crutch and something was wrong with his face.

He struggled to think of a name and then it came to him: Robert. They had been in the same year at school and he had been called up at the same time as Hébrard. They had travelled on the troop train together and Robert had been amongst those billeted at Castignac. Hébrard remembered him as a bit of a clown, tending to show off to the others.

'Hello… Robert,' he said, trying not to stare. 'So did you.'

'Yes, but not all in one piece. Still, at least I didn't run away from the war, not like you,' Robert said. His tone was bitter. He didn't wait for any answer but walked on.

Hébrard was stung by the encounter, but not surprised. He left the war memorial and made his way to the vintner's premises where his mother had told him that Eugène's parents still lived above their shop. They had known him well as a boy and it made it easier that, aware he had come to see his family, they were expecting him. After the brief incident with Robert, he began to fear that they, too, would upbraid him in some way, the more so because he was still alive and they had lost their son.

Eugène's father, busy arranging a new display of bottles in the shop, recognised Hébrard immediately and called his wife down. He was a burly man with a beard and a broad girth, across which ran a watch chain, as Hébrard remembered from years ago.

'Hébrard, my boy! You haven't changed that much,' M. Vigneron said, clasping him warmly. 'I hear you're married now and working on a farm in the east.'

Hébrard nodded. 'Yes, I'm just here for my father's funeral.'

'Well, you know what happened to Eugène, of course.'

'It must have been a terrible shock for you. I've come to give you my condolences.'

'Thank you. Oh, Hébrard, it's kind of you to call. We heard you were back.' Mme Vigneron had appeared in time to hear Hébrard's words and came over to welcome him. 'We're so proud of Eugène. He came home on leave when he could, but he was a good soldier. Did you know he was promoted?'

'No. He did well,' Hébrard said. His parents had never been proud of him.

He was feeling awkward about standing there alive. It made little difference that some years had passed since Eugène's death. From the grief that his parents obviously felt, it might only have happened yesterday.

Mme Vigneron, a thin woman with a lively face, looked at him closely and her manner became less formal.

'He wrote and said that you disappeared, Hébrard! We didn't know what had happened to you for a long time. Then your mother said you were on a farm on the other side of the country and I told Eugène when he came home on leave.'

'I couldn't go with them to the front. I couldn't bear the thought,' he said. 'I tried to tell Eugène on the journey. He understood, but he was determined to go on.'

Mme Vigneron, her face crumpling, brought out a white lace handkerchief and dabbed her eyes. 'Oh, how I wish he'd listened to you! I hated the war, but he came home twice on leave. He wouldn't say much about what it was like. Then we had a telegram. It arrived after the armistice. We had just started to think he was safe when we received it.'

'He was our only boy and I'm going to have to sell the business when I can't carry on anymore,' M. Vigneron said, as his wife recovered herself.

Eugène's parents had aged and seemed smaller than Hébrard remembered. He realised that he was lucky to have a brother. Without Philippe, he would have had to return to the family farm or see it sold to outsiders. Yet it would have been unthinkable to sell it when it was his mother's home. Having a brother had given him more choices in life.

They talked for a little longer, about Eugène's name on the war memorial, about a letter praising his courage from his commanding officer, about Hébrard giving the farm over to Philippe on the death of his father. A silence fell and there was nothing more to say. It would have been tactless to talk much about his own life and family in the circumstances. Afterwards, he was grateful for their welcome but couldn't help thinking that his visit showed up their terrible loss and his own discomfort at how he had saved his skin.

The following day, saying goodbye to his family, he took the train back to St Martin des Remparts. He was glad he had made the journey, seen his mother, talked to Philippe about the farm and seen Eugène's parents, but the discomfort he felt about deserting had grown during his visit and he was longing to return to Castignac, see Nicolette and the girls and let the past go, if that was possible.

Part Three

Chapter One

After Ian

I AN HAD DIED THE day after my visit to the museum during that summer holiday at Castignac. The two incidents might have seemed quite unrelated, but there could have been a connection, if his death had resulted from curiosity about Castignac's past, curiosity that I also felt, but hadn't yet done much about.

Waiting for Angela and Jenny to return from the hospital that evening, we struggled to answer Stephen's question about why Ian had climbed the staircase, knowing it might not be safe. No-one knew the answer for certain.

'I *told* him it was likely to be dangerous,' Graham said. 'I told everyone,' he added with a sigh.

Graham had said that more than once. We didn't need the ruined farmhouse and no-one had thought to do anything about the staircase. We had no children with us to protect from danger and had assumed that the adults, having been warned, would be sensible. Graham wasn't thinking about repairs for it: there was enough to do in the main house. Whatever it might once have been, the ruin was no more than a kind of folly, a talking point. It was silent evidence of the past life of the farm.

'Well, yes, but we all know he was keen to see the view from the pigeon loft. Maybe he thought that the staircase would be safe and the rest of us were being too cautious. After all, Jacques thought it was all right,' I said, remembering my conversation with the old farmer at our party the previous week.

'So you told everybody. You said Jacques hadn't been up there recently, though, so what would he know about how safe it was?' Graham said.

'Surely you're not blaming me? I only repeated what Jacques said. I didn't encourage Ian to do anything. Besides, Ian talked to Jacques about the old farmhouse.' I heard my voice sounding high and strained.

'Of course I'm not blaming you, Tessa,' Graham said.

He gave me a mollifying smile, but I felt accused and began to fear that some careless remark of mine had led Ian to his death.

We sat around after we had finished eating, keeping each other company, talking now and again, but mainly sitting in silence in the growing dark. It was late when we saw the lights of the car and heard it pull up to the house and the engine die, then listened to the sound of Angela and Jenny's footsteps as they came round to the terrace.

Jenny looked drained and didn't want to talk. Lily offered salad, but Jenny wasn't hungry, even though she hadn't eaten since lunchtime. It was a relief that the light was fading because it was so hard for us to look at each other.

'I'm going upstairs because I need to phone Ben and Kate. I'll see you in the morning. Good night,' she said.

'Let me make you a cup of tea to take up with you,' Lily said.

Jenny agreed to that and they left the terrace together. Angela was hungry and helped herself liberally to the remains of the supper.

'What's the news?' Stephen said, hardly giving her a chance to swallow a mouthful.

'We had to wait around for a long time before a doctor saw us. She had examined Ian. She asked a lot of questions and said that he died from multiple injuries, including hitting his head as he landed on the flagstones.'

Angela paused, but nobody spoke, so she carried on.

'There's a problem. The doctor refused to give Jenny a medical certificate, which she needs in order to register the death. Even though we argued that Ian's death was purely an accident at home, with no suspicious circumstances, she wanted an inquest. She questioned us about the possibility of suicide, but Jenny is quite certain it wasn't and I'm sure she's right. It was helpful that I was there and could translate, but I'm sorry there's going to be an inquest. It will be such a trial for Jenny, but she'll have to go through with it. There'll be an autopsy first.'

Lily came back from the kitchen and slipped into her seat. With all the windows in the house open, we could hear Jenny climbing the stairs to her bedroom, her feet stamping heavily, as if to make sure that she was safe, or perhaps it was just from exhaustion. Angela told Lily about the inquest.

'That's a shame. It might mean more publicity than a simple accidental death. I've been imagining red-top headlines and being doorstepped,' Stephen said.

'Stephen! How can you think of yourself at a time like this?' Angela, never normally critical of him, looked tired and drawn.

'Because I have to be aware of how the media might see anything I am involved in, as you well know,' Stephen said.

'It's absolutely dreadful for Jenny and their two. I expect she's phoning them now,' Lily said. 'They'll probably turn up here tomorrow.'

'There was a torch in Ian's pocket,' Angela said. 'He'd clearly planned to explore the pigeon loft.'

'Why take a torch? Aren't there windows up there?' Stephen said.

'Yes, but there's no electricity supply and it might have been quite dark at first, with the shutters closed and only the pigeonholes letting in any light,' Angela said.

'What happens after the inquest?' Graham said.

'Jenny will be given a death certificate and she'll register the death at the town hall. Then she'll have to arrange for Ian's body to be sent to England for burial or cremation at home. The doctor thinks it likely they'll hold the inquest soon, within the next few weeks,' Angela said.

'If only he'd clung on and saved himself,' Lily said.

'Yes, but he didn't, and it was the staircase that betrayed him,' Angela said. 'It probably all happened in seconds and the poor man had no chance. Look, it's terribly upsetting, but there's no escaping it. I'm going to bed. I'm so tired. We'll have enough time tomorrow to help Jenny and to think about the impact of it all.'

She got up from the table and went indoors, leaving us to clear away the plates. I was taken aback. Angela was the keystone in the arch of the group, always encouraging and helpful. I had never seen her crushed before.

I went to bed thinking I would always remember that day as one of the worst in my life. Apart from the terrible loss of Ian for Jenny and as a member of our group, I hadn't even begun to work out what it meant for everyone else, except for one thing. A huge question mark, if not a full stop, was hovering over our future at Castignac. Yet I knew then that I didn't want to give it up. I wasn't quite sure why, but it was beginning to mean a lot to me.

In bed that night, I kept seeing Ian's body lying on the flagstones. I tried hard not to think about the horror of his last few seconds, but I couldn't escape the images. Mark cradled me in his arms and I slept, but I woke in the small hours, crying out from a nightmare about falling from a height into depths I couldn't see. I disturbed him and he woke up. He didn't say anything, but he hugged me.

At that moment, I desperately wanted to tell him that I loved him. I'd never said so before, being uncertain of his response, that he wouldn't welcome it because of his wretched aversion to commitment and would edge away from me. Apart from that, the timing was awful. I couldn't let him think that I was taking advantage of the moment, of people wanting to be close to each other in order to face a terrible event. I didn't want my declaration of love for Mark to be forever linked to Ian's death, even if he welcomed it, so I stayed silent.

Mark went back to sleep, but I couldn't do the same. I lay awake for hours, trying not to toss and turn, with the events of the previous day running in my head. I tried hard to recapture that last moment of ordinariness before I discovered Ian's body, when we were still enjoying the holiday and coming to the end of yet another perfect day.

I could only remember snatches of it: watching a lizard on the terrace in the morning; conversation over lunch about Didier's slowness in checking the staircase to the pigeon loft; writing postcards while Mark went off to read outside; going for a swim to cool down; Jenny coming up to me in the pool to ask if I had seen Ian, before we all began to discuss his whereabouts over an early evening drink and I had found him.

I was disinclined to face people the next morning and wanted to be back at home, safe in my small, low-ceilinged flat where such a terrible accident would have been impossible. How I had welcomed the high, wide spaces of the Castignac house and its ruin, compared to my cramped London life. Yet how dangerous they seemed now.

'I'm tired,' I said to Mark as we scrambled out of bed.

'I didn't sleep well either, and I want to go for a long walk to clear my head,' he said.

'All right. I'll wait until we know more about Jenny's plans, in case she needs us.'

'Well, I won't go off without you, not after yesterday,' he said.

I was grateful for that.

It was a grey morning. Jenny was pale but calm. She admitted that she had barely slept, and she seemed to be still in shock. Her thick, chestnut hair straggled, and her face was too pale for someone on a summer holiday in southern France. The others, too, had slept badly. Looking round the table during breakfast, it was obvious that we all felt wretched. Jenny received a text and told us that Kate was flying over at lunchtime. Ben was away on a business trip that would prevent him from coming to Castignac straightaway, but Jenny had managed to speak to him on the phone.

Just as we were finishing breakfast, a knock at the door announced two policemen. We knew that French police carried guns, but, even so, my eyes went straight to their holsters. It was mildly shocking to see armed men in our house, but everything was different now.

The policemen visited the ruined farmhouse, with Angela and Jenny. Mark and I went across with them. After examining the building, they asked us to leave everything there untouched. They took one of the broken spindles for testing.

Angela escorted the police back to their car, while Mark, Jenny and I stayed behind. Jenny was still looking around and we didn't want to leave her there alone. She stepped carefully around the bloodstain and craned her neck up at the staircase.

'I wonder if Ian saw a better view of the mountains from up there,' she said.

'Maybe. The shutters are closed now, but he may have opened them to let in light and to see the view,' I said.

Mark peered at one of the pieces of wood lying on the ground. We had been too preoccupied with Ian the night before to examine them closely.

'Termites have done that. Look at this,' he said, pointing at the crumbling end of the spindle. 'Ian may have leaned on the railing for a moment, as he came out of the pigeon loft, just to look around as he'd never been up there before. Because it was rotten, the slightest pressure made it give way and there was nothing for him to hold on to.'

'Why didn't it happen on his way into the pigeon loft?' I said.

'Well, it could have done, if he'd leaned on the railing at that stage, but it looks as if he went in there because the entrance to the pigeon loft is open. There may not be any damage in the steps themselves,' Mark said.

Jenny nodded. 'I just want to see better,' she said, putting a foot on the bottom rung of the staircase and beginning to climb. We were too far below the top for a clear view.

'No!' Mark called out. 'It's far too risky. You might want to go up there, to see what Ian saw, but not before the railing is repaired. The staircase will need testing.'

Jenny ignored Mark and continued to climb. She was at the top of the first flight of steps when Mark started to follow her. He grasped her shoulder from behind.

'Jenny, come down. It's too dangerous!'

I was aghast. There was an awful moment where I thought she might ignore Mark and struggle out from under his grip, so that he would have to manhandle her down the staircase, or worse, that some terrible accident would happen to them both, but fortunately she turned round and realised what she was doing. She was crying as she looked at Mark, but then she recovered, heaving a sigh and returning to ground level.

'I'm sorry, Mark,' she said as she stood on the flagstone floor once again. 'I shouldn't have done that. I don't know what came over me just then.'

'It's all right. You're not yourself,' he said, giving her a quick hug and looking relieved that the moment had passed.

'Let's go back,' I said, wanting to escape from the ruin before anything else could happen.

'I need to collect Kate from the airport, but I don't feel like driving,' Jenny said as we walked back to the house.

'I'll drive,' I said.

That afternoon, I drove with Jenny to the airport at Carcassonne. Amongst the passengers coming though the arrivals gate, her daughter Kate was easily recognisable as a younger version of Jenny, with a plump face and chestnut hair and wearing clothes from her shop. She burst into tears as soon as she saw Jenny.

Back at Castignac, Jenny and Kate retreated upstairs. Kate was a student, in between summer jobs, and fortunately able to stay as long as necessary. She was a comfort to Jenny in a way that the rest of us couldn't be and I felt relieved by her presence. Ian had been a fond husband and father, and his loss was going to distress the small family greatly.

I couldn't prevent my mind from leaping ahead, even as I criticised myself for selfishness at such a time. Everything seemed so fragile in a way that it hadn't before. Would Jenny leave Castignac now that she had lost Ian? Would the group break up and sell the house? Most of all, I was afraid that Mark would decide it was all too much. What had been, for all of us, an escape from the pressures of ordinary life, was fast turning into a nightmare. Castignac was no longer the heaven away from home that we had wanted from the beginning, but it was tied up with Mark in my mind. Our best times, almost our only times for the year we had owned Castignac, had taken place there. I hated the thought but couldn't help feeling that losing it could lead to losing Mark.

'I'm wondering if Ian knew something we didn't know,' I said to Mark when we were alone. 'That could be why he went into the pigeon loft, to see something there.'

'Even if you're right, we've got no way of finding out because we can't do the same, at least not at the moment,' Mark said.

Mark was right. The pigeon loft was now quite inaccessible and any investigation of it would have to wait. Besides, we were all still in shock and there was the inquest to think about and Ian's funeral.

Angela rang Marianne and told her what had happened, so she would hear it from us first and not from gossip in the town or from the local newspaper. A journalist who kept an eye on events at the police station and the mortuary had already been on the phone to us. With Jenny's permission, Angela had given her a brief account of Ian's death and we were expecting to see an article in the local paper.

Jenny was waiting for a date for the inquest. She couldn't arrange Ian's funeral until afterwards and she was in a kind of limbo. We all drew together in an effort to help her and Kate, as much as we could.

'I might show Kate the staircase,' Jenny said at breakfast time the following morning.

'Won't that be upsetting for you?' I said quickly, remembering Jenny's attempt to climb the staircase the day before.

'It's all right, Tessa. We won't do anything silly,' Jenny said. 'That was a moment of madness yesterday, not the real me.'

I nodded. Jenny was basically a sensible and level-headed person. She and Kate clearly wanted time together and so we left them in the house. Stephen and Angela drove off to Carcassonne, and Graham and Lily set off to visit a nearby Cathar castle. Mark and I headed south, at last free to go for a long walk.

Chapter Two

Towards the Mountains

Passing through St Martin des Remparts, we noticed that the grey cloud of the early morning had thinned and blue sky was appearing. It would be a bright, warm day. Beyond the town, the countryside was the strong green of high summer, the earth bare where crops had been harvested. Ahead of us a flight of small birds swooped and fluttered in the air and the trees, full of invisible birds, appeared to be singing. Woods, fields and streams surrounded us. Butterflies, flashing a wide range of colours, danced in the air, while crickets jumped around our feet. The crackle of dry grass underfoot mixed with the sound of birdsong. The air smelled of summer, dry and slightly scented with hay.

Others in the group liked to say that the countryside around Castignac was like that of England fifty years ago for its wildlife and flowers. I was too young to know, but I did notice much more birdsong and a much greater profusion and variety of wildflowers in rural France than I had ever heard or seen in England. For all our sadness, I was entranced.

Neither Mark nor I wanted to talk much at first. I was wishing that time would roll back so that Ian would be alive again and events could turn out differently. I had never wanted to undo anything so much as the afternoon of his death, impossible as that would have been.

Mark and I exchanged stories of the few people we had known well and lost. For me, there was only Aunt Jessie, who had left Jackie and me the money behind my share of Castignac. She had lived nearby and I had been fond of her as a child. Mark had suffered the loss of his father from a heart attack not long after he left school and a close friend of his had been killed in a road accident only the previous year.

'I'm afraid of what will happen now, that Ian's death will lose us the house in some way,' I said later, wanting Mark to disagree and assure me that there was no connection between the two.

'It could happen, say, if Jenny wants to leave and you can't find a replacement.'

As the clouds disappeared, the mountains came into view along the horizon. Bare ridges here and there contrasted with snowy peaks, even in summer.

'I like seeing the mountains from a distance,' I said, catching up with Mark on the narrow path. 'I can almost feel myself flying towards them. I don't like heights or anything to do with climbing. I simply want to lose myself in looking. Maybe it's because they're here on some days and not others, and they look different from one season to another.'

He nodded. 'Just looking at them takes you to another world.'

'I don't like them close up. We drove into them one day last summer, on the holiday when we found Castignac, but they became too big and hulking.'

'You might like to be amongst them if you got to know them. Anyway, I don't think we'd reach them today, no matter how fast we walk, so you've nothing to worry about,' Mark said. 'They're quite a sight, aren't they?'

'Ice-capped, clear, remote, unattainable, just as I like them,' I said dreamily.

We sat by a stream to drink coffee we had brought with us and then carried on until lunchtime, when we stopped again for our picnic. High up on a hillside, looking over a valley, we were still facing the mountains. After lunch, we took advantage of the fact that there was no-one about to make love on a grassy patch beyond the path. I felt better afterwards and Mark did too.

Later, we continued walking. The path rose and fell, the mountains remained in the distance and the sun was high in the sky. We didn't see another person all day. Occasionally we heard distant farm machinery, but we were too far from any roads for sounds of traffic. Our view near at hand was of meadows and scattered copses, with the occasional herd of cows.

'It's idyllic,' I said. 'This is why I like having Castignac, for the countryside and the space, as well as because we're in France. It's so unspoiled.'

'It's nice countryside,' Mark said.

His tone of voice was measured. Was he afraid that I would try and persuade him to join Castignac? I wasn't going to ask him again. If he changed his mind, he only had to tell me. Besides, there was a new factor now, the chance that the Castignac group would fall apart.

Mark began to talk about his work in Lebanon, how the project was coming to an end and what the possibilities were for him in future. The rise of Islamic fundamentalism meant that increasingly few Middle Eastern countries were safe for him to work in.

'Why not find a job in France, near here?' I said. 'You can speak French well and perhaps you could stay at Castignac. I would come to see you here.'

'I rather think the French have plenty of engineers of their own.'

'England, then?'

His tone was dismissive. 'I wasn't thinking of leaving the company I work for and nearly all their projects are abroad.'

'We could see more of each other if you worked in England.'

I was trying to sound casual. Yet Mark was like a mountain on the horizon, keeping his distance. Would he ever get over his marriage?

'We could, but I don't,' he said, with a note of finality. He looked up into high, blue sky. 'Is that a buzzard up there? See the way it glides and turns? Look, there's a bunch of crows mobbing it. They can be so aggressive.'

I watched the buzzard wheeling above us and listened to its mewing cries and the harsh cawing of the crows. Mark was as independent as a buzzard and he liked to imply that I was independent too. Did he think I was mobbing him?

We passed through St Martin des Remparts again on our way home. The plane trees on the main avenues were in full leaf, their fiercely pruned branches shielded by green. Quite a few people were about in the main square and Jacques Lordat was sitting alone on a bench. He was one of the older men often to be found on the wooden benches dotted around the square. He was easy to recognise because he was taller than many of the other old men, his head the highest in a row on a bench or waiting for his turn in a game of *boules*. His weather-beaten face was topped by a hat and he had a brawny frame and strong, handsome features.

I went up to him. *'Bonjour, M. Lordat,'* I said, in my best, almost my only French. I wouldn't have approached him if I had been on my own, but Mark spoke good French and could translate for me.

'Bonjour, mademoiselle,' Jacques said.

He obviously recognised me from the party and he knew about Ian. He offered his condolences and Mark translated. Through Mark, I replied that it was a terrible shock.

'I wonder if Jacques was sad to leave Castignac,' I said to Mark as we continued on our way.

'I expect he misses his old home, if he lived there all his life,' he said.

We returned late to Castignac, with aching legs. Angela was in the kitchen, cooking. She said it made her feel better to be doing something. Mark and I were starving and glad of the meal when it was ready. In our absence, Jenny and Kate had visited the ruin and had appreciated time to themselves to talk about Ian and the devastating impact of his death.

Jenny and Kate spent most of Kate's visit sitting alone together or going for walks, remembering Ian. At mealtimes, they told us many stories about him. They were not sad all the time. Many of their stories were heartening or simply funny.

I contributed something Ian had said about renovating Castignac. He had been telling us gleefully about how he didn't like decorating.

'Our bedroom at home had a dark blue ceiling when we moved in twenty years ago and it's still there,' he had said. 'It can carry on reminding us of the night sky, for all I care. I might even paint a moon and a few stars on it one day. I don't want to spend my holidays decorating. I suppose I wouldn't mind wielding a paintbrush now and then, just to show willing.'

I didn't like decorating either and it had amused me at the time to hear what Ian thought about it.

'Ian was on a one-year contract at the university and never knew whether it would be renewed until the last minute, so he was looking around for alternatives. He fancied making a name for himself as a freelance writer of articles,' Jenny said, during one of the conversations about him.

'What sort of articles?' I said.

'About changing ways of life in southern France, how the modern world is making an impact on a rural economy, or even local history, with photographs, of course. So many magazines and journals are on the market these days that he thought it would be possible, especially with Castignac as an example. There wasn't much chance of tenure where he taught because botany is almost finished as a subject. The new plant science that has come along is different and he hadn't caught up with it. He was pretty sure that he would soon be looking for another job. He fancied becoming a freelance writer, after all those years of being an employee. He was going to write in English for the English market or even in French for the French market.'

'I know someone who's trying to make it as a freelance writer, but it's not easy unless your subject is finance or business. Maybe Ian was planning an article about Castignac,' Angela said.

'Yes, maybe, although he didn't say anything about it to me on that day. I know, because I've been over and over it in my mind, trying to piece it all together,' Jenny said.

'Supposing he thought there was something in the pigeon loft he could write about? That might have overcome warnings about safety. Maybe that's why he didn't tell anyone what he was doing that afternoon,' I said.

'Yes, but what could be up there? Pigeons aren't that interesting and it's not the only pigeon loft in France,' Stephen said, with a hint of impatience. He gave the impression of wishing that he had never asked why Ian had climbed the staircase. The question seemed to have taken root in everyone's mind.

'The view of the mountains, of course,' Angela said. 'It'll be better from higher up.'

'I don't know,' I said. 'His death seems a bit of a mystery to me.'

'That's one thing that it isn't,' Stephen said, his tone reprimanding. 'It's a tragedy, especially for Jenny and her family, but it's not a mystery. It is, quite simply, an accidental death, but one with consequences.'

'For Jenny, certainly,' I said.

'And for the rest of us. I'm in two minds about keeping the house now,' Stephen said, and Angela nodded. Clearly they had been talking about selling Castignac, but I didn't want to do that. I decided that ignoring the subject might cause it to go away.

'It's such a shame, as we were just getting to know Ian,' I said.

Everyone still felt both shaken and puzzled. It meant that we covered the same ground more than once.

'Could Ian's death have been suicide?' I asked at the end of one evening meal, after Jenny and Kate had left us to go upstairs. Angela stood up and began to clear the table. The plates clattered as she stacked them up.

'I don't think we'd be having this conversation if Jenny were here. It's rather silly,' she said, striding off to the kitchen with a full tray.

'Yes, speculation like this would upset her,' Lily said. 'What has happened is bad enough, without trying to make it even worse.'

'I'm not trying to make it worse. I'm just trying to understand it, that's all. Shouldn't we be asking if there's more to it than meets the eye?'

I was abashed that Angela and Lily, older, more worldly and experienced women, had joined forces against me.

'Don't forget that there's going to be an inquest,' Stephen said.

'I've never thought Ian was suicidal, Tessa,' Angela said sharply, returning from the kitchen. 'Don't go asking Jenny, though. We went through all this with the doctor and you'll upset her even more if you try to put her through it again.'

'I was just thinking about possibilities,' I said.

'Tessa, that's enough for now, unless you have anything definite to say or any evidence to put forward. You've been reading too many thrillers,' Stephen spoke firmly.

That was a low blow. It was true that I read thrillers. I had one on the go at the time. It had been lying open, face-down, in the sitting room since the day of Ian's death, because I hadn't had the heart to return to it. It might have been gripping beforehand, but no novel could match the drama around us.

There was no evidence that Ian had been suicidal. Mark said it was pretty obvious to him that it was an accident and no-one else seemed to think otherwise, except perhaps the doctor who ordered the inquest.

'Well, if there is more to it than meets the eye,' Angela said, in a less irritable voice, 'we may never know the answer. We may have to assume that Ian's wish to see the view from the pigeon loft got the better of him when he was alone there, with no-one giving him advice. I'm not sure that there is any mystery.'

'We all feel Ian's death more keenly because he died when we were here together. If he'd had some kind of accident in London which didn't involve us, we would be sad, but not so affected,' Lily said, and everyone agreed.

'You mustn't sow doubts in people's minds without good reason, Tessa,' Mark said afterwards, when we were alone.

'All right. I promise to shut up, but I'm still puzzled.'

I happened to find myself alone with Lily as we were clearing up the lunch things the next day. It was almost inevitable that we returned to the subject that was preoccupying us all.

'I feel dreadful about it. I know Graham is wedded to his decorating, and it's true what I said about enjoying making new friends, but I'm not sure if I want to carry on with the house now,' Lily said.

I nodded and sighed. The chances of holding on to the house would certainly be slimmer if Lily were wobbling as well as Stephen and Angela. Graham would follow her if she wanted to leave because it was obvious how much she mattered to him.

'Perhaps it's best to wait and see. If Jenny wants to carry on, then I should feel a bit of a wimp if we were to leave the group,' Lily said, and I agreed.

Mark said later that he was sorry some of the group were thinking of selling the house so soon after buying it. He liked Castignac increasingly. It was becoming the place where we spent most of the little time we had with each other. Mark didn't have to attend to any of the problems with the house, but he took an interest and made useful contributions to discussions about it.

Mark and I went for a swim on the last full day of that summer holiday, with the sun sparkling on the water. I didn't know where the others were. We all lacked the energy to talk to each other much, apart from conversations about Ian. Even the meals together, previously so light-hearted, were becoming an ordeal.

'I'm going to miss you,' I said.

'It's nice to be missed,' he said lightly, swimming off from the side of the pool where we had been treading water.

'When are we going to meet again?'

I spoke to his back, sure that he heard me, even though he was half-submerged. He turned round at the end of the length and swam back to me.

'I don't know.' He was shrugging his shoulders and smiling.

'Don't you have any idea about your next leave?'

I knew that I sounded clingy, but I couldn't stop myself. I wanted something to hold on to, especially as I was feeling shaken by Ian's death.

'I might get a few days off at Christmas. Or I might be in London and you might be here. You put yourself at a distance with your house in France,' he said.

'Oh, poor you! Poor Mark, forced to have holidays in France! And I don't put myself as much at a distance as you do.'

He splashed me and the swim ended in laughter.

'I'm sorry, Tessa. That was unkind, especially after the holidays I've enjoyed at Castignac,' he had the grace to say.

The next day, Mark and I parted at Carcassonne Airport with the wish to meet again, but no definite plans. He was flying back to London, on the way to his job in Lebanon.

Jenny and I drove back to London the day afterwards. Three of us had driven down and only two of us were returning, but everything had seemed strange since Ian's death and it was better than Jenny having to make the long drive back on her own. She couldn't wait at Castignac until after the inquest because she needed to get back for her business. Her partner, she explained to us, was much better at dressmaking than running the business side and she didn't dare be away for too long.

The journey of about nine hundred miles offered plenty of time for us to think and talk. Jenny didn't mind doing her share of the driving as she said it helped to take her mind off

Ian's death. She was sad, but there was no sign of collapse while she was driving.

We took two days over the journey and needed petrol on the morning of the second day. We stopped at a small garage as we left the town where we had stayed the night. An attendant filled the car and I paid, after enquiring about the cost, as it was my turn. He took my money and brought the change back to the car.

'This is ten euros short,' I said.

I couldn't speak French, but I could add up. Jenny translated for me.

'No, it's the right change,' he said.

It wasn't. An argument began, in French, between him and Jenny. He was unmoving, but so were we. Meanwhile, a small queue was forming behind us and one car hooted.

Jenny was in the driver's seat and I was next to her.

'Don't move,' I said, and Jenny nodded.

We sat and waited. Afraid of losing custom, the attendant gave in and fetched the right change, refusing to give it to me and throwing the notes into the car. Only when I had picked them up and we were satisfied did we move off, with the attendant shouting rudely at us as the cars behind continued to hoot.

Instead of feeling pleased that we had stood our ground, I felt shaken and quite unlike my normal self. Fortunately, Jenny was calm. I sat quietly beside her and recovered while we continued the journey.

Later we talked about why the incident had rattled me so much.

'It wasn't frightening,' I said.

Jenny agreed. 'No, but perhaps it's because you've been trying to help me since Ian's death and haven't allowed your own feelings to surface. We've all suffered from it, not just me and my children.'

'Yes. Even though I didn't know him well, it's still been a shock,' I said.

The rest of the journey was uneventful and I returned home to tell Jackie in full the sad story of Ian's demise. She was upset that the friendly and good-humoured man she had met at Castignac shortly beforehand should have had such a terrible accident.

Chapter Three

Deciding to Sell

THE FRENCH AUTHORITIES MOVED fast on the inquest. It was held in September, less than a month after Ian's death, but we didn't all need to go. Jenny, who had returned to England at the same time as the rest of us rather than stay alone at Castignac, attended with Kate and Ben. The rest of us made short signed statements about who we were, our relationship to Castignac and what we had been doing on the day of the accident. Angela translated them into French and Jenny submitted them, verified by the notary, to the coroner in advance of the inquest. These statements weren't required, but we thought they might be helpful. The French coroner also heard the evidence of the emergency services, the doctor who had examined Ian and the police.

In France, Jenny kept in touch with Angela, who rang everyone with the news of the verdict. It had been an ordeal and she had struggled with the language, but people had been kind and helpful, the hearing hadn't taken long and had been straightforward. The verdict, of accidental death, was a huge relief to Jenny and to all of us. There was no longer any question of Ian having been suicidal and she could now obtain a medical certificate, register the death at the mayor's office in St Martin des Remparts, arrange to bring Ian home and hold the funeral.

Angela sent me a text one morning as I was getting ready for work. Marianne had alerted her to a report in *La Dépêche*, the regional newspaper. It was based on the interview Angela had given to the journalist in France and it included the inquest verdict. It was quite straightforward.

Mark was away in Lebanon, but everyone in the Castignac group attended Ian's funeral. Jenny, Kate and Ben invited people back to their house afterwards. Talking to funeral guests who hadn't been to Castignac, I was aware they were shocked at the fatal accident, but also curious about the house.

'The way you've all pooled resources, renovating the house together and sharing a holiday home is impressive,' one friend of Jenny's said to me. Others, listening, agreed.

Normally I would have lapped up the praise, but I couldn't help doubting it then. I suspected that the guests were at best uncertain about the idea of sharing a house and were thinking that Ian would still otherwise be alive. No-one dared to say so, but I felt the death removed any claim we could have to success with Castignac.

'Why didn't you put a barrier at the bottom of the staircase saying "No Admittance"?' one guest asked Graham, in the closest anyone came to criticism.

Graham glared at him. 'Because we're not children and everyone had been told that it wasn't safe.'

Jenny rose to the occasion by being calm and approachable.

'Ian's absence will leave a big gap in the group,' I said to her and she nodded.

I had liked Ian's sense of humour and enjoyed his knowledge of wildflowers and his interest in Castignac's past. I wasn't sure what Jenny thought about Castignac after losing Ian and didn't want to pester her, but she soon made it clear.

'Are you going to Castignac at New Year, Tessa?' she said.

'I hope so. I don't yet know if Mark will be able to, though. What about you?'

Jenny sighed. 'I'm torn. I'm not sure if I can bear to go back to the place where Ian died and be there on my own, although I wouldn't have to go into the old farmhouse.'

'You won't be completely alone if you go when someone else is there. Why don't you and I go at the same time?'

'Thank you, that's thoughtful. I'd be without Ian, of course, but I'm without him anyway. He loved Castignac so much, as I do, that part of me wants to go back.'

'It sounds as if it's too soon for decisions. You've got so much to think about now and it's only a holiday home. Put it on the back-burner for a while.'

She smiled then. 'You're right, Tessa. What a sensible thought. I'm going to bury myself as much as I can in work. I've always enjoyed sewing and now I find it consoling.'

We all met a couple of weeks after the funeral, at Stephen and Angela's place, to discuss Castignac. I was the last to arrive. Looking around the room, I felt that the group was too small and too solemn. Ian almost seemed to be there, not just when people mentioned him, but because I kept seeing his face and hearing his voice.

We had barely begun to talk about the house when Stephen cut across something that Graham was saying about renovations.

'Angela and I have been thinking that we should sell Castignac.'

'Really? Why is that?' I said, eyes wide. I had feared the question of selling would arise again and was prepared for it, determined not to meet him halfway.

Graham echoed me, while the others looked at Stephen expectantly.

'Angela and I have been talking about it since the accident,' Stephen said. 'Ian's death has destroyed something for me. I don't feel relaxed there anymore.'

His change of heart made it obvious how much we all depended on each other. Until now we had been doing something together, with all the emphasis on sharing the house. We had had only minor disagreements of the kind that could be easily resolved. I was afraid that, if we were to pull apart, it could be messy or contentious.

'I've had some adverse publicity. A journalist in the constituency thought it would be in the public interest to look into what I was doing during the summer and he's found out about Ian's death. Remember it was reported in the local paper in France? Now there's a piece in one of the local papers here. Jenny knows about it already, because I thought I should tell her. Here's a copy.'

Stephen was flourishing a newspaper clipping as he spoke and I took it from him. The article was topped by a picture that had clearly been snapped when he was unaware and it made him look furtive.

Local MP In Mystery Death Drama

Local MP Stephen Hart and his wife Angela were embroiled in a mystery death on holiday this summer. Escaping to the house they own in the south of France, they were expecting no more than a quiet break from parliamentary and constituency business when tragedy struck.

One of the friends on holiday with them died suddenly from a dramatic fall in a ruined building on the property.

French authorities have declared a verdict of accidental death, but the mystery remains of why the friend, Ian Kemble, a constituent of Stephen Hart, chose to climb a staircase he had been warned to avoid and which had been attacked by termites.

And this raises the question of whether, if an MP can afford a house in France, MPs' salaries are too high.

'This article is cobbled together from the local newspaper report in France. It's exactly the sort of thing I didn't want to happen and it's firmed up my decision to sell Castignac. You may have noticed I've had to say something on social media. I frankly don't want to do anything to endanger my standing in the constituency or in the Commons, especially given the fragile hold that politicians have on public affections these days.'

Stephen sounded weary and irritated and I found the change in his manner unnerving. Surely, if he were so worried about publicity, he shouldn't have bought the house in the first place? And it was highly unlikely that a finger would be pointed at him for Ian's death. Except that he was nearby at the time, it was nothing to do with him. Yet stories could be easily twisted.

He was looking serious, with no sign of his usual smile. I could see he was afraid that the article might grow into doorstepping and other pressure from the media. I was glad that my obscure life ran no risk of anything like that, but at the same time I didn't like what he was suggesting at all.

'It's such a shame. I love the house and if it were just me, I wouldn't sell, but Stephen has to think of his career,' Angela said.

'I want to sell. I wasn't sure at first, but I've been thinking of it increasingly,' Jenny said.

That was news to me, but no-one questioned Jenny. It was only too understandable that she might wish to leave Castignac.

'I love it there and I don't want to sell,' I said. 'Couldn't we delay the decision to give us a chance of enjoying Castignac? After all, we've put so much into it and we might feel differently in six months or a year.'

'Good idea, Tessa. I'm reluctant to sell. I'm just getting into my stride with decorating the house and I love the countryside,' Graham said.

Everyone looked at Lily, who had been silent so far.

'I'm upset by Ian's death and inclined to think we should sell,' she said.

I doubted Graham would insist on having his way, if Lily wanted to sell. He always seemed to put her first.

'I don't want to delay,' Stephen said in reply to my suggestion. 'I'd like to get on with putting the house on the market as we seem to have a majority in favour of selling.'

'What a pity. There's so much I want to do there,' I said, unwilling to give in. 'We haven't found out about the history of Castignac or explored the area properly—'

'Nonsense, Tessa,' Stephen said, interrupting me. 'Look, you have a flat in London, but I've never heard you talk about the people who used to live there, so why all this interest in the history of Castignac? It's a farmhouse. Farmers lived there. Why does it matter who they were? Their history is in the past.'

'Not quite,' I said. 'We don't know for certain, but Ian might have lost his life because of curiosity about Castignac's past.'

Jenny turned a stricken face towards me, burst into tears and fled the room.

'Now look at what you've done!' Angela said, frowning at me. Her reprimand made me feel terrible and I was tempted to do the same as Jenny.

'I'll go and apologise,' I said, getting up and leaving the room with as much dignity as I could summon.

I found Jenny in the kitchen, drying her eyes, and I apologised for my insensitivity.

'It's all right, Tessa. I probably shouldn't have come. I was in two minds about it, but I knew Stephen and Angela were going to suggest selling, so I thought I should be here for the decision. And what you said is perfectly reasonable. I'm all right now, so let's go back in and face them.'

We joined the others, both of us apologising for the scene.

'So, are we all agreed, except Tessa?' Stephen said.

Everyone, except me, nodded. We had agreed, when buying the house, that any dispute would be resolved by majority decision.

'What will happen to the group now?' Lily said. 'As we're going to sell the house, I suppose the whole thing will come to an end. It's a shame, though. I was enjoying it and I love France.'

'It is a shame,' Stephen said, as if he weren't causing the break-up of the group, but the decision was made. Angela promised to phone Gilles in the morning and ask him to put the house on the market.

It was hard to believe that the early excitement, not much more than a year ago, of owning a house in France had disappeared so quickly. It was a low moment and I was tempted to feel sorry for myself. I could hear Jackie and my friends saying that I had fallen in love with a man I scarcely ever saw and now I loved a place that I was going to lose.

Angela rang a few days later to tell me about her conversation with Gilles.

'When I asked Gilles to put the house on the market, he tried to argue me out of it! He says Castignac will be difficult to sell, despite the work we've done on it, because of Ian's death on the property. He even said something about it not being the only death.'

'That's right. Do you remember that Marianne told us about a hanging in the ruined farmhouse?' I said.

'Oh, yes. I'd forgotten about that with all this going on. But if it's hard to sell, perhaps we'll have a few more holidays there.'

I liked that thought.

'And Gilles isn't the only person in the town to be upset about the sale. Marianne is sorry that we're going after such a short time. She said, "Oh no! I'm losing my English," when I rang to tell her, as if she's going to lose status in the town!'

'But did Gilles agree to try and sell it?'

'Oh, yes. He didn't refuse outright.'

'It's a pity more of us don't speak better French,' I said, thinking that too much was resting on Angela's shoulders.

'If Stephen's French were fluent, I would still be the one doing things. He's good at delegating, as he likes to say, and because he's rarely at home, I have to pick up all the pieces. I'm becoming a real grass widow,' Angela said.

'You sound fed up,' I said. 'That's not like you. Is it because of Castignac?'

Her reply was frank. 'I know it's awful that Ian died, but I don't want to sell Castignac and Stephen does. I can't stand in his way, just because it's my chance to get away from it all. You know, not just my job, but the constituency.'

'I don't want to sell either, but we're in a minority, at least at the moment.'

I was glad of my job and its ability to absorb me at work. I took refuge in the petty squabbles and everyday problems of the library in a way that I'd never done before. I breathed in the ink and paper smell of books and told myself that I preferred it to the smell of old stone. What had been irritating or merely dull before was reassuring.

My imagination had created a chain of events. It was a short chain of three links, with each one leading to the next: Ian's death, selling Castignac, losing Mark. Selling Castignac might not lead to losing Mark, but it had become the place where we met and it was bound up in my mind with him.

I didn't like the uncertainty of not knowing when I would see Mark again. In bad moments, I felt I was pretending to have a relationship that didn't exist. Would we ever see much of each other? I brooded over the scene in the swimming pool towards the end of our summer holiday and how close it came to being a quarrel.

I sent Mark a text about our decision to sell Castignac and asked when we might meet up again. He replied quickly but briefly.

Hi Tessa. Sorry about Castignac. It can't be much fun. Have been cooking local food and will do same for you next time. But v. busy now and next few months. Mark xx

That was depressing, with no suggestions for seeing each other. Doubts flew into my mind. Was Mark cooking for a new girlfriend? Had he dismissed me? Our Castignac group must have seemed frivolous when he was providing the essential service of a water supply to people. And now we were selling the house too soon. I hadn't looked ahead much but had assumed we would keep it for some years.

Despite trying to take refuge in work, I wasn't getting along with the head librarian. She breathed down my neck all the time and was often irritable. It didn't help that she caught me writing a personal email one day. Much of my job involved dealing with the public, but during a quiet moment, the head librarian loomed up behind me and starting reading what was on my screen before I was aware she was there. It wasn't even lunchtime, when I might have had an excuse for doing something personal at work.

Mark's message had left things so much in the air that I couldn't concentrate properly on my job. Not having a plan to see him made me start to fear that it was all over. The head librarian made some crisp remark about how I wasn't paid to conduct my personal life in work time and asked what I was doing about arranging a meeting with library users who had heard rumours about cuts to the library and were demanding a meeting with staff.

I hadn't finished my email, but I pressed send because it was the quickest way to get it off the screen in a crisis.

Hi Mark,

I'm at work, so must be brief. How about a last visit to Castignac at New Year? You said Castignac makes it difficult for you, but I know you don't like going to England at the moment, so I'm thinking of a last visit to the house. I would like to know when I can see you again.

Tessa

I failed to add any sign of affection in my panic and I forgot that he had mentioned cooking a Middle Eastern meal for us.

When the head librarian had gone, I looked at my reply and cursed myself for being a wet blanket. The poor man was in a desert somewhere and I was moaning. I wondered about adding a more cheerful rider but decided it would look too clingy. It wouldn't do to give in to him too much. I would simply wait for his reply.

It was obvious now that Mark was keeping his distance in more ways than one because his reply to my email was a long time coming. A week later, his name popped up in my inbox. I hesitated before opening his message. Was this going to be goodbye? Whatever it was, it was short.

> Hi Tessa. Thanks for inviting me to Castignac again. It's a great place, but I'm saying no this time. Let's cool it for a while. I'm very busy now anyway, as you know, and holidays are the last thing on my mind. Mark xx

I was both furious and upset. I almost banged back an angry one-liner, but I managed to resist. I wasn't going to reply yet, perhaps not ever. I needed to calm down, but I could hardly concentrate on my work that day as I mulled over whether cool it for a while meant for good or whether I should take it literally and if so, for how long.

Mark's few words seemed to be saying that he didn't have time for me at the moment, or did he mean at all? And did he need more space to get over his marriage, when it had ended two years before? This was becoming ridiculous.

All he had ever told me was that his marriage had failed because his wife was unfaithful to him. Some instinct had told me to say as little as possible when I heard that. He hadn't used her name. He never had and he had never referred to his marriage again except as something he needed to get over before making any further commitment. It was obvious that the failure had hit him hard, but whilst I was sympathetic, I was also feeling increasingly impatient.

Had he had enough of me? Had he met someone else, some Lebanese woman who had stunned him so much with her exotic beauty, Eastern perfume and silken garments that he had started cooking meals for her? Jealousy stabbed, and it didn't occur to me that such a woman would be far more likely to be cooking meals for him than the other way round, as he was in her country. I only wondered how a librarian from south London, with or without a share in a house in France, would be able to compete with that.

I bristled. He wasn't the only one with commitments. I could be busy too. I decided to let a period of silence occur. If he didn't contact me then I would know where I stood. I had some pride.

Life would be dull without Mark and without even the prospect of seeing him, but I began by being determined not to let it get me down. I breezed about for a few days, until I found myself alone with Jackie one evening.

'Look at this lovely house in France, rather like yours,' she said, passing a magazine across to me.

We were having a rare evening at home together. Jackie spent most of her spare time with Phil these days, but he was doing something late at school that night.

Glancing at the picture, I saw yellow stone walls, a red-tiled roof, duck egg blue shutters, white hibiscus and a turquoise pool, all sparkling under blue skies. Outside our London flat, a gloomy evening in early November, made darker by the hour falling back the week before, had descended. I was overwhelmed by a longing to be at Castignac with Mark. Yet it didn't look as if we would be going there together again and not just because we were selling up.

I had told Jackie briefly about Mark's last email and now I poured out all my misery. She was sympathetic and didn't try to persuade me that everyone would turn out well, even though that was happening to her and Phil.

'Before Ian's death, Mark was enjoying Castignac, the group was beginning to gel nicely, Didier had done the repairs and the party was successful. Now it's all going into reverse. We're selling Castignac and Mark has disappeared with no plans for us to meet again. I was expecting years of holidays there. I saw myself, and Mark, feeling at home there, getting to know the area better and having favourite places,' I said, passing the magazine back.

'I'm not surprised you're selling, after what's happened. Who would want to buy into a house where someone died so recently in such a horrible way?' Jackie said.

'You don't have to say so. At least it happened in the ruin, although people won't understand that, if they haven't seen the set-up,' I said, with a sigh.

'Why does Castignac matter so much? I mean, it's a great place, but it's only a holiday home,' Jackie said.

'I'm not sure. I feel something is unfinished, or hardly started, and I suppose it's all tied up with Mark in my mind,' I said. 'If things are going wrong with Mark, I want Castignac to work, so that at least one thing in my life is going well.'

'Your life isn't that bad. You've got a good job,' Jackie said.

'Not really,' I said, telling her the story of the reprimand about the email, which I had skipped over before.

I stood up and decided to cook. I felt like doing something active and simple. In the kitchen, I made us a quick meal and opened a bottle of wine. Jackie and I usually only did that on a special occasion or at weekends, but solace was needed.

I felt better after talking to Jackie and I resolved to put Mark behind me. I would act as if he had gone from my life. At least he wasn't in London, or living with me, so it shouldn't be difficult, because I saw so little of him anyway and he played no part in my day-to-day world. Our lack of time together should come to my aid.

It wasn't so easy because there were reminders of him. Any thoughts of Castignac contained Mark; so did plans for travel and even walks by the Thames. I went out with one or two other men, but with no great interest on either side. It wasn't surprising, when I found it hard to sparkle.

Part Four

Part Four

Chapter One

Brigitte

B RIGITTE WAS CUTTING WAXED paper for wrapping up the butter, which her mother Danielle was making. They were in the dairy, a small outbuilding on the north side of the Castignac farmhouse, near the milking shed. It was relatively cool in there, and its whitewashed walls and white tiles made it seem even cooler. On a hot summer's day, such as this one, that was welcome.

When the butter was ready, Brigitte would weigh out half kilo portions on brass scales, pat each one into shape with wooden bats and stamp it. The stamp was simply the name Castignac written in a circle, as on the stone placed at the entrance to the farm. She would then wrap each portion in the greaseproof paper and stack them to await the Monday market.

Brigitte, now fourteen, had left school. She was bored with cutting the paper and was gazing out of the window at fields and trees, wanting to be out of doors. A movement outside led her to crane her neck to see what was happening. Her father was struggling with Rose, the oldest of the farm horses. Rose was lying on the ground and Jean-Louis was pulling on her halter, trying to make her stand up.

'Look at Rose, *Maman*. She'll die if she can't get up!'

They both knew that a horse shouldn't lie down for too long after a pleasurable roll on the ground.

Danielle stopped churning and peered out of the window with Brigitte. 'Oh, I can't leave the churn now. The butter's just beginning to come. Where's Hébrard?' Danielle said.

'I don't know. I'll go.'

Brigitte went to the aid of her father before Danielle could call her back. Between them they pulled at Rose's halter. Rose was trying hard, her hooves scrabbling on the ground, and at last she was able to stand up.

'You've got a bit of strength in those muscles now, girl,' Jean-Louis said to Brigitte, patting Rose's neck to soothe her after her struggle.

Brigitte was flushed and excited from her success and her father's praise, which was rare. She didn't even mind being called girl, although normally she disliked it because it made her feel that she wasn't good enough. Her father only used her name when he was annoyed with her.

Brigitte loved her father and was desperate to earn his approval. Until the incident with Rose, nothing had ever seemed so difficult. She had always known that he wanted a son. Yet Jacquot had died of scarlet fever when he was little more than a baby and Brigitte, a girl, had come along instead. There were no photographs of Jacquot, only the story about his death that Brigitte had grown up with. He wasn't talked about much, but he was never entirely absent.

Despite loving him, Brigitte had been fearful of her father as a little girl. He had seemed remote and strict. He was out in the fields with Hébrard all day long and often didn't arrive home, at least in the summer, until after she had gone to bed. She spent her early years largely with her mother and grandmother, and then was at school for much of the time. Her grandmother died when she was ten, but even when the small family was reduced, Jean-Louis didn't take much notice of his daughter.

Her mother was determined to make Brigitte work all day once she had left school. Brigitte had other ideas but dared not cross her mother. She wanted to go into the town and meet her friends, but there was no easy escape, because Danielle was stern. She had been brought up to work hard on the farm where she had grown up and she was bringing up Brigitte in the same way. Danielle met any disobedience with a good slap.

There was always laundry to do, the house to clean, butter to make and prepare for the market, bread to knead, cakes and pies to bake, and much more. The list was endless, and Brigitte longed for brothers and sisters to share the work, but in vain. Sometimes she would escape to Nicolette's cottage, where Marie and Jeanne seemed to have more time to play, but Danielle would come over and drag her home again with sharp words.

It didn't help that for years now there had been something called the Depression, which meant that her father had to sell his wheat and other crops at a low price, and her mother made less on her market stall because people didn't have the money to pay for the farm produce. Even so, they still had to pay taxes, which her father grumbled about constantly. The government gave him nothing back, so why should he have to pay them?

Everyone said that times were hard, but Brigitte couldn't remember when they had been any better. There had been a war before she was born, so times couldn't have been better then. Some of the old people in the town liked to think that things had been better before the war, but that was history. At least the Lordat family had a roof over their heads and food in their mouths. They weren't poor. People in the town with barely a roof or a job were poor, but not the Lordats.

Brigitte's bedroom had been hers as long as she could remember. It was a good size and furnished with a daybed, a dressing table, an old chest where she kept her treasures, a wardrobe with a mirror and a couple of wooden chairs. On the floor was a large rag rug. Her mother had tried to replace the daybed with what she called a proper bed, but Brigitte had insisted on keeping it. A comfortable mattress covered its hard surface.

What she liked best about her bedroom wasn't the furniture, but the view from her window of St Martin des Remparts and the hills and mountains beyond. She always began the day by gazing out of the window, only dragging herself away at the sound of her mother's impatient voice. She liked to play a game with the flawed old glass in the windowpanes. She would sway from side to side and whatever she was looking at would change shape, making grotesque patterns. The spire on the church would wriggle or trees would shiver.

It wasn't the view or the game with the old glass that occupied her attention on the summer evening after she had helped her father with Rose, although she spared the town a glance. Alone in her bedroom, she flexed the muscles of her arms. She was showing signs of the strong young woman she would like to become. After the incident with Rose, she thought she had found a way to show her father that she mattered. She would help him in the fields. Why had she never thought of that before? She had been too busy being under her mother's thumb. Things were going to change.

There was no persuading her back into the house after that. She would milk the cows and lug the churns into the dairy for Danielle to make butter or for collection by the local milk depot, but that was all. Every spare moment, she was with the animals or out in the fields with Jean-Louis or Hébrard.

There were plenty of boots around the house that she could wear and she could plait her thick hair to keep it out of the way, but she lacked the clothing for the change from house to field. Skirts and dresses quickly became muddy in the fields and restricted her movement. Danielle complained about the mess Brigitte was in and the extra work it meant for her in doing the laundry.

Brigitte went to the broom cupboard in the kitchen after getting up one morning. She rummaged through the ragbag that was hanging there and scattered old clothes over the floor.

'What are you up to now?' Danielle said irritably, seeing the floor heaped with the contents of the ragbag.

'I want some trousers. I can't work in the fields in a skirt all the time,' Brigitte said.

'Well, you won't find any trousers for women in there or anywhere here. We wear skirts.'

'Oh, they don't have to be for women. Any trousers will do. Oh, look. Here's an old pair of *Papa's* trousers. I'll wear them,' Brigitte said, holding them up. They were worn and patched because the Lordats wore all their clothes until they were threadbare, except for Sunday best, but Brigitte didn't care. They were trousers.

She changed into them there and then, rolling up the trouser ends to fit her shorter legs and pulling in the waist with a belt she found hanging on the back door.

'You look like a scarecrow,' Danielle said grumpily.

She didn't insist on Brigitte returning to skirts and Brigitte knew that the grumpiness wasn't just about her clothing. Danielle had been looking forward to having her daughter at home now that she had left school. She had even said so, during Brigitte's last term, but Brigitte had abandoned her mother. With her father clearly pleased to have his daughter's help on the farm, there was little her mother could do about it.

On Sundays, however, Brigitte put on her best dress and went to church. On Mondays, she wore a blouse and skirt and went to the big, weekly market with Danielle. They harnessed Rose to the cart piled with goods and drove into the town. Brigitte loved the sounds and colours and thronging of people in the market and enjoyed selling their goods.

She liked running into old school friends in the town and there was always the chance of seeing Gilbert. She had met him at school and he was also the son of Guy, one of Nicolette's seven brothers. Brigitte liked Gilbert, and her only regret on leaving school was that she might not easily see him again. Yet he usually made his way to the Castignac stall on Mondays and even sometimes on Thursdays, when there was a farmers' market, a much smaller affair, where Danielle liked to set up her stall as well.

Gilbert was a friendly, easy-going boy with neatly cut, dark hair and a ready smile. He was the same height as Brigitte, who was tall for a girl. He had a way with Danielle, whom he teased about her stall, with a running joke that she could never have made all her goods within a week, even with Brigitte's help, and that she must have a secret team of people working all night on the farm.

'Let me take Brigitte for a walk. She needs the exercise,' he said to Danielle after his first few visits to the stall.

'All right, but only for a look round the market. Make sure she's back in half an hour,' Danielle said, mollified by his attention to her.

'Come on, Brigitte! Let's go and see the knife sharpener. Dad has given me some tools for him to work on,' Gilbert said, patting his backpack. They went off together.

Gilbert was comfortable with himself and didn't seem to be afraid of anyone. It became a habit for them to go around the market together on Monday mornings, always with the permission of Danielle, which Gilbert made sure to obtain.

'You're good with *Maman*,' Brigitte said. 'She's so strict, but you seem to have a way of getting round her.'

'So do you,' Gilbert said. 'At least, from what you told me. You escaped her apron strings to work in the fields.'

'That's true,' Brigitte said, with a feeling of satisfaction. She had a lot to do on the farm, but she felt much happier now she had taken matters more into her own hands. The farm was her life. She didn't want ever to leave it. A woman could be a farmer, just like a man.

August was a busy month with the wheat harvest. The wheat fields had changed from the brown of bare earth to the green of growing plants and finally to golden ripe wheat, rustling in the summer breeze under blue skies. As usual, everyone was helping. Hébrard, with his family, and Joseph, with his family, were there, along with Jean-Louis, Danielle and Brigitte.

Gilbert came on Brigitte's invitation, because Jean-Louis wanted all the help he could get. As Gilbert arrived at Castignac, panting slightly from the walk uphill, he laughed, seeing Brigitte in trousers for the first time.

'Don't worry, Brigitte. I'll never mistake you for a boy, with all that hair and your...'

He stopped and Brigitte could have sworn that he blushed. She laughed. It was true that she was growing up. Her breasts were noticeable now, monthlies had come the previous year and men were starting to look at her in a way that wasn't always welcome. Gilbert was all right, though. She welcomed his attention.

It took several days to cut the three wheat fields. They used the tractor and the two carthorses on alternate days. The reaper cut the wheat as it did every year. Brigitte joined in with enthusiasm, all the while anxious to impress her father.

The best part came at the end when the wheat fields were cut. On the morning of the last day of the harvest, Jean-Louis and Brigitte brought the *monastère* into the garden. Danielle added chairs and piled the *monastère* with food and with wine that they had bought on tap. When the harvest was in, everyone feasted until late in the evening.

'You did well, girl,' Jean-Louis said to her over breakfast the next morning.

'But don't call me girl,' Brigitte said, scowling. 'I've got a name.'

She had never dared to snap at her father before and wondered if she had gone too far.

'All right, Brigitte,' he said.

In September came the turn of the potato crop that Jean-Louis had planted that year.

'I'm going to borrow Joseph's digger today and attach it to the tractor for getting up the potatoes tomorrow,' he said one morning.

'I'll help,' Brigitte said. 'I can be behind the tractor and pick up the potatoes with Hébrard.'

'All right, my girl. Make sure you're up in time, because I'm starting straight after milking,' her father said.

'I'll be up with the lark!'

'See that you are.'

Brigitte was out in the field at dawn the next morning. Jean-Louis had borrowed the digger the night before to make sure of finishing the potato field in a single day. He hitched the digger to the tractor and drove to the potato field with Brigitte walking beside him.

Brigitte clambered down and took up her position behind the tractor. Hébrard turned up with two baskets and gave one to her. Jean-Louis inched the tractor forward along the first row and the potatoes seemed to spring to the surface of the earth, where they lay, pale and round, the cleaner ones glistening and others clinging to clumps of earth until it was nudged off as they were gathered up. Brigitte and Hébrard picked up the potatoes, filling their baskets and emptying them into the wooden box on the tractor.

It was hard work, and Brigitte's back was aching before long, but she was determined not to give in. Standing in the row, legs wide and bending down to pick up the potatoes, she filled and emptied her basket again and again while the tractor inched ahead. She was greatly relieved when, after they had finished a number of rows, Hébrard called a halt. He had a thermos flask and gave Jean-Louis and Brigitte hot coffee.

They carried on for the rest of the morning, until they saw Danielle appear with a basket. There was to be no lunch in the kitchen that day because Jean-Louis wanted the potato field finished by dusk, so the Lordats ate bread and cheese and fruit while Hébrard produced his own lunch, packed for him that morning by Nicolette.

There was something that Brigitte wanted to do, for its own sake and as a relief from bending down to pick up potatoes.

'Let me drive, *Papa!*' she said after lunch. She had never driven the tractor before, but it looked easy at such a slow speed.

'All right, but just to the end of the row. I don't want you trying to turn it round,' Jean-Louis said.

Brigitte climbed into the driver's seat and he showed her how to turn the engine on and put it into the lowest of many gears before he jumped off. She drove along the whole row, inch by inch, while Jean-Louis and Hébrard picked up potatoes behind her. It was a beautiful summer's day; she felt like a queen until the row ended and she climbed down to let Jean-Louis take the wheel. He let her drive along several rows that day, a welcome break from being bent double over the crop.

Hébrard's daughters, Marie and Jeanne, came along to help pick up potatoes but were too young to be allowed to drive the tractor. The job was done by dusk and Jean-Louis took the digger back to Joseph after Hébrard had taken a share of the potatoes for his family's use and Jean-Louis had given a similar amount to Danielle.

Brigitte became an expert tractor driver, turning the machine round at the end of a row and changing gears. Later in the year, she helped harvest beetroots and carrots. Everyone liked Danielle's wood-smoked beetroots. With their skin wrinkled and their taste matured from wood-smoking, they disappeared quickly from the market stall.

Chapter Two

Danielle

Danielle stood in the kitchen at Castignac, sighing with irritation at the taste of the butter she had found on the kitchen table. The weather was hot in August, but the butter needn't have gone rancid. Brigitte, charged with clearing up after last night's meal, had left it out, instead of putting it in the cool of the larder. It wouldn't have mattered so much before the war, but with the cost of things and all the rationing in place now, every scrap of food counted.

By 1942, Danielle was sixty, stouter than in her youth, her face lined and her hair, still tied in a bun, now grey. At Brigitte's age, Danielle had been married, with her life mapped out. Her mother had taught her everything that a farmer's wife needed to know and heaven knew that Danielle had done her best to pass the knowledge on to her own daughter.

She had not succeeded. Brigitte was a scatterbrain around the house, with her way of treating domestic work as if it were beneath her. Yet she had to learn, because she, too, would be a farmer's wife one day. That was the hope of Jean-Louis and Danielle, but exactly when it would happen was in doubt. Brigitte had certainly let that nice boy Gilbert slip through her fingers.

Hardly any men were about these days because of the war, and Gilbert had disappeared as soon as it started, first into the army and then, after the armistice, no-one seemed to know where he was. He was probably hiding out in the maquis, escaping a labour camp. Brigitte was twenty-four now and time was passing. She ought to marry someone who would be willing to come and take over Castignac, but the war seemed to have put anything like that on hold. If she didn't find a husband, the farm might have to be sold. What a calamity that would be, with Jean-Louis' habit of pointing out that it had been in the family for over four hundred years! That was the trouble with having only one child, and a girl at that. If only little Jacquot had lived, it wouldn't matter so much what Brigitte did. Everyone knew that a farmer's best years came when his sons were old enough to farm with him.

After all these years, Danielle didn't dwell on Jacquot, but she couldn't entirely forget him. His death from scarlet fever at the age of two had occurred over twenty-five years ago and after that she had simply got on with life. There had been no time for moping. Brigitte had come along later, of course, but that was all. Jean-Louis had been stricken at the loss of Jacquot and his disappointment had grown with the birth of a girl and the lack of any further children.

Yet he, at least, was pleased at the way Brigitte had turned out. As careless as she might be in the house, she had certainly done her best to make up for being only a girl. She had scarcely been seen in the dairy or the kitchen, except for meals, since the day she gone out into the fields to help her father with Rose, the old horse, long dead.

Danielle now made the butter and cheese on her own or with Nicolette, who had become a skilled dairymaid. She tasted the butter in the dish again. It was rancid. With another sigh, she picked up the dish and carried it out to the pig bin. The pigs weren't fussy and would eat it, mixed in with their swill.

The years between the wars, when Brigitte was growing up, hadn't been easy, what with the Depression and poor prices for their wheat and other farm produce, but Castignac had survived. It had even featured in the regional newspaper, *La Dépêche*, one year. A photograph of her and Jean-Louis standing outside Castignac had appeared as part of an article about farming and they had been given a copy. Hébrard and Nicolette's girls, Marie and Jeanne, had been Brigitte's close companions during those years, but they had left Castignac now and were married and living in the town.

This war had come so soon after the last one that people said it was all one war with a break in the middle. Of course, it had affected Castignac, even though they were far from occupied France. Both Jean-Louis and Hébrard were too old to be conscripted and food rationing affected a farm less than it did people in the town. Castignac's milk, bread, butter and jam, cheese, and vegetables kept them all well-fed. Then there were various meats, like bacon, ham, sausages and joints for a good roast on Sundays. Danielle was proud of their farm produce. They sold it for the best price they could get and didn't have to buy much food. Trade was easy for a farm so close to the town and they also sold produce on the black market, as everyone did, although they simply called it helping out a neighbour or a friend.

So many young men were prisoners of war that it was hard to find farm labour these days, and who knew what was going to happen before the war ended? Jean-Louis scorned the Vichy government for giving in to the *boches* so easily and Danielle agreed with him. There would be no protection if they decided to tear up the armistice.

Danielle returned to the kitchen to set out their breakfast on the scrubbed pine table that occupied the centre of the room. She brought out bowls for coffee from the wooden dresser that took up most of one wall, cut slices off a big loaf of her home-made bread, and found fresh butter and jars of jam. Jean-Louis and Brigitte, out on the farm since dawn, were always hungry by breakfast time.

She spooned chicory into a jug, poured in water she had heated up on the range and stirred. Real coffee was even harder to obtain now than before the war, but they had never bothered much with it and were used to the chicory substitute.

Brigitte came into the kitchen. She was wearing her usual shirt and trousers, these days run up for her by a seamstress in St Martin des Remparts and not the hand-me-downs she had worn when first working with her father. Her thick dark hair was tied back, as it always was when she was working, and her face with its strong features was brown from her outdoor life. She had been milking the cows.

'Marguerite's last calf was born dead and she's due to have this one any day now, so I'm keeping an eye on her.'

Brigitte made light of the butter incident when Danielle tackled her about it. Jean-Louis joined them and they began the meal. He was worried.

'This drought is doing us no good on top of a poor harvest. The vegetables are behind.'

'Our produce is fetching a good price in the market,' Danielle said, not to be cast down.

'Yes, but the supplies we need are now much more expensive because of the war.'

'At least we can grow a variety of crops, not like the Mediterranean side, where they're limited to vines and olives,' Danielle said.

Brigitte had quite a different concern.

'More people are coming down from the north. Paulette says someone needs a bed for the night. Only for a few days, so she can rest up before she goes on to Spain. Is that all right, *Maman*? I told *Papa* and he agrees,' she said in between mouthfuls.

Danielle was taken aback. People had been escaping the *boches* since the beginning of the war, but they never had anyone to stay at Castignac. And there was Brigitte, ganging up with her father again, so that Danielle was always the last to know anything. It had been like that ever since Brigitte had started working with him in the fields. Despite the good company of Nicolette, Danielle sometimes felt lonely.

'But who is it?' she said.

'I don't know, but I told Paulette we could offer her a bed for a few nights. She'll be safer here, out of the way, than in the town. Police and officials are always sniffing around down there.'

Paulette was a friend of Brigitte's from the town. Danielle had heard about people arriving from the occupied zone.

'You mean a refugee? Because of the war?'

'Yes, a Jewish woman. They're imprisoning Jews, sending them off to prison and I don't know what else. She's from Paris.'

Danielle had never been to Paris. Like everyone she knew, she thought of Parisians as rich people from the other side of the country. The only city she had been to was Toulouse and that rarely, with Jean-Louis, to buy farm tools and equipment. Before the war, they had occasionally made a day of it, taking the farm truck. She had always been impressed by the shops with their impossibly expensive goods, but she hadn't liked the noise and crowds and had been glad to return to the peace of Castignac. Now, with the war on, they didn't have the money for a visit to Toulouse.

'Oh, I don't know... if she's from Paris, she'll look down on us,' Danielle said, discomforted.

'*Maman*, she's on the run! She'll be glad to be safe,' Brigitte said.

'I don't want a stranger staying in the house. You never know what might happen,' Danielle said.

'She can sleep in the old farmhouse at this time of year,' Jean-Louis said, finishing his chicory and holding out his bowl for more.

Danielle filled it from the jug on the stove. Jean-Louis was undisputed lord of his farm and not one to be deterred from letting a stranger spend the night there, whatever anyone might think, but she had another objection.

'Won't we get into trouble with the authorities?'

'They won't know. Look, *Maman*, you're always telling me about billeting twenty soldiers at once in the last war. This is only one woman, tired from a long journey, probably with little money. She needs help. We must do our bit.'

Danielle thought back to the soldiers billeted with them during the last war at the request of the army. One of them had been Hébrard, who had turned out to be such a blessing.

'All right, but you must look after her, make up a bed out there. And it's just this once,' Danielle said.

Brigitte's warm smile made Danielle feel, for a moment, that she had her daughter back.

It was washday, a Monday, and Danielle was boiling the laundry in the copper and putting it through the mangle, before hanging everything out to dry and then preparing lunch. She had just finished her chores when the refugee arrived. Accompanied by Paulette, whose large family meant that she didn't have space to shelter anyone, she looked pale, thin and exhausted. Paulette handed her over but didn't stay.

Anna was her name. She was little more than a girl, younger than Brigitte and grateful to the Lordats for taking her in. She joined the family for lunch, telling them in a quick, bright voice about the occupation of Paris and her escape.

'They've made life so difficult for us. There are so many jobs we can't do and places we can't go to and now we have to wear the yellow star. But the worst thing is the roundups. I only escaped because I was staying with a friend that night.'

Danielle was horrified. 'What about your family?'

'They were taken – my parents and my younger brother, to a place in eastern Paris. I went there to try and see them, but I was too late. They've been sent to Germany. That was when I knew I had to escape.'

Anna's face crumpled as she spoke and Danielle saw desperation under her bright manner.

'How did you manage to cross into the unoccupied zone?' Jean-Louis said.

'I didn't have a permit. I was lucky to get a ride in a truck. The driver hid me in the back,' Anna said.

Anna's experiences belonged to a different world from Castignac. Danielle shrank from what she had told them and didn't want to hear any more.

Anna slept in the ruin with makeshift bedding which Brigitte gave her. She only stayed for two days and was then off, heading further south with a lift that Paulette had arranged to a safe house and to meet a guide who would take her over the Pyrenees.

They never heard what happened to Anna, but, despite Danielle's insistence, she wasn't the only person they sheltered. By 1942, a thin stream of refugees from the occupied zone was turning up in St Martin des Remparts. Castignac was in demand as a refuge. Jean-Louis, instinctively against any kind of authority, said it cost them little and sided with Brigitte, but Danielle had her limits.

'I don't want the war in my kitchen,' she said when Brigitte wanted to shelter someone else. 'People can stay in the ruin and you take their food there, but I don't want to be bothered. Is that understood?'

'Of course, *Maman*.'

By chance, Danielle was shopping in St Martin des Remparts when the Nazis arrived on a wintry morning in November 1942. They were now occupying the whole country because they feared an Allied invasion from North Africa. A long column of vehicles drove into the square and officers jumped out, barking orders. Danielle and the few people out and about on that cold morning stared at the invasion. They were not surprised, because they had heard news of it on the radio, but they muttered to each other in disgust.

To date the war had affected people in the unoccupied zone mainly through forced labour, food rationing, lack of supplies and rising costs. Life was harder than it had been, but the occupation had kept its distance and Danielle had only once or twice glimpsed Nazi soldiers in passing. Seeing this arrival, she knew that any freedom had vanished. The only consolation was that at least Castignac was outside the town and the two families there would be able to keep away from the Nazis.

Continuing with her shopping, Danielle watched the invaders organise themselves. Whispers began to spread that they had found the mayor and ordered him to come up with a list of billets and plenty of space to conduct their rule of the town and surrounding countryside. There was no doubt that they intended to be firmly in charge.

Danielle had learned to drive the farm truck as soon as Jean-Louis had bought it. Petrol was scarce and expensive now, but she had driven into town that morning and parked outside the central square. Loading her few purchases into the truck, she caught sight of a Nazi officer looking up at Castignac. The treacherous sun had broken through clouds and was shining on the windows of her home. Beckoning two soldiers, the officer jumped into one of their cars and the men climbed in behind him.

A few minutes later, Danielle found herself in the extraordinary position of driving up to Castignac behind the Nazi car. Any hope she might have had that they would drive on was dashed when their car stopped at the entrance to the house. The officer climbed out and banged on the front door. Jean-Louis and Brigitte were away at the other end of the farm that morning and there was no sign of Hébrard or Nicolette.

Danielle parked the truck and got out with her shopping. Adjusting her bun, she walked over to the officer, who turned to face her. She didn't quail. He was much taller than she was, but she looked him up and down, from his shiny boots and his crisp uniform to his peaked cap and waited, her face as stern and unsmiling as his. She didn't know more than a single word of German, but she was damned if she was going to use it. He would have to make himself understood.

'We want rooms, one for me and two for our men. And there's a gun to set up,' the officer said, in halting French.

Danielle understood immediately that her greatest fear was realised. The war had finally come to Castignac and she dared not refuse the demand. She nodded and beckoned the officer to follow her into the house. She left her shopping in the kitchen and took the *boche* upstairs where she indicated three bedrooms he could use. Brigitte would have to move out of her room facing the town, because a machine gun, trained on St Martin des Remparts, was going to be placed there.

Leaving the soldier to settle in with his men, Danielle set off to find Jean-Louis and tell him what had happened. She had trudged over several fields before she found him clearing a stream.

'I saw the *boches* in town this morning and now they have come to Castignac and are demanding three rooms in the house. I couldn't refuse,' she said to him.

Jean-Louis was in his sixties now, still a strong man devoted to his farm. Danielle worried about him because he was easily cast down. She had first noticed it years ago after the accident when a car had frightened the horse he was riding. The loss of his brothers in the last war, then Jacquot's death and the lack of any other sons had added to his gloom. She knew he wouldn't take the news well.

'Nothing like this has ever happened here before.' He put down the shovel he had been using and looked aghast.

'It's because they want to install a gun and train it on the town.'

At lunchtime, Danielle spoke to Brigitte in a low voice. 'Castignac can't be a refuge anymore. It's too dangerous now they are here. You must tell Paulette and anyone else.'

'Of course, *Maman*.' Brigitte was sobered by the events of the morning.

The officer made sure that the mayor was aware of the position of the gun and word of its arrival spread quickly. Any sign of rebellion would lead to swift and sure reprisals. Whereas people were accustomed to glancing casually up at Castignac from the square of St Martin des Remparts, they now began to do so with a measure of unease. The Castignac families, both well-established in the town, became aware of this change from remarks, whether serious or jesting, that came their way. Such a divide had never happened before, as far as anyone at Castignac knew. Neither the Lordats nor the Montvals liked it.

Chapter Three

Hébrard

IN THE YEARS SINCE his death, Hébrard hadn't forgotten Eugène. Gritting his teeth over the Nazi invasion of his country in 1940 and then of his adopted town two years later, he remembered his vow, made at the time, to atone for deserting in the last war. This war had come close to him now and he would fight in the only way possible. He would join the resistance in St Martin des Remparts.

By the end of 1942, the voice of resistance, uncertain at first, was growing stronger in France. Hébrard was in his late forties by then, a big, physically fit, quiet man, sure of himself after his rocky start in the last war. He had lived at Castignac for nearly thirty years and knew the area well. Through Nicolette and Pierre, he had come to know many people in the town. People had accepted him and he was now well regarded, a key figure on the farm, with a local wife and a family.

Hébrard sat in his accustomed seat at the bar where Pierre worked one evening soon after the arrival of the Nazis. Pierre was serving customers whilst having a glass of red wine with Hébrard. He was still able to find wine for a favoured customer. They had been good friends for many years and played *boules* together when Hébrard had time.

'They've taken over Castignac and trained a machine gun on the town,' Hébrard was saying.

Pierre, always at the heart of local news, already knew that and nodded. 'They're stealing our food and supplies, leaving us practically nothing,' he said in disgust.

News of the ways in which the Nazis were taking the cream off the top of the local economy was travelling fast around the town. Hébrard was well aware of how much Pierre hated the Nazi occupation.

'If there's anything I can do to help get rid of the pests...' he began, his own voice no more than a murmur.

Pierre was interested. 'You can join our group. We're already collecting information to pass on to the Allies and planning surprises for the *boches*,' he said quietly.

No-one else in the café could hear them. The occupation was already revealing who could and could not be trusted, and it was wise to ensure that listening ears heard nothing. There were collaborators and Nazi sympathisers in St Martin des Remparts as there were everywhere.

Hébrard nodded. 'Tell me where and when and I'll be with you if I can,' he said.

Pierre nodded and reached for the bottle to refresh their glasses before quietly giving Hébrard details of a meeting.

Hébrard joined the resistance group which Pierre led and found that he already knew some of the members, middle-aged men like himself. In addition, there were three young women, who were friends and had been drawn into the group by their leader, Suzanne, one of Pierre's many customers. Young men had vanished from the town. They had either been sent to work camps in Germany or had disappeared into the maquis, the scrubland beyond the surrounding farms.

The group met in the evenings, always somewhere different, with details of the meetings passed by word of mouth. Hébrard told no-one at home what he was doing, not even Nicolette. It was too risky with a houseful of Nazis next door and Nicolette keeping in regular contact with her large family. She was trustworthy, but it would be unfair to burden her with his secret when anyone could make a slip of the tongue. Castignac people simply thought that Hébrard liked to go down to the town for a drink after work more often these days or, if they thought differently, had the sense to keep quiet.

'My brother Raymond wants to join us,' Pierre said one evening as a meeting of the group began.

Hébrard stiffened, ill at ease because he had never liked Raymond. 'How does he know about it?'

'He doesn't, but he asked me what he could do to help with resistance. He's probably guessed I know more than I've been letting on. It's a bit surprising because he's never shown any dislike of the occupation, but I'm prepared to vouch for him.'

Hébrard didn't want to come between the brothers, especially as Pierre was a good friend, so he didn't stand in the way and nor did the other members of the group. Raymond began to attend their meetings. He volunteered information from time to time, but he didn't offer to do much and privately Hébrard not only thought that he was useless, but also that he knew too much about what the Nazis were doing. The town had been even fuller of rumours than usual since their arrival, but Raymond spoke with authority. Still not wishing to cause trouble between the brothers, Hébrard kept his suspicions to himself.

The winter that year was extremely cold, like the previous winter. Hébrard was glad to have the resistance work to take his mind off the weather. There was less to do on the farm in the winter and time could hang heavily.

The group was busy. The young women organised a demonstration against the town hall for complying too enthusiastically with Nazi orders, producing and distributing leaflets for it. Others put together what information they could about the occupiers' movements and passed it on to Allied contacts that Pierre had made. They organised hiding places for local Jewish people, who were now being hunted down, imprisoned at a concentration camp near the village of Le Vernet d'Ariège, not far from Pamiers, and sent away, no-one knew where. The resistance group was too far to the north to guide people across the Pyrenees, but, as Castignac had done before it was occupied, they provided shelter for men and occasionally women who were travelling south or north and in need of help, either a bed for the night or a meal and some rest before they continued on their way.

Encouraged by small successes, the group began to think more ambitiously. In the summer of 1943, Pierre spelled out a plan.

'They're using the railway and the roads for taking produce and materials east to Germany. We're going to try and disrupt that. We can blow up the railway line.'

'Even better, destroy the road bridge. They can replace railway tracks easily, but with the road bridge being high above the river, repairing it would be a big operation,' Suzanne said. Short, curly hair surrounded her lively face and she was eager for action.

'You can't do that! You'd cut Castignac off from the town!' Hébrard said immediately.

The only way into St Martin des Remparts from Castignac,

unless he went for miles around, was across the road bridge over the river. The same was true for several other farms and nearby villages. The farmers needed to sell produce in the market, and they and the villagers purchased supplies from the town.

'Hébrard is right,' Pierre said. 'We can't possibly blow up the road bridge. It'll have to be the railway tracks. The *boches* use the railway to transport produce and supplies just as much as they use the roads. I've started collecting explosives, but we need a safe house not far from the railway line to store them.'

With the Nazis in possession, Hébrard couldn't offer Castignac, nor even the cottage where he and Nicolette lived, as a safe house, but he had an idea that might be helpful.

'There's an old shepherd's hut at the southern end of the farm, not far from where the railway line crosses a road. The railway bridge would be a good place to blow up. The hut is on our land, but we don't have any sheep these days and it's not used anymore. Of course, it's under the noses of the *boches*, but they never go near it. I'll have to square it with Jean-Louis, but he's a sympathiser and if he agrees, I can show you how to get there unnoticed.'

'Thanks, I can take a look at it with you,' Pierre said.

'How are you getting explosives?' Suzanne said.

Pierre grinned. 'I have a contact at the stone quarry. They use dynamite. He can't give me more than a couple of sticks at a time because it would be noticed, but we can slowly build up enough to put the railway line out of action, without killing anyone.'

Everyone knew the stone quarry which had supplied much of the building material for the town. Jean-Louis had told Hébrard that the stone for Castignac had come from there. Nearly a hundred years later, the stone quarry was still in use.

'Don't we want to kill the *boches*?' Suzanne was impatient.

'If we kill them, there'll be reprisals. People here won't thank us for that, especially if far more of them are killed as a result,' Pierre said.

Suzanne muttered something about reprisals for blowing up the railway line, but she gave way. With some misgivings, the group agreed to go ahead with Pierre's plan.

Jean-Louis was still fuming at the presence of the Nazis at Castignac and willing to help the resistance.

'All right,' he said, when Hébrard asked him about using the hut to build up a store of explosives. 'Of course, it's risky, but the hut is inconspicuous and far away enough not to attract attention. They don't go anywhere near those fields. But be careful.'

'They won't know anything,' Hébrard said.

A day or so later, Hébrard and Pierre wended their way along footpaths shielded by tall hedges to the hut, pushing open the wooden door. A single window gave some light and they could see it was empty apart from an old table. The hut had only one room and sat low on the ground. Over the years, it had taken on the colours of the countryside around it and its roof was covered in moss so that it was barely visible from a distance. Surrounding brambles added to the impression of neglect. That it was on a farm occupied by the *boches* might be an advantage, because people would be less likely to show any curiosity about it.

'It's ideal,' Pierre said. 'We'll need to be careful not to be seen coming here, but we'll store the dynamite on this table, wrapped up against damp.'

Hébrard pointed out the nearby railway bridge and took Pierre over to it. They stood underneath, on a path which connected a nearby village with the town.

'It'll be easy to climb up from here,' Pierre said, pointing to the gradual slope of the earth to the railway line. 'We'll put the dynamite on the middle of the bridge. It'll cause much more damage than anything on the ground.'

The railway line which ran through St Martin des Remparts was the one on which Hébrard had travelled from Orthez in 1915 and which had taken him on his visit ten years later to the farm where he had grown up. Blowing up the line would deprive people of an important form of public transport, but damaging Nazi supply lines was vital in winning the war.

'We're doing it under their noses,' Pierre said with suppressed glee one day as he and Hébrard added to the store of dynamite and closed the door of the hut behind them.

Slowly the supplies accumulated in the disused shepherd's hut. One day in September 1943, Pierre decided that there was probably enough dynamite for the job. There was one difficulty, which they had been aware of for some time. None of them had any experience of using explosives.

Pierre had contacts with a group of *maquisards* and had sent several messages asking for help. One evening, when Hébrard arrived at a meeting in Pierre's small house, his friend introduced him to a stranger. Albert was a young man from St Martin des Remparts, a former soldier, who understood explosives. He had joined a local group of *maquisards* in order to escape being sent to a labour camp and he would help the group with the sabotage of the railway bridge. He would stay with his parents in secret for the next few days, until the job was done.

Pierre took Albert on a reconnaissance trip to the railway bridge and to see the supplies of dynamite which Albert pronounced sufficient. A date was agreed for the explosion and that it would occur at night after the last train of the evening and before the first one of the next morning. Suzanne was put in charge of making anonymous telephone calls to the station at Pamiers, in one direction, and Limoux, in the other direction, alerting staff. Timing was important, both to avoid accidents to French trains or their passengers and also to avoid any action by station staff or the police aimed at preventing the explosion.

Pierre, Hébrard and Albert had to work fast on the night, carrying the explosives to the railway bridge on foot after the last train had passed through and securing them in place. They worked by the light of torches used only when necessary, such as on a dark night with only a sliver of moon. When everything was ready, Hébrard and Pierre retreated, under instruction from Albert, who remained on the bridge to light the fuse.

Hébrard and Pierre were uphill, crouching down in scrub and cursing thorns, when they heard a loud explosion. In the moonlight, they saw clumps of brick and metal tracks flung upwards and then heard the sound of debris falling to the ground. They waited in the silence that followed, expecting Albert to appear, but there was no sign of him.

'Where is he? Something's gone wrong,' Pierre said.

'We must find out. We've got a few minutes before anyone comes,' Hébrard said.

They ran towards the explosion, calling as loudly as they dared for Albert, but there was no reply. Under what had been the railway bridge, they looked up and saw that it had largely gone. They stumbled over lumps of brick and torn railway tracks at their feet. Then, by the footings of the bridge, Hébrard trod on something soft. He shone his torch briefly.

Albert was lying there, his neck at an odd angle, although he seemed otherwise untouched. They knew at once that he was dead, but they weren't sure what had happened, whether Albert had been blown up when making his escape or had fallen from the bridge and broken his neck on landing.

There was no time to talk. Hébrard slung the body over his shoulder and carried Albert towards the town. No-one had yet arrived at the scene and they were able to leave unseen. Pierre knew where Albert's family lived and they made their way to a small house in a back street. They knocked at the door, but there was no answer.

'They've gone to bed,' Pierre muttered, picking up a handful of small stones and flinging them at an upstairs window. He had to repeat the action several times before the window opened and a man's voice demanded to know what in the devil's name they were doing.

'It's Pierre from the café. Albert's had an accident,' Pierre said.

Albert's father came downstairs and unlocked the door. At the sight of his son's body, his expression changed from one of annoyance to distress.

'I'm so sorry,' Pierre said, as Hébrard carried the body indoors, placing him carefully, as directed, on a sofa.

'What happened?' Albert's father said shakily.

Pierre explained quickly, emphasising Albert's desire to be part of the action and his devotion to the cause of ridding France of the occupier.

'But what on earth am I going to say to his mother? She's asleep upstairs,' Albert's father said.

'I'm so sorry,' Pierre said again. 'We have to go now, but I'll come and see you both tomorrow.'

With the success of the sabotage overshadowed by Albert's death, Pierre and Hébrard said little to each other before they parted. Exhausted, Hébrard climbed the hill to Castignac and slipped unseen into the cottage. Entering the bedroom, he saw that Nicolette was awake and worried. She was standing by the window in the dark, peering out, but she turned round as Hébrard came in.

'Oh, there you are! I was woken up by a loud noise and I saw you weren't here. The noise must have woken the soldiers, and Jean-Louis and his family as well, because there are lights on in the house. What happened? What have you been doing?'

There was no point in pretending he didn't know what had happened, and he gave Nicolette a brief explanation.

'Poor boy,' she said of Albert, as she and Hébrard got into bed.

He yawned. 'Yes, that's the worst thing. It will be hard to think of the operation as successful.'

'I watched from the window as the officer ran into the yard, jumped into a car with two soldiers and drove off.'

It was a sign of resistance that no-one at Castignac used the names of any of the Nazi soldiers billeted there.

'The group will be safe so long as no-one betrays us,' Hébrard said.

'You can't deceive me, Hébrard. I knew you were up to something. Lately you've been gone from Castignac much more than usual.'

'Mmm.' Hébrard was too tired to talk.

The next day, in answer to her questions, he told Nicolette about the resistance group and their activities. He swore her to secrecy.

'I thought as much,' she said. 'You could have told me before now. I know how to keep a confidence.'

Hébrard acknowledged that she did. 'I didn't want to burden you, but I'm glad you know.'

'Be careful. I don't like to say this of my own brother, but I suspect Raymond. I've heard he's been talking to the *boches*.'

Hébrard's disquiet about Raymond peaked. 'He certainly doesn't pull his weight in the group. He left the railway job to me and Pierre.'

He decided to keep a sharper eye on Raymond and to warn Pierre. Later that day, he heard that soldiers had been knocking on doors, consulting informers and collaborators, and dragging suspects to the town hall in their search for the saboteurs. No leads emerged. No-one who was questioned admitted to knowing anything about the explosion on the railway line.

The Nazi authorities in St Martin des Remparts were furious about the loss of the railway line and ordered repair of the damage. They were further annoyed to discover that this was going to take some weeks owing to a shortage of bricks and metal tracks. Any peaceful aspects of the occupation vanished and a harsh, angry mood prevailed in the town.

The day after the explosion, the machine gun was fired from Castignac. No warning was given to anyone except the Nazis themselves, who made sure to be well out of the way. Danielle, with the cows in the cattle shed, was almost kicked in the face as the animals registered the shattering noise by becoming restive and stamping their feet. She had never heard the gun in action before but identified the sound at once.

Bullets spat at the town for what seemed a long time and the habitual peace was shattered for the second time in twenty-four hours. People ran indoors screaming at the dreadful rattle. When they emerged into the silence afterwards, they discovered several bodies and some severely wounded people on the side of St Martin des Remparts nearest to Castignac. Chunks had been gouged from buildings in the path of the gun.

Hébrard, out in the fields, heard the machine gun as well. He was shocked by the callousness of the revenge. Apart from Albert, no-one had been killed in the blowing up of the tracks and the response was overdoing things. He was upset about Albert and wanted to talk to Pierre but had as yet had no chance. His only satisfaction came from a private feeling that he had tried to avenge Eugène's death and compensate for his own desertion in the last war.

The firing of the gun wasn't enough for the Nazis. They wanted the saboteurs and threatened to fire it again unless they were given names within twenty-four hours. They offered a reward for information.

That evening, the resistance group met in the house of one of the members. Raymond was absent and Pierre didn't know why. Twenty-four hours had passed since the threat to fire the gun again and group members were nervous. They discussed the death of Albert in low voices, still uncertain as to whether he had been blown up or had fallen from the bridge after lighting the fuse. Pierre had been to see his parents and had tried to persuade them that their son had died fighting for a noble cause. The railway had been put out of action for some time and so the mission had succeeded, but it was hard to feel triumphant, given Albert's death.

Hébrard was uneasy. 'They're going to fire the gun again unless someone comes forward. I've been thinking that perhaps I should—'

Pierre cut across him. 'There's nothing we can do except lie low. It would be foolhardy to give ourselves up.'

'Then people will die in the gunfire,' Hébrard said, lighting a cigarette.

'Can't we ask Albert's parents to show them his body and say it was all his work and he killed himself in the process?' Suzanne said.

'No,' Pierre said. 'Definitely not. They wouldn't believe he did it alone and you'd be putting his parents in grave danger.'

Before anyone could reply, a loud knocking at the front door startled them.

'Police!' Pierre said, jumping up. No friend or neighbour would knock like that.

The knocking came again, even louder this time. Someone opened the front door and several Nazi soldiers entered, shouting orders to everyone to stay still. Pierre, Hébrard, Suzanne and the two other young women in the group were caught before they could escape. Handcuffs were applied and they were all thrown into the back of a van. Doors were slammed and the van drove off.

Chapter Four

Brigitte

B Y CHANCE, BRIGITTE WAS in her bedroom late on a November morning in 1942 when the Nazis arrived. She had come indoors for a thicker jacket as the day was getting colder. Looking out of the window, she watched, with horrified fascination, as Nazi soldiers arrived by car. Downstairs again, she saw three of them move into the house and take over some of the rooms, including, to her great annoyance and disgust, her bedroom. She had only a few minutes to clear it of her personal things.

'You're not to talk to them!' her mother said in a loud whisper on the day the Nazis moved in.

'All right. I won't, but, *Maman*, my bedroom!'

'You didn't expect us to give up our room to them, did you? There are two of us and only one of you! Besides, they wanted the best view of the town for their gun.'

Brigitte watched the installation of the machine gun

covertly from her new bedroom door down the corridor. She was frightened of the soldiers with their boots, loud voices and most of all, their big gun. Local hunters carried rifles when going out after boar, but this was much bigger. She heard the soldiers grunting and, for all she knew of their harsh language, swearing, as they brought it upstairs and placed it in her bedroom. In her new, much smaller, room, she tried to forget the gun but remained aware of its silent menace. She didn't need an order from her mother to keep as much distance as she could from the soldiers.

Months passed and Brigitte grew used to the presence of the invaders as she went about her duties on the farm. Sometimes she had to prepare food for them, but it was her mother who had any direct dealings and Brigitte, out in the fields or with the animals most of the time, could simply ignore them. She never looked at them and didn't try to learn their names or anything about them. They ate separately in the dining room, sitting around the *monastère* and waited on by Danielle.

What Brigitte later called the hatred in Castignac, that she always thought so unjust but could do nothing to stem, appeared in the town and grew with the use of the machine gun after the sabotage of the railway tracks almost a year after the occupation of the town had begun. What with the rationing as well, life was harsh. She had an idea from something that her father had said inadvertently that Hébrard had been involved in the sabotage, but she knew better than to ask questions.

When Danielle and Nicolette set up their stall in the weekly market in St Martin des Remparts the day after the machine gun had been fired on the town, Brigitte was with them. She had been terrified by the use of the machine gun, but she braved going into town because she liked serving at the market stall and there was always the hope of meeting a friend, even though it would no longer be Gilbert.

The women from Castignac expected the usual queue to form, yet people passed by on that morning, avoiding eye contact, going to other stalls. The cheese, butter and bacon, jams, tarts, fruit and vegetables that they brought to the market were well known and well liked locally, even though much less was available than before the occupation because the Nazis at Castignac took a good share of the produce before it left the farm.

'Where's the queue? No-one is buying,' Nicolette said to Danielle and Brigitte after they had been standing behind their stall for some minutes.

'They're buying all right, but not from us. Look at old Mme Grimbaud there. Her basket is full. She's been to other stalls this time. And M. Fayard who always does the shopping for his family because his wife is disabled. He's over there, buying from another stall. They normally come to us,' Danielle said.

Raymond came up to their stall. Seeing his plump form and satisfied air, Brigitte felt uneasy. She had nothing to pin on him, but she knew that Nicolette suspected that this brother of hers was a collaborator. He certainly didn't object to the occupation the way that the rest of Nicolette's family did, and he always seemed these days to be able to lay his hands on good food and supplies when everyone else was struggling.

'How are you doing today?' he said.

'Badly. No-one's buying from us. It's odd, because we always sell out, especially now that we've got less to sell,' Nicolette said.

'It's because of the gun,' Raymond said. 'They're blaming it on you.'

'We didn't fire it!' Danielle was aghast.

'No, but it's in your house. That's enough. I know because I've heard people talking.'

He passed on, without buying anything from the Castignac stall. But for Nicolette's other relatives, who remained loyal, the Castignac women would have sold hardly anything that day. Despite the privation caused by rationing, it was clear that some people were boycotting their goods. The laden cart that they brought to market, which usually bounced back empty, was almost as full on its way home that afternoon.

That evening, Nicolette's brother, Guy, turned up at Castignac. It was late, but Nicolette wasn't at home and he was looking for her. Hébrard hadn't come home and she was worried that something had happened to him. Her girls were asleep and she had come over to ask if Danielle knew anything. Brigitte was there too.

'Hébrard and Pierre have been arrested,' Guy said. 'I've just heard what happened.'

He was the same height as his brothers, Raymond and Pierre, but thinner and more muscular than Raymond, and stronger-looking than Pierre. He was Gilbert's father and Brigitte had known him quite well for some years. She had none of the suspicions about Guy that the Castignac families had of Raymond.

'Arrested! Where are they now?' Nicolette said.

'I don't know. They were taken away in a van. I don't even know if they are still here in the town,' Guy said.

There was nothing more he could tell them. Nicolette thanked him for making the journey and he left.

'You'll have to ask the *boches*,' Danielle said to Nicolette when the three women were talking about the arrests afterwards.

'You mean go down to their offices in the town? Will they even speak to me?'

'No, let me ask the officer here. The way I look at it, they owe us a lot, as they treat Castignac like a hotel and give nothing back.'

Nicolette gave her a hug. 'Oh, thank you, Danielle. I'm desperate to know where he is.'

Danielle was as good as her word. When she next saw the officer, instead of avoiding him as she usually did, she marched straight up to him and told him that Hébrard and Pierre had been arrested, and they had no idea where they had been taken. She expected to be rebuffed, but the excellence of the food at Castignac and the comfort of their quarters there worked in her favour. The officer made her repeat her request more slowly until he understood her.

'They have gone to the camp at Bram,' he said in his slow French.

Danielle knew the nearby town of Bram, although she never had any call to go there. A concentration camp had been established outside the town.

'How long for?'

'I don't know.' He shrugged and strode off to his car.

Danielle had to be satisfied with that. She sent Brigitte over to the cottage with a message for Nicolette. Brigitte liked Hébrard and missed him. She had known him all her life and he had always been kind to her; much kinder, she thought, than her own father who was strict and, since the beginning of the occupation, much grimmer even than before.

'Thank you, Brigitte, and please thank Danielle. I hate to think what's happening to them, but it's a help knowing where they are,' Nicolette said.

'How did the *boches* know where Hébrard and Pierre were? Did someone betray them?'

'I've been wondering that. I hate to say this, but I suspect my brother.'

'Raymond?'

Of all Nicolette's brothers, Raymond would be the suspect. He was the outsider in the family, always at odds with everyone else.

'Yes. He was in their group, but he wasn't arrested and I know he talks to the *boches*.'

'What can you do about Hébrard?'

Nicolette sighed. 'I don't know. Nothing, I suspect. I don't know anyone influential who could get him released. And he won't be there long. From what I've heard, Bram is just a transit camp.'

The people in the town were relieved that arrests had been made in connection with the sabotage of the railway line because it might mean that the Nazis would no longer fire the gun.

Everything changed in the early months of 1944, when a new Nazi soldier arrived at Castignac, a young, blond, good-looking man, who smiled at Brigitte the first time he saw her and continued to smile as the days and weeks passed. She tried to ignore him, because of her mother's often-repeated command about not talking to the *boches*, but one day she found herself responding to his smile. It had been so long since any man showed an interest in her, because all the young men had disappeared, not simply Gilbert. She turned away quickly, but too late. She was sure the *boche* had seen the twitch of her lips.

He could speak better French than the other soldiers and when he called her *mademoiselle* and asked her the French for some object or another, she couldn't resist replying, as long as her mother was out of earshot.

He was stiff and obedient in the presence of his superiors, but she watched him and the other soldiers kicking a ball round in the farmyard and she could see he was good-humoured.

'What is your name?' he said to her in French one day.

She replied without thinking of her mother's strictures. 'Brigitte.'

'Oh, yes, a pretty name. We have that name in German too. *Birgitta,*' he said. 'My name is Siegfried and I come from near Munich in Bavaria. I live with my parents in a village outside the city. At home, we are like you living on the farm outside the town.'

He sounded like an ordinary person, someone she might know. Brigitte didn't spend a lot of time with local men. Jean-Louis had been keen for her to leave school as soon as she could. At the age of twenty-six, she was busy working on the farm, still helping her father with the crops and the milking, but also feeding the hens, making butter and cheese, and cooking with her mother. Her time was more evenly divided between her parents than it had been during the years when she had rebelled against her mother and gone out into the fields to join her father.

Brigitte went to the old ruin with a scoop and a bucket to get feed for the chickens every morning before collecting the eggs. It was used only as a store, although Jean-Louis had told her that a long time ago, in his grandparents' time and before then, it had housed the family and their animals. His grandparents had built the new house over eighty years before. Everyone knew the date of 1860 on the house.

Siegfried must have been watching her and following her, because, one morning, he arrived there just after her.

'Let me help you,' he said, taking the scoop from her and filling her bucket with the chicken feed.

'Thank you,' she said.

She thought of refusing and snatching the shovel back as her mother would have wanted, but she didn't. He was so polite and chivalrous that it would have seemed rude, so she did no such thing, even though he was the enemy. They walked to the chicken coop together, with Siegfried asking her for French words for things around them: the chestnut trees, the pigeon loft and the jackdaws.

'*Les chataignes, le pigeonnier, les choucas,*' Brigitte said. She had gone too far by then to refuse to speak to him.

After that, he caught up with her often as she went to the ruin for the chicken feed. She didn't see him every day, because some days he was busy down in the town, but she saw him often enough for her to look out for him and even to miss him on the days he wasn't around.

She grew used to his jokes and to his miming when the words weren't there. He made her laugh. She was nervous at first in case her mother saw them, but Danielle didn't mention any transgression, so that, after a while, Brigitte relaxed.

One day, in the shelter of the ruin, he took the feed bucket from her and began to kiss her gently. She didn't push him away. Although her head was full of what her mother would say, her body was saying something quite different. Sensations that she didn't know were possible were aroused in her for this man who was no longer a stranger. He didn't persist but let her go with a smile like a promise, and they went back together to the coop and fed the chickens. He helped her collect the eggs, just as he often did, and they walked back to the house together.

'Brigitte! I saw you talking to that young *boche*. I've told you before to keep away from them. No good will come of it,' Danielle said on her daughter's return to the kitchen that morning.

Brigitte knew what was coming next. She had been taller than her mother for some years, but Danielle didn't hesitate. The slap on her face stung. Brigitte put her hand to her cheek protectively but said nothing.

She didn't care. Her heart raced now when she saw Siegfried and she wanted him to kiss her again. No local boy had aroused such feelings in her since Gilbert years ago. Her mother might spend all day slapping her and telling her not to speak to Siegfried, but she wasn't going to listen. She lay in bed at night in her small room at the back of the house and imagined his kisses.

Although she loved the farm work, she was beginning to resent the amount she had to do. There was much more now that Hébrard had gone because her father was being stubborn and refusing to replace him. As well as working in the fields, Brigitte had to deal with the pigs, milk and look after the cows and goats, and see to the hens.

Yet it was springtime. Crops were growing, leaves were bursting out, it was warmer and birds were singing. Brigitte's heart was light as she went about her work, thinking of Siegfried's touch. Much of the time, Siegfried was busy being a soldier, on parade or dealing with people in the town. She didn't know exactly what he did and she didn't ask. She didn't want to think that he was part of the hated occupier. It was the year after the blowing up of the supply train and, although nothing else so dramatic had happened, relations between St Martin des Remparts and the Nazis continued to be poor.

Brigitte wanted the handsome young man with a smile playing on his lips and the gentle hands with which he held her. When he was free, he sought her out and they went to the ruined farmhouse together even when the chickens had been fed. They kissed and played amongst straw bales and sacks of feed. It was such fun being with Siegfried in their special place. The fear that her parents would appear and reprimand her diminished as time went on and they weren't discovered. Her parents were too busy on the farm to worry about what she was doing unless it was staring them in the face.

Siegfried chased her from one end to the other of the ruin one day. No-one would have been likely to see them from the outside. He was asking for a kiss and she played at refusal. She ran up the staircase to the pigeon loft, screaming with laughter. He didn't try to follow her.

She stood at the top, leaning on the railing and laughed at him. The door to the pigeon loft was behind her, but it was heavy and hard to open, and she knew the floor was covered in pigeon droppings, so she didn't want to go in there. Besides, there was no other way out of it. There was only one way to go and that was downstairs again, but Siegfried was standing at the foot of the staircase.

Siegfried's mood had changed. He was no longer laughing and teasing. 'Come down. I won't chase you again, I promise,' he said, his face serious now. He held out his arms to her in a plea.

She couldn't resist him and came down slowly, her laughter dying as she saw the intensity in his face. Siegfried gathered her in his arms and kissed her as gently as the touch of feathers at first and then more urgently. He carried her over to where new bales of hay were stacked on the ground and laid her slowly down, caressing her all the time. Brigitte responded to his touch. She spared a second to reflect that she wasn't disobeying her mother, who had never in so many words forbidden her to do this wonderful thing, even though its wickedness outside marriage was well known. Amongst the haystacks, his hands were busy with the fastenings of her overalls and her underwear, and she, a wearer of trousers, knew how to help remove the ones that he was wearing. Almost before she knew it, they were in heaven. They were breathless and panting as they finished.

Brigitte's passion for Siegfried soared after that. Months passed and they met in the ruined farmhouse on many more occasions. Brigitte was so excited about Siegfried that she didn't think about precautions and he never mentioned the subject. They were both clever enough at concealing their passion that her mother didn't suspect what was going on and even expressed her pleasure that Brigitte had become more biddable lately. She was disguising her affair with Siegfried by performing her duties in the house with greater efficiency and speed.

Everything came to a halt one day.

'One of our soldiers has been killed by a Frenchman!' Siegfried said to Brigitte one afternoon as he returned to Castignac from St Martin des Remparts. 'There will be reprisals, you'll see.'

Brigitte was taken aback, as much by the tone of his voice as his words. She had never seen him angry before and she hardly recognised the loving man she knew in the tight-lipped soldier who faced her now. She backed away in silence.

'Someone in the town has killed a *boche*,' she said to her parents that evening.

'What happened and how do you know?' Jean-Louis said. He was in his chair in the kitchen, where they were about to have something light to eat as was their custom in the evening.

'I don't know what happened, but I saw Madeleine today,' Brigitte said, referring to a friend.

She had seen her friend that day and allowed her parents to think that was how she knew about the death of the Nazi officer. It was easier than incurring Danielle's wrath by mentioning her conversation with one of the Nazis at Castignac.

'They won't take it lying down. There'll be trouble,' Jean-Louis said.

He lapsed back into the silence that had become habitual in recent years, but the family at Castignac shivered, anticipating reprisals, remembering the use of the machine gun the year before.

Over the next day or so, details of the killing reached Castignac. It had been an opportunistic shooting by a young man they scarcely knew. He had taken a hunting rifle, belonging to his father, and gone out early to shoot rabbits. With food so scarce, a rabbit or two for the pot was always welcome. Seeing a Nazi standing alone on the bridge over the river early in the morning, he had taken a chance and killed him with a single shot.

The young man was caught and shot that day, but ten hostages were taken on the day after the shooting and kept under guard overnight.

Going shopping for her mother early the following morning, Brigitte unexpectedly witnessed the death of the hostages. They were taken to the central square and made to stand in a line. Amongst them was a young man Brigitte had known as a boy at school. She was glad she was too far away to catch his eye because it was obvious what was going to happen next. She wanted to run, but her feet wouldn't move. Soldiers with pistols stood in front of the hostages. On the order of an officer, they pointed them and fired. They kept firing until all the ten men were down and even afterwards when there was a movement. Only when they were sure all the men were dead did they stop. Silence descended, punctuated by a long wail and then screams as families came forward to claim their dead.

People going about their business in the square had watched, horrified by the sight.

'Poor devils. They'd done nothing wrong,' a man said.

'They think they're teaching us a lesson, damn them,' a woman said.

They were standing next to Brigitte. 'It's terrible,' she said, and words seemed to fail her. She backed away and, despite the weight of her shopping bag, ran up the hill to Castignac, hardly stopping on her way home and collapsing into the kitchen to gasp out her story to her mother and Nicolette.

'They're losing the war, that's why they're so vicious,' Jean-Louis said at lunchtime, when the family was gathered in the kitchen, discussing the dreadful event.

'Remember when they fired the gun before? They'll do it again,' Danielle said.

Brigitte knew her mother was referring to the machine gun in her bedroom and that she meant that the death of ten hostages might not be enough revenge for the Nazis furious about the shooting of their officer.

That night was quiet. The next morning, Brigitte was up and dressed, preparing to go downstairs, when voices from her old bedroom caught her attention. Siegfried and one of the other soldiers billeted at Castignac were standing on either side of the machine gun. She dared not go too close, but she imagined what they were doing. She hovered in the doorway of her new bedroom, hardly daring to move. When the harsh rattle of the gun broke the silence, she covered her ears and ran downstairs to the kitchen where she and Danielle could only exchange frantic, terrified glances.

The noise of the machine gun firing on St Martin des Remparts seemed to continue for a long time before it stopped, and a deathly silence followed. There was no birdsong. The jackdaws and pigeons who were loudest at Castignac had been silenced, and nothing seemed to move for some minutes. The sounds which the family were accustomed to hearing from the town were no longer audible, as if the day had given up. Brigitte was horrified that Siegfried, who made such sweet love to her, should do such a terrible thing, and she kept well away from him that day.

Chapter Five

Brigitte

THE FIRING OF THE gun caused the deaths of six people, including two children whom Brigitte knew. When Siegfried followed her to the ruined farmhouse the day after she heard the dreadful news, she turned on him. She was so shocked and angry that she lost any fear of the gunner.

'You killed innocent people and *children* with your gun! How could you?'

His French was good enough by then to understand her.

'I had to obey orders. I'm a soldier and there's a war on. Don't forget that one of our soldiers was killed.'

'You can't have me as well as fire your gun!'

She brushed away the hands that sought her and ran out of the ruin and along the path to the main house. Catching her breath, she slipped into the kitchen, telling Danielle that she was upset about the deaths but not daring to mention Siegfried. She could not love a man who killed children so heartlessly. There was something else as well. The hatred of Castignac would be worse now that the gun had been fired again. It was almost as if the family had given the order to fire it.

During the autumn of 1944, as the Nazis were being chased out of France, Brigitte continued to keep away from Siegfried. Once he understood that she meant what she said, he seemed to accept it and didn't attempt any force.

One morning, she realised, with some alarm, that she was late with her monthly. Day after day it didn't come. She had heard of women missing it because they were underfed in the occupation, but that wasn't true of her. Food on the farm was no longer plentiful but it was sufficient. She wasn't starving. She had to accept that she was pregnant. She didn't know what to do, so she did nothing, except try to conceal her condition from her mother. The one person who could advise her was the last person who should know.

'I'm carrying your baby!' she said to Siegfried in an angry whisper when she saw him on his own outside the house a week or so later.

He looked at her but said nothing, only nodded. Then he gave a slight shrug, turning away from her. He didn't offer to help her or to take her with him back to Germany. Nor did she ask him to. Castignac might be hated now, but no matter how much she had loved and wanted him, she would never give up her home to go and live with the enemy in a defeated country where she couldn't speak the language. He may have thought it better for her to stay on her farm with her family than risk life in a Germany that was losing the war; he may simply have wanted to obey orders and leave with no complications or he may not have cared what happened to her. Brigitte avoided him after that and didn't speak to him again. She never knew what he was thinking about any future they might have had. She carried on working on the farm, knowing she was pregnant, but putting off the day when she would have to tell her mother.

It was clear that the war was coming to an end. One autumn morning, news came up to Castignac that French resistance forces were approaching the town. Everyone waited, dreading a battle and longing for the Nazis to go. Brigitte watched the Castignac Nazis covertly and saw them begin to pack up their belongings and equipment. The family stayed out of the way. Jean-Louis was busy in a distant field. Danielle and Nicolette were churning cream to make butter.

A last, defiant, burst of gunfire sped from the house just before the Nazis' departure. Brigitte, occupied with the pigs, heard the noise and stood listening, hands clasping her cheeks in horror. She crept closer and saw the Nazis leave the house with their baggage and pack their two cars. Siegfried, bringing the gun downstairs with one of the other soldiers, was the last to climb aboard. He turned and saw her watching the departure. He raised a hand to her, but Brigitte kept her hands clasped firmly at her side. One by one, the cars drove away.

Brigitte stood rooted to the spot. She would never see Siegfried again, but she was joyous that the Nazis had gone. At last Castignac was free. She ran to tell Danielle and Nicolette, and the three of them hugged each other with delight. When Jean-Louis turned up for lunch, the women greeted him with the news and a smile took years from his careworn face. They celebrated with a glass of *hypocras* from a bottle kept for exactly that moment.

Yet Brigitte was still fearful because she knew what was going to happen next. Danielle, free of the hated Nazis after nearly two years of the occupation of her home, looked around her with fresh eyes on the following morning and noticed a change in her daughter.

'Brigitte, look at you! Don't think I can't see what you've been trying to hide, deceitful girl!'

Brigitte was five months pregnant by then and it was becoming impossible to hide it. She felt relieved that her mother knew at last, even though it meant another slap across the face.

Danielle's fury reached the rafters, and Nicolette, Marie and Jeanne soon heard Brigitte's news. Jean-Louis was out in the fields at the time, but his face turned to thunder when he found out. All the years of Brigitte helping on the farm might never have happened. He growled at his daughter.

'You've let us down, you and your *boche*. It's as bad as using the machine gun on the town. People already don't want anything to do with us and you've made it worse by your sluttish behaviour. What do you mean by bringing a German baby into the house? Didn't you think the occupation was enough? I've a good mind to throw you out.'

Brigitte was horrified at her father's last words. She had nowhere to go. No-one would welcome a homeless, pregnant girl, especially when food was so scarce and she needed to eat for two. Danielle, listening, intervened.

'No, you won't throw her out. She's staying here. She's our daughter!'

'She's not my daughter anymore. If only we'd had a son, there'd be none of this nonsense and I'd have someone to leave the farm to! Or if she had married a Frenchman instead of opening her legs for that *boche*, then she could have had a son to carry on the farm, but not like this, never like this!'

Jean-Louis's face was twisted in anger and disappointment, but Danielle stood her ground. Hands on hips, she took a deep breath and faced him.

'She *is* your daughter and if she goes, I go. Now, out of my kitchen, both of you. I've got work to do.'

Danielle seized a large wooden spoon as if she meant to go into battle with it. Jean-Louis and Brigitte left the kitchen in different directions, not speaking to each other. Brigitte stopped working with Jean-Louis after that and spent her time in the kitchen and the dairy.

Nothing more was said about Brigitte having to leave home, but Danielle lost no time in pointing out that her *boche* had abandoned Brigitte. She said so the morning after the confrontation with Jean-Louis when she and Brigitte were alone in the kitchen.

'But he had to go when the soldiers left,' Brigitte said, pausing in her kneading of the dough with which she was making bread.

'Did he ask you to go with him? Did he say he would send you money for the baby?'

'No, nothing like that.'

Danielle was chopping vegetables for lunch, but she pointed her knife at Brigitte with a flourish. 'You see! He just wanted his way with you and now he's left you in the lurch. He didn't care about you.'

Brigitte shaped the dough into a ball and left it to rise. The calm and purposeful movements of her hands didn't betray the sinking of the heart she felt at Danielle's words. They remained with her and she began to see truth in them. Later that day, she took over her bedroom once again, trying hard to forget that it had hosted the machine gun which Siegfried had fired on St Martin des Remparts. All in all, he wasn't the good German she had loved.

In the coming days, Jean-Louis's temper improved a little, with the help of a welcome event. Brigitte was the first to find out. Her pregnancy was beginning to be tiring and she was gazing out of her bedroom window, playing idly with the distortions created by the old glass, late on an autumn afternoon. Through the glass, she saw a dark, moving streak. A clearer pane showed a tall, gaunt-looking man stumbling towards Castignac. His face was too far away to see, but something in his appearance told her she knew him. Staring hard as he drew closer, she recognised him. He was turning towards the cottage, but Nicolette wasn't there. She was in the dairy with Danielle. Brigitte ran downstairs screaming.

'Hébrard! It's Hébrard! He's come back. Nicolette, Nicolette, he's back!'

In the dairy, Nicolette, both hands clasping the churn, let it go and turned round, amazed. She and Danielle rushed outside, with Brigitte on their heels. Catching sight of Hébrard, Nicolette ran up to him and threw her arms around him, crying with joy and relief, while Danielle and Brigitte stood back, trying not to look, waiting their turn to welcome him home.

No-one had had any news of Hébrard or Pierre or the other people who had disappeared on the night of the arrests the year before. The butter had to wait. Jean-Louis was called, and Danielle and Brigitte did their best to prepare a feast in the kitchen.

'We were taken to a prison camp in Bram that night,' Hébrard said.

'We knew that, because Danielle found out from the *boches*,' Nicolette said.

'But it was only a holding camp. We were transferred to the camp at Le Vernet, near Pamiers, the next day. I was taken to a room and interrogated. I admitted to my name, which they knew, but I refused to say anything more. The man in charge began to rage at me, then he set the guard on me, with a whip. An hour later, with the threat of worse to come, I was taken back to my cell. I didn't see Pierre or the others. For weeks, I saw no-one, apart from my interrogators and the guards who brought food fit only for dogs. I did exercises in my cell to try and keep fit. It was awful being cooped up like a chicken when I'm used to the outdoor life. The interrogations stopped at some point. I can't remember exactly when, because my memory's bad now. I didn't tell them anything they could use or give anyone's name.'

Hébrard looked exhausted and sipped at the glass of brandy and milk that Danielle had given him.

'I began to be allowed out for an hour a day into a yard. Other people were there and once I saw Suzanne from our group. I went towards her, but she shook her head and turned away. She didn't want to acknowledge me. She might have denied everything or given names and information away. I don't know. There was never any sign of Pierre or the other two. When I was released two days ago, because they're closing the camp, I found out about Pierre. He had died soon after we were imprisoned and he's in the cemetery there. I'm sorry, Nicolette.'

There was a silence in the kitchen. Hébrard put his arm around Nicolette as she took in the news of her brother's death.

'Raymond didn't come to the meeting that night, so he wasn't arrested,' he said.

'No,' Nicolette said. 'He's been in St Martin des Remparts all the time, as usual.'

'Someone told the police where we were. Was it Raymond? Did he betray us?' Hébrard said.

'He denies it, of course, but we're pretty sure that he did betray you. He was seen talking to the *boches* more than once. They might even have given him money because he appeared flush after you were captured. The brothers and I don't speak to him now,' Nicolette said.

'Pierre should never have let him into our group. He paid with his life,' Hébrard said.

Nicolette nodded, tears in her eyes.

'How did you get here?' Jean-Louis said.

'Walking and thumbing lifts where I could. There's not much traffic on the road, but I flagged down one or two cars, which took me most of the way.'

'You're a brave man, Hébrard, and it's good to see you back,' Jean-Louis said.

Jean-Louis was short of labour on the farm, although Hébrard was never as strong again as he had been. The other members of the resistance group, also released from prison, made their way back to St Martin des Remparts. Pierre was the only casualty, much missed by Hébrard after many years of friendship and by Nicolette and her family.

Brigitte stayed at Castignac, working hard throughout her pregnancy, trying to show her parents how useful she was. She made little headway with Jean-Louis, who remained stern towards her and rarely addressed her directly.

When Brigitte's waters broke, she called for her mother, and Danielle asked Hébrard to drive down to St Martin des Remparts to fetch the midwife. Jean-Louis was at the other end of the farm that day and, in any case, it was better to keep him out of it. It was winter and Hébrard was able to spare the time. There was some delay, because the midwife was attending another case, but he returned with her eventually, to Danielle's great relief.

Brigitte's baby was born in January 1945 on the daybed in her bedroom, with the midwife in attendance and Danielle toiling up and down the stairs, fetching towels and hot water. It was an arduous birth and the baby was big enough to cause the midwife to exclaim about his size.

Afterwards, with her baby in a wicker cradle given to her by Nicolette, Brigitte was exhausted. Feeling weak, she cried for

Siegfried. He had been gone for four months by then and she had no hope that he would return. She hated him for firing the gun on the town, but she had loved him and she was sure that she would never see him again. He would never know his son.

People in the town shunned Jean-Louis and his family as collaborators. The older ones began to remember what they had forgotten years ago, that Hébrard had been a deserter during the last war. Mutterings arose about Jean-Louis's German grandson.

Brigitte called the baby Jacques, in memory of the brother she had never known. Danielle was pleased and the choice of name helped to reconcile her to the baby, but Jean-Louis took no pleasure in his grandson. Brigitte, determined to change his mind, took the sleeping baby up to him and dropped him in her father's lap after lunch one day.

'Please look after him for a minute, while I go upstairs to fetch something,' she said.

'No. Ask your mother,' he said, pushing Jacques away.

Jacques woke up and started crying. Brigitte, afraid that Jean-Louis would drop the baby, took him back.

Both Danielle and Brigitte noticed that Jean-Louis was keeping away from people. He had never frequented the bars of the town, but he stopped going into St Martin des Remparts unless he couldn't avoid it and became more and more morose. The farm was struggling by then, because he had slowed down. He was in his mid-sixties, by the end of the war, but by no means an old man. Danielle confided to Brigitte that she was worried about his mood. He was still strong and fit, but he didn't have the will to do as much as before. The others were doing most of the work.

One day, Jean-Louis didn't turn up for the mid-morning breakfast with the family. Danielle was puzzled because that had never happened before.

'He won't be far, because he never leaves Castignac without saying where he's going,' she said to Brigitte as they cleared away their breakfast things, leaving Jean-Louis' place laid.

'Shall I go and look for him?' Brigitte said.

With Jacques to look after and Jean-Louis unreconciled to him, she had continued to confine herself to the house and dairy.

'There's no need. It's probably a sick animal. He'll be along soon enough,' Danielle said, turning her attention to some risen dough and starting to knead it.

At lunchtime, there was still no sign of Jean-Louis.

'We'd better go and look for him,' Danielle said, as she and Brigitte finished their meal.

They began to search the outbuildings and the fields, hoping that Jean-Louis was immersed in some task and had forgotten the time. Because it wasn't used anymore except as a store for grain and hay, no-one thought at first to look in the ruined farmhouse. Brigitte even trudged over to the old shepherd's hut on the other side of the farm to see if her father was there, but there was no sign of him.

Later, coming into the kitchen with fresh butter she had made that afternoon, Brigitte heard Danielle shouting. Hébrard was there with her.

'It's Brigitte's fault. It would never have happened but for her. How could he put up with the son of a *boche*?'

'What do you mean?' Brigitte said, surprised to see her tough and practical mother in tears.

Danielle didn't reply but sat down and clasped her head in her hands. Hébrard came towards Brigitte and put an arm around her.

'I'm sorry, but your father has taken his life.'

He told Brigitte what he had just said to Danielle. She had questioned him about Jean-Louis's whereabouts and he had started looking for him. He, too, hadn't thought to look in the ruin at first, but not finding Jean-Louis anywhere in the fields, he had begun to search all the buildings systematically. He had found Jean-Louis hanging from the top of the staircase to the pigeon loft. He had climbed up and used the Swiss army knife that he always carried to cut the rope and let the body fall to the ground in order to save Danielle and Brigitte from the sight of the hanging body. Leaving Jean-Louis, he had gone to the house where Danielle was in the kitchen, setting out food for the high tea the family had in the evening.

Danielle was weeping and Brigitte sank into a chair in shock. When Danielle had pulled herself together, the three of them went over to the ruin, taking a cart to bring back the body. They placed Jean-Louis on the *monastère* in the dining room. It hadn't been used since the Nazis had left.

Danielle went to the church in St Martin des Remparts to speak to the priest the next day. She returned distraught.

'He's refused to bury him in consecrated ground! I wasn't going to pretend it was a natural death, so I told him the truth. Everyone knows that suicides are refused a church burial, but I thought it worth asking. Think of all the years I've attended the Sunday service and added to the collection! And Jacquot is buried there. He should be next to Jacquot.'

'What are we going to do?' Brigitte said.

'We'll have to bury him on the farm. The priest will come up – he promised to do that, at least. I went on to the town hall to report the death and apply for a death certificate. That's all I could do. But it's shameful!'

Brigitte was upset about Jean-Louis's death and sorry that the priest was making her mother suffer. She had to put one thing right, though.

'It's not my fault that my father took his life. You mustn't say that,' she said to Danielle.

Danielle looked at her daughter, puzzled. 'I didn't say that!'

'Yes, you did. When Hébrard was in the kitchen yesterday, telling you what had happened. You said it was my fault, that *Papa* didn't want the son of a *boche*. Well, Jacques is going to be French and it's not my fault that *Papa's* dead. I won't have it on my conscience.'

Danielle nodded. 'Maybe I did say something, but I was upset.'

Brigitte had to accept the closest that her mother would come to an apology.

Searching around the farm, Hébrard found an old paving slab which he shaped into a tombstone and on which he carved Jean-Louis's initials and dates.

'I shouldn't be admitting this, but I carved my name on the wall of the pigeon loft forty years ago when I first came here,' he said to Danielle and Brigitte when they praised his lettering.

'We can probably forgive that,' Danielle said.

'I always felt grateful to Jean-Louis for taking me in during the Great War, instead of turning me over to the authorities,' Hébrard said, in an unusual burst of confidence.

'That was a long time ago, but God bless the day you came to us,' Danielle said warmly.

Hébrard drove to the town in the farm truck to see an undertaker and came back with a coffin in the back. Picking up a spade, he went to the south of the old farmhouse and slowly dug a grave. It was hard work in his weakened state, but he persevered until the hole was as deep as he was tall. Danielle laid out the body, refusing help from Brigitte.

Later, with the priest, Danielle, Brigitte and baby Jacques, as well as Hébrard and his family in attendance, Jean-Louis was buried. Hébrard placed the stone in the ground, standing it like a tombstone so that the lettering could be seen. It was soon covered in ivy and barely visible, but everyone at Castignac knew where it was and Danielle would sometimes pull away the choking strands.

The death of Jean-Louis meant that Hébrard was the only man at Castignac. Because he wasn't as strong as he had been, and because Danielle and Nicolette were older now, much more of the farm work fell to Brigitte, while Danielle looked after Jacques. Brigitte learned to manage the farm with the help of Hébrard and his family: planting and harvesting the crops; looking after the animals; making butter, cream and cheese; and keeping bees for honey. Leaving Jacques with Danielle, Brigitte and Nicolette went to the market every week for provisions and ran their own stall, selling butter and cheese, sausage, bacon, jam, honey, and even soap that Brigitte made from goats' milk.

The hatred arising from the Nazi presence at Castignac and the shame of Jean-Louis's death hung over Castignac after the war. Danielle, Hébrard and their families bought supplies and animals for the farm and sold their produce, and Nicolette was often in touch with her family, apart from Raymond, but otherwise they tended to keep to themselves. Brigitte became known as a collaborator by people who wanted to make an enemy of her. Gilbert hadn't been seen for years and Brigitte had no idea what had become of him.

Brigitte made a garden at Castignac where there had never been one before. Buying plants in the weekly market, she grew roses, hydrangeas, trumpet flowers, marigolds and hibiscus. She planted some wisteria seeds beside the terrace after Jacques was born. Paulette had a flourishing mauve wisteria growing over a metal frame in front of her house and she had given Brigitte some seeds. Hébrard made a frame of metal posts and the plants sprang up, covering the frame within a few years. Brigitte also bought two small date palms from a Moroccan stall in the market and planted them outside the front door of the house.

Part Five

Chapter One

A New Staircase

T HE DECISION TO SELL didn't prevent all of us visiting Castignac at New Year. We couldn't keep away, because it might have been our last visit. Jenny and I shared a rented car for the journey from Carcassonne.

'No Mark this time?' she said, as we met at Stansted.

'No, he's working,' I said.

'Oh, poor you, but never mind, I'll keep you company.'

The journey from Carcassonne took us along tree-lined avenues, with shadows of tree trunks striping the sunlit road. The countryside was flat at first, with vineyards on either side of the road. Then we climbed towards hill-top towns crowned with churches. The best sight of all was of the mountains. We crested a hill at one point to see the Pyrenees on the horizon ahead of us, under a clear, blue sky. Nearing St Martin des Remparts, we saw the spire of the church appearing amongst the treetops.

Castignac was beautiful in a different way in the winter, standing quietly in the large garden with its shutters open in welcome. The house looked bare without geraniums in flower, yet the colours of the roof and walls still glowed when the sun shone, while the bare chestnut trees around the ruin created a delicate pattern against the sky. Bertrand had pruned the wisteria to within an inch of its life after the leaves fell in the autumn, but there was a promise for the coming year in its snaking trunks and branches.

Marianne wasn't there when we arrived, but she was expecting us and had prepared the house. She had turned on the heating and even left us some candles as a New Year present. We lit the candles in the dining room and they helped us to forget that the house was cold. The weather in south-west France could remind us of an English winter and the heating was only taking off the chill.

The others were curious about Mark's absence but accepted my explanation. Only Jackie knew how things stood with us, so there was no need to say any more. Some weeks had elapsed since his text about cooling things, but a certain obstinacy, or a remaining faint hope, had prevented me from saying to anyone, beyond Jackie, that Mark and I were probably finished.

Around the dining table that evening, we talked about selling Castignac. Angela had spoken to Gilles.

'He was overwhelmed by interest after the house went on the market. People flooded to see it, but he's dashed any hopes of a quick sale or any sale. No-one has asked for a second visit or put in an offer. He says it's all because people are curious about Ian's death. Everyone's asked to see round the ruin, especially after an article in the local paper saying we're leaving because of that,' Angela said.

'So we're not getting anywhere?' Graham said.

'No-one's seriously interested in buying. They just want to see where Ian died. It's idle curiosity and my impression is that we've become a talking point in the town. Some of the people Gilles has been showing round haven't even got a house to sell! He's fed up because he's wasting his time. We're a tourist attraction without an entrance fee. It might be hard to sell anyway, but no-one wants to buy a house where there was a death,' Angela said.

'Ian didn't die in the house,' Stephen said.

'No, he didn't, but Gilles said it doesn't matter. He died at Castignac, on the property, which includes the ruined farmhouse,' Angela said.

'The property includes the ruin now, but there was no mention of it when we first came to see Castignac,' I said.

I began to nurse a hope that we might not be able to sell Castignac after all, or at least, not for some time. If the others were determined to sell, we could put the price down until someone made an offer, but I would be the last person to suggest that. I decided to keep quiet. Everyone knew I wanted to keep Castignac and it was better to wait for Stephen and the others to change their own minds. Circumstances might argue my case for me.

We relaxed into the New Year holiday with short walks in freezing weather and long, hearty meals. Jenny turned to me after breakfast one morning and asked if I would come to the ruined farmhouse with her.

'I've been avoiding it, but I want to go there and to see for myself if anything needs to be done, rather than leaving it to the rest of you. I also want to see how I'll feel there, but I don't want to go on my own,' she said.

'Of course I'll go with you, Jenny. Just say when.'

She looked relieved. 'Thanks. Let's go now and then it's done.'

The others were still sitting around over breakfast, debating how to spend the day, when Jenny and I took the path to the ruin, our boots crunching on almost-frozen mud. It was a foggy morning and we could barely see ahead. The tops of the trees had disappeared. The ruin loomed up out of the fog and we entered the courtyard, making our way slowly across to the pigeon loft. We could hear pigeons cooing high above, their soft calls punctuated by the sound of squabbling jackdaws, but we could hardly see any birds.

I breathed in the smell of stone and felt the peacefulness of the old farmhouse. Looking down at the flagstones, we saw only a faint mark of the bloodstain. There was no sign of the spindles which had been lying on the ground, but the broken railing at the top of the staircase and the open entrance to the pigeon loft remained as obvious signs of Ian's fall. Marianne had cleared up what she could after the inquest.

Screwing up our eyes and craning our necks, we peered into the gloom.

'I don't like the way that entrance is gaping open or the sight of the broken railing. I don't want it left like that,' Jenny said. 'And there's something else. I want to go up there and see what Ian saw. I can't help feeling that he knew there was more up there than the view of the mountains. I want to know what he knew.'

'Well, I've had similar thoughts and I'd like to do that, too, if we can get the staircase repaired, although, with the house on the market—'

'Let's go now. I've seen enough,' she said, walking quickly away.

On the path back to the house, we stood for a moment, taking in the view. The mountains were appearing through thinning fog and beginning to be clearly etched against the skyline, with thick snow on their peaks and white fingers stretching down their slopes.

'Even though the house is on the market, I'd like to pay for repairs to the staircase, and I want to go up there and see what Ian saw,' Jenny said later, telling the others about our visit to the ruin.

'Yes, let's do that. Now that we're back here, I'm curious too,' Stephen said.

We all seemed to feel Ian's curiosity. I was no longer the only one, apart from Ian, who wanted to know more about Castignac. In London, we had been too far away to do anything about it, but it was different now that we were at the house.

Angela lost no time in giving Marianne a message for Didier and we were pleasantly surprised to see him arrive with his assistant, Philippe, the next day. They were driving an impressive-looking vehicle with a hydraulic lift on the back. It was the kind of thing that the town hall employed to prune plane trees. Graham called it a cherry-picker. After smiles and handshakes all round, Philippe drove the machine round to the ruined farmhouse and we followed them on foot. The generous proportions of the building allowed him to position the vehicle so that Didier rose up next to the staircase.

With Philippe in the driving seat, operating the hydraulic lift, we watched as Didier ascended and conducted his examination. It didn't take long. He came down saying that only the railing at the top was infested.

'We can treat the wood of the whole staircase with a chemical to deter termites, once we've repaired it. Philippe and I will do the repair, but it won't be until after you've left. I'm sorry I'm so busy, but you're not staying long and I can't drop what I'm doing for any longer,' Didier said.

We were disappointed, but no-one suggested going up to the loft in the cherry-picker. It would have taken a lot of manoeuvring to lift us all up there one by one and I wasn't sure anyone fancied the ride. I didn't. It was frustrating to have to wait, when our curiosity had been whetted, but there was no choice and Didier had at least put himself out that day. It would be springtime before we climbed the staircase.

Back in London, after New Year, when I was almost certain that I would never hear from Mark again, I received a text from him. I felt a mixture of excitement and alarm at seeing his name on my phone screen and I hesitated before opening the text in case it was goodbye, but I had to know. No amount of effort had enabled me to dismiss him from my mind.

> Sorry for silence. Is Castignac sold yet or can we go for a last time? Missing you. Mark xx

Hope flared in me. I sensed a change of heart in that word "missing", even though it would be months before we met. I considered sounding busy or casual, but in the end I said that we hadn't yet sold the house, that another visit to Castignac might be possible and that I had missed him too.

Mark and I arranged to meet at Stansted Airport and fly to Carcassonne for the Easter holiday. I had taken a week off work and he had leave from his project in Lebanon. As the day of seeing Mark drew nearer, I became more and more nervous about it. I wasn't certain if we would regain our old ease together. We had almost quarrelled in the summer and he had drawn back since then. It was months since we had met. My efforts to move on in life had led me nowhere. I still loved him and wanted to be with him, but it scarcely seemed to be a relationship: I wanted more than Mark could offer and he was too enmeshed in his past. Jackie and a number of my friends gave me the benefit of their advice and my head was in a whirl on the way to Stansted.

Despite all that, I had learned something from Mark's standoff in recent months, a kind of independence that I may have lacked before. I felt stronger in myself. I could deal with this and if necessary, I would face the end of the relationship calmly. I hadn't done well so far, but I wasn't going to carry on forever seeing Mark only when we were on holiday. I could meet someone else if I had to. I told myself that I was attractive and that thirty-five was not old.

This turmoil lasted all the way to the airport, but it was extraordinary how, on seeing Mark, it vanished. He stood out from the crowd, not for height, which he lacked, but by some instinct that I possessed for his presence. He looked delighted to see me and a huge smile welled up from within and broke out over my face as he took off his rucksack to give me a proper greeting. I breathed in the clean, fresh scent of him as we hugged and I felt his warm solidity. I drew back from his embrace to examine him properly.

'You look well, brown from the Lebanese winter sun and your outdoor life, and you're thinner,' I said.

'You don't look so bad yourself,' he said, and then relented. 'No, Tessa, you look great, and it's lovely to see you!'

He did look pleased to see me. Waiting for the plane and also during the journey, I was struck by a difference in his manner. He was less inclined to warn me off and more at peace with himself. I was different too. I was full of resolutions, even if they weren't all consistent. I wanted to be less demanding of him, yet I also wanted my feelings to count. I told myself that we would have a holiday with no strings and let the future look after itself. I wasn't sure I could manage that, but I would try.

'I thought we were finished when you sent that email about cooling it. I imagined you'd been lured away from me,' I said.

He laughed. 'No, it wasn't that. I mean, there's no-one else, if that's what you want to know. I needed some space and I wasn't living up to what you wanted. I was too busy to get away at New Year, but I still want to see you.'

I had rented a car for us. On the drive from Carcassonne, we crested a hill at one point to see the mountains along the horizon beyond the hills, still at their winter best, icy and glittering in the spring sunshine. A mist of new green leaves covered hedges and trees. I exclaimed at the early signs of spring as if I had come from the equator, instead of Britain, where spring was surely as beautiful as anywhere in the world. Mark, living in what I thought of as a desert climate, was more justified in being entranced. The car swung off the main road to St Martin des Remparts, taking a smaller road to Castignac, and we were soon at the house.

It was still too early in the year for geraniums, but the shutters were flung open in welcome. Castignac was waking up after the winter. The chestnut trees were coming out and the wisteria was in flower, its mauve blooms a bright patch of colour in the garden.

Mark and I lost no time in disappearing upstairs to our room after a swift greeting of the others, who had arrived before us. With the bedroom door closed, we made love with a new kind of excitement, getting to know each other again and admitting we had missed each other. We were back together again, but I was hoping it would be different now.

Didier hadn't repaired the staircase in the ruined farmhouse. When Angela spoke to him, his excuse was that he needed to talk to us more about what we wanted.

'It's obvious,' Graham said, when we gathered over a drink in the early evening. 'We ask Didier to replace the railing so that we can get up there safely.'

'That's a minimal approach,' Stephen said. 'What do you think, Jenny?'

'I like the idea of a metal spiral staircase. I'd feel safer with something new,' she said.

She passed around a catalogue that Didier had left in the house for us.

'I know it's more expensive, but I can't bear the thought of another accident. I'm willing to pay the whole cost myself. Ian had life insurance and I can afford it,' she said.

'That's generous,' Stephen said. 'We should do anything that will help you and I'd like to pay our share.'

Jenny was grateful for Stephen's offer and everyone else agreed straightaway to do the same. We couldn't say no to Jenny after what she had been through.

Didier was busy and couldn't do the work before the end of our holiday, so there was a further delay. It would be the summer, now, a year since Ian's death, before we could see the pigeon loft. With no offers on the house, it was beginning to look as if we would be coming again.

Angela called in at Gilles's office on the square one morning when she was shopping.

'I wanted to check on the sale of Castignac, but there's no news,' she told us later. 'As we know, the interest that followed putting it on the market has died down and there's no sign of any offer.'

'What does he say about why it's so difficult to sell?' I said.

'Oh, the same as before, that people might have been put off by a death on the property, but also that the market is slow at the moment.'

'I'm glad it's not selling. The more holidays we have here the better,' I said.

The more time I spent at Castignac, the more I didn't want to sell the house, but Stephen was still determined on the sale and resisted any attempts to discuss it.

Chapter Two

Graffiti

MARK HAD TAKEN A month off for the summer and, on my invitation, was planning to spend three weeks at Castignac. My job was quieter in the summer and I had arranged to take the same three weeks off work. In less busy moments at work, I would close my eyes and see St Martin des Remparts lying in its valley and Castignac gazing down on the peaceful town. Whenever life in London became tense or tedious and frustrating, I would see the two of us walking towards the mountains.

Stephen and Angela, Mark, and I arrived one day in late July, with Jenny. Graham and Lily were due to arrive a few days later. It was a sunny afternoon and Marianne had made sure the window boxes were decked with red geraniums again. We had chosen a slightly earlier holiday this time because Jenny wanted to avoid being at Castignac for the anniversary of Ian's death. Parliament was in recess and the school holidays had begun, so Stephen and Angela were free to come at the same time as the rest of us.

Doves were nesting in the wisteria. I sat beneath them on the terrace on that first afternoon of the holiday and saw how the two young ones perched together in the afternoon heat, shielded by leaves and the last of the hanging flowers, cocking their heads, their pinhead eyes bright. They fluttered wings and fanned tail feathers, pecking out down which floated through the lazy air. They were too young to give the querulous screech of adult doves, but they whistled softly for their mother, struggling with each other on her sudden arrival, plunging into her open beak for food.

The young doves were in danger from more than one direction. A cat who came into the garden stared up at the nest with yellow eyes, and Marianne told us that she had watched the doves grow and was waiting for them to be big enough to eat. She laughed at our horror. She might have been teasing about the doves, but I knew that any pigeons she caught would have gone straight into the pot.

I didn't sleep well that first night. A storm was brewing and I could hear wind wailing down the chimney in our bedroom and screaming around the roof of the house on a high, ghostly note, as if frustrated at meeting a solid object it couldn't simply whistle through. I lay awake, trying not to toss and turn too much because I didn't want to wake Mark. A repeated bang somewhere made me snuggle down in bed. It was sometimes hard to tell if a sound came from inside or outside, and I didn't want to leave the warmth of the bed and hunt around the house in the middle of the night to secure a swinging shutter.

An owl hooted repeatedly, a quavering sound nearby. I imagined it sitting in one of the chestnut trees, calling for a mate, and I heard a response from further away. The calls added to the ghostliness of the night, but I loved the sound. I never heard owls in London.

When I did sleep, it was fitfully. At one point I was falling down a flight of stairs, yet I never seemed to reach the ground. When I eventually landed, I found myself amongst a great patch of the hanged man orchid, with all the men waving their arms and legs at me, each face shielded by a hood, like a gang of city youths descending on a victim. I woke up in a sweaty panic and was reassured to see early dawn light edging the half-open shutters of the bedroom and Mark on his back beside me, snoring lightly.

The seven of us congregated on the terrace before the evening meal the next day and Stephen opened a bottle of sparkling wine. It was a beautiful summer's day and a kind of peace seemed to have descended over Castignac for the first time since Ian's death.

'Do you realise that two years have passed since we first sat on a terrace and talked about buying a house in France?' Angela said, passing around a bowl of olives.

'Yes, we thought you were joking at first about sharing a house and we grilled you mercilessly about the idea, remember, Stephen? Then we had that mad week of house-hunting. It's obvious, looking back, that the whole business was relatively smooth,' Jenny said. 'The problems only began afterwards...'

She stopped, looking stricken.

'Ian's death could have destroyed us, but instead it's brought us together,' Stephen said.

I was surprised. These were not the words of a man trying to leave Castignac. Was Stephen changing his mind?

'With everything that's gone wrong, I've never failed to love Castignac. And it's given me so many new interests – the house, wildflowers, countryside, French language and history, not to mention the company of all of you...' I said.

'It's your holiday home, but perhaps it's only now becoming a place to relax in. You all wanted a kind of heaven here, but it's not just heaven. It's a place with its own climate, people, history and of course, you brought yourselves and your lives. I tried to escape from myself by working abroad when my marriage cracked up and yet I couldn't escape. I had to live with the same old me,' Mark said.

He looked around at us. I wished that he had spoken as openly to me, but I was pleased to hear him sounding more at peace with himself.

'I brought my disappointment about not climbing higher on the political ladder,' Stephen said, in a rare admission.

'I wanted a holiday home, some space to breathe, away from school and away from the constituency,' Angela said.

Stephen turned towards her and I wondered if she had ever said as much as that before. Angela had a career in her own right, but there were times when she felt the need to escape from the demands of Stephen's political career.

'I wanted somewhere that Ian and I would enjoy together,' Jenny said, and a short silence followed as everyone nodded.

'We wanted to spend our holidays in France and to have a new interest in life,' Lily said.

Angela turned to me. 'What about you, Tessa?'

'Oh, it's quite simple. I wanted somewhere to enjoy holidays and an escape from London,' I said lightly. I would have added more had Mark and I been alone together.

Mark glanced across at me and I felt something shift between us. We had learned how to secure time to ourselves, either by staying in our room, which was big enough to have a sitting area by the window, or by exploring the countryside, or sloping off to our favourite café in St Martin des Remparts, where I might try to understand an article in a French newspaper, with Mark on hand to help.

At that moment, I wanted nothing more than for everyone else to disappear so that the two of us could be alone. It was impossible. There was the meal to get on the table and Mark was cooking. He took his glass of wine into the kitchen and I followed. Except for the occasional query about the food, we cooked together in amicable silence.

Over the meal, conversation drifted to the party the previous summer. We talked idly about the party guests.

'I wonder what Jacques thinks of seeing his family farm turned into a holiday home for foreigners,' Lily said at one point.

'He's never said what he thinks of us,' Angela said.

Stephen was dismissive. 'He probably thinks we're from another planet. After all, we don't have anything in common with him. Anyway, it doesn't matter because it's our house for the present.'

I hastened to ward off another discussion about selling the house because I didn't want us to come up with any new ideas for it, like reducing the price.

'We do have something in common with him. We have France and we have Castignac. He must know a lot more about it than he's told us so far. And remember my impression that he misses it.'

Another thought struck me. 'Jenny, do you remember Ian talking to Jacques for ages at the party? I could tell he was asking lots of questions, but I don't remember him saying anything about the conversation afterwards.'

'He only said that they'd talked about the ruin. He asked Jacques about its history, I think.'

'Maybe Jacques told Ian something we don't know.'

'I can't remember that he said anything else afterwards,' Jenny said.

Angela came to Jenny's rescue. 'Oh, not again, Tessa, stop it. You're always stirring things up.'

Remembering the animation in Ian's face as he had talked to Jacques, I was beginning to think that we had overlooked something important. The party had taken place only a few days before Ian's death and the two could be linked. I was silent for a few moments while the others talked. Angela had found a jewellery stall in the market that she and Jenny both liked and they were comparing purchases. I liked jewellery too. It would have been so easy to brush aside what Ian knew and discuss necklaces and so forth, but something wouldn't let me.

'Angela, there could be something in this. We must go and see Jacques and ask him what they talked about.'

'The party was a year ago. He probably won't remember the conversation and you really ought to let it rest.' Angela's green eyes flashed a warning.

'I can't. Look, he's always in the square. I say *bonjour* to him but I daren't go any further. I'm taking lessons, but I'm not at the stage yet where I can chat to an old French farmer with a strong accent! Come with me tomorrow and we'll speak to him, please. It'll only take a few minutes. We've got nothing to lose and we can't do it without you, because you know him best out of all of us. We might find out something important,' I said.

'There's no need for flattery,' Angela said.

She was silent and I had the sense not to push further, but let the conversation move on, this time to painting. Many artists had found their way to St Martin des Remparts and the shops were full of their work. The setting of the town in the valley, its stone buildings with their tiled roofs, had inspired Lily to take up painting in watercolours again, something she had done at school and not allowed time for since.

The next morning, Graham cycled into St Martin des Remparts early, before anyone was up, and bought our breakfast. He wasn't a man to be found lazing in the pool or sunning in a deckchair. I was in the garden when he returned with baguettes tied across the back of the bicycle and croissants in the basket on the front. I complimented him on looking French, even though it was too hot for a beret.

It was a beautiful, sunny morning under a pale blue sky and innocent clouds. The air was still fresh and we had breakfast on the terrace. Finishing a croissant, Angela stood up.

'Well, come on, Tessa, if we're going, let's get moving before it's too hot,' she said.

I leaped to my feet. Jacques would have been hard to find on market day, with the town under siege from people from surrounding villages, but fortunately it was an ordinary morning. We parked the car and did our shopping first, but once it was packed away, Angela was prepared to hunt for Jacques.

'Why are you now so sure that he knows something? You didn't think of talking to him before,' she said as we walked around the square in the shade of the colonnades.

'Talking about the party reminded me that Ian had spent a long time with Jacques and I began to think Jacques might have told Ian something that led to the accident. We might find out something useful,' I said.

As one of a number of old men who spent their days in the main square of St Martin, Jacques was not hard to find. The old men played *boules à pétanque*, they talked for hours in cafés while nursing drinks and they took part in a tractor parade as often as possible, but they always seemed to spend part of every fine day sitting on one of the wooden benches placed at various points around the main square. Here they were visible to anyone and could see what was going on. I scanned the square.

'There he is,' I said, pointing to where Jacques was sitting alone on a bench, reading a local newspaper, just as I wanted him to be. It meant we avoided being a nuisance by separating him from cronies. He looked like a man who had spent a lifetime out of doors and didn't want to be shut inside now. He was as brown as a nut, although a hat shaded his eyes. He always wore a hat and I suppressed a mischievous thought about whipping it off to see whether the top of his head would be as white as a peeled egg underneath.

Angela and I sat down on either side of him before he looked up from his paper.

'*Bonjour, mesdames.*'

'*Bonjour, Jacques,*' we said, and then Angela took over.

The conversation went on for some time, with Angela probing and questioning, and Jacques replying. I listened, trying to catch words here and there and generally failing. Jacques seemed to run words together, with his strong southern French accent, but I understood his last remark.

'Now, if you will excuse me, it is time for lunch.'

Angela thanked Jacques and we went back to the car, leaving him striding towards a café. I had the distinct impression that he was trying to escape from us.

'Lunch? It's not yet noon,' I said, looking at my watch and seeing the hands at half past eleven.

I made Angela repeat the conversation in English, word for word. She hadn't understood everything, but she had grasped the essence.

'Do you remember coming to our party last summer?' she had begun.

'Of course, *madame*, I remember it well. It was the last time I saw the old place,' Jacques had said.

'And you know that one of us died not long afterwards?'

'Poor man. Everyone knows that. A terrible accident.'

'You talked to him at the party.'

'Yes. He asked a lot of questions about the old farmhouse, especially the graffiti. He wasn't interested in the new house at all.'

'He died because he fell from the staircase to the pigeon loft. We'd told him not to climb it because it might be unsafe and we're curious about why he did.'

Jacques had stiffened and sat more upright at that point. 'Well, he asked me about it, but I didn't tell him it was safe. It's not my fault he died, *madame*. That is what I said to the police after his death when they came to see me.'

'No, of course it isn't your fault, Jacques. No-one is blaming you.'

He had relaxed then and she continued her questions.

'What do you mean by the graffiti?'

'They're just graffiti, *madame*, in the pigeon loft, but your friend was excited when I mentioned them. They were left by soldiers who were billeted there on their way to the Great War. Your friend said that meant that they were a hundred years old and people would be interested because of the centenary of that war. I haven't been up there for years and never think about them, but I mentioned them to your friend because he was asking me so many questions about the old farmhouse. No-one's ever been interested in it before.'

'Why do you think Ian went up there, when he knew it might be dangerous?' Angela asked then.

'To see the graffiti, *madame*, I'm sure of it, because he was so interested when I told him about it. But I didn't tell him the staircase was safe, only that it was safe as far as I knew and that I hadn't climbed it for years. My hip wouldn't let me, and anyway, there was no reason to. I didn't use the pigeon mess as fertiliser the way that we used to in the old days. I didn't need to. Fertiliser is cheap.'

'Why didn't you tell us about your conversation with Ian?'

'There was no need for me to say anything, *madame*, when he could tell you himself.'

'He didn't tell us anything.'

'He could have done. The graffiti are not important. You bought my big house, not an old ruin. Besides, I thought you might blame me for his death.'

'There were termites in the top of the staircase, in the railing. That's why he fell.'

'I had no idea about that when I was talking to him, *madame*. I only read it in the paper after he died.'

'We're not blaming you for the accident, Jacques. It was only that we didn't know why he went up there, but I think we have a better idea now.'

'Well, that was fascinating, I must say,' Angela said to me, as she finished her account of the conversation. Her earlier impatience had vanished. 'So Ian knew about these graffiti in the pigeon loft. He obviously thought he was on to something and he didn't tell us about it because we would have warned him off the staircase again.'

'Jacques didn't tell *us* about the graffiti, although you and I spoke to him at the party. Also we didn't know that the police had spoken to Jacques. They could have told us what they found out from him.' I couldn't help feeling aggrieved.

'Don't forget I had to translate your conversation with Jacques at the party, so that slowed things up, whereas Ian's French was pretty good. And Jacques may have felt easier talking man to man. As for the police, they were investigating for the inquest. They probably didn't think of telling us anything.'

'Jacques wanted to get away from us,' I said.

'Yes. Probably not because of the graffiti.'

'No. It's because of Ian's death. He's right that it wasn't his fault, but he didn't want to talk about it because he feels uneasy. I can understand that. We all felt terrible about Ian's death and it wasn't our fault.'

Chapter Three

The Pigeon Loft

Back at Castignac, the others surrounded us, wanting to know what we had found out. Angela relayed her conversation with Jacques for the second time.

'But why was it so urgent that Ian couldn't wait for Didier to check the staircase?' Stephen asked.

'Ian loved the ruin and my guess is that he wanted anything in the pigeon loft to be his discovery. Remember I told you that he was thinking of writing some articles about the area? He might have thought that the graffiti would make an article, especially now, during the centenary of the First World War,' Jenny said.

A short silence followed. No-one wanted to say that Ian had made a terrible mistake, but we must all have been thinking that.

'We need to go up there and have a look for ourselves,' Stephen said.

Everyone agreed. Angela phoned Didier and pointed out that it was six months since we had asked him to repair the staircase and that we weren't prepared to wait any longer. What she would do otherwise she didn't say, but her voice on the phone was firm.

Angela's phone call fortunately coincided with the cancellation of another job and Didier was able to move fast. He came along to Castignac with Philippe and the cherry-picker within a couple of days and removed the old staircase, arranging to chop it into logs for our fireplace.

The new spiral staircase, which Didier had already ordered, was installed quickly. At one point, we noticed that some of the shutters in the pigeon loft were open. Didier was up there, checking the soundness of wooden beams before our visit.

As we collected at the foot of the new staircase, Didier appeared at the loft entrance. He rattled away and Angela listened intently, still finding him a challenge to understand, but getting the gist that it was safe. We could climb up and only had to watch out for pigeon droppings. Any morbid thoughts were banished by the job of conquering my fear of heights, and I forced myself upwards.

Light was coming in through the pigeonholes, high up on the walls and in one or two places where roof tiles were missing, as well as through the one set of shutters that Didier had opened. We struggled with the rusted fastenings of the remaining shutters. They squeaked and moaned as we tugged away until, one by one, they gave up and more light streamed in.

We were now at the highest point of Castignac, several metres higher than our house and we were distracted by the entrancing sight before us. It was a sunny day and to the south, beyond the hills, the blue Pyrenees stretched hazily across the horizon. Vestiges of snow clung to the tops here and there, even though it was summer. I had that feeling again of flying towards the mountains, into another world. I leaned out of the window and lost myself in gazing at them until the rising sound of voices behind me drew my attention.

We were standing in a square room under a tiled roof which rose to a point created by wooden beams. The walls were plastered but bare of paint, and the wooden floor was hardly visible under a thick carpet of pigeon droppings. Above the plastered walls, just under the roof, was a layer of wooden planks, pierced by a pattern of pigeonholes.

Pigeons were gazing down at us from their perches on beams. They were cocking their heads and cooing softly as if commenting to a neighbour on the strange creatures appearing unexpectedly in their midst. High up in the roof were spectacular cobwebs, great nets and swags of them, bristling with dust, untouched by any broom.

'They're beyond your reach, Angela!' I said, looking up at them.

'What a great room for a party!' Stephen said.

'And this is valuable compost,' Didier said, pointing to the pigeon manure. I understood that.

'Look at this graffiti!' Mark was peering at the wall nearest to him.

Cut into the bare plaster, alongside the windows facing the main house, were the names of soldiers that Jacques had told us about, carved with the point of a knife or some other sharp object. Facing the garden, I traced the most prominent name with a finger. Eugène Vigneron had written in a fine cursive script, an educated hand. Under his name was his birth date, 4th July 1895 and his place of birth, Orthez.

He had added *Classe 15*, which could have meant 1915. That would have made him at least twenty and put the date of the billeting at 1915 or later. In large letters, he had written *soldat*, obviously an important word to him and 59 *BP*. Underneath was the word *infanterie*, which even I could guess meant infantry and then, in large, clear letters, *St Martin des Remparts, Ariège*. Some of the lettering was a little ragged, perhaps because he was carving plaster. I could imagine perfect handwriting on paper.

Mark was already checking his smartphone and looked up from it as he spoke. 'Orthez is a town in the department of Pyrénées Atlantiques, near Bayonne. Eugène was a long way from home,' he said.

A minute or so later, he looked up from his phone again. 'Pyrénées Atlantiques was formerly Basses-Pyrénées, which explains the BP of the graffiti. There would have been no need to spell it out as everyone where he came from knew what it meant.'

'And he wrote St Martin des Remparts out in full because it was new to him,' I said.

Eugène Vigneron would have been able to look at our house as he was carving into the wall of the pigeon loft. He had chosen that view for his work, rather than the mountains on the other side, perhaps because he liked looking down on the house. It might have seemed a solid, reassuring presence when he was on his way to the trenches. Had he thought it would be a great adventure, or was he scared? He might have left the graffiti in case of his death, so that there would be some record, not set in stone, but at least in plaster; or he and the others might just have been bored, cooped up, perhaps for days, waiting for a train to the front. They might have simply done it, as people had left graffiti for centuries, because they could.

'Here's another one, in perfect writing, but he's only left his name. Hébrard Montval,' I said.

Examining the plaster all around the loft, we found other names and markings, but no-one had written as much as

Eugène Vigneron or as neatly as Hébrard Montval. Patches of plaster were missing here and there, and splashes of pigeon mess on the walls obscured some of the names, but not to any great extent. They seemed fresh and might have been carved only a day or so ago. I felt as if I were standing there with the young soldiers who had been billeted in the ruined farmhouse almost a hundred years before. I looked down at my feet.

'It's only pigeon shit, not the mud from shell-holes or trenches,' Mark said, reading my thoughts. 'So soldiers were brought together and then transported from southern France to the Western Front?'

'That's pretty well what Jacques told us,' I said.

Soldiers from all over France had fought in the trenches in the First World War. It looked as if St Martin des Remparts had been a place where those from south-west France had met to travel to the Western Front. There had once been a railway station in the town and although I knew from a second visit to the museum that it had closed in the 1970s, trains would have been the main form of transport at the time of the First World War. I was touched by the thought of Eugène and Hébrard and their fellows staying in the ruin on their way to the trenches.

Making my way slowly around the loft, examining the graffiti, I noticed something else. I almost missed it because it was lower down than the soldiers' names and fainter. It showed the kind of gibbet that children draw when playing hangman, but with a hanging flower, not a man. It was drawn with a pencil and the writing underneath it was in a simpler, more modern style than the careful italic of the soldiers' handwriting.

'It's a hanged man orchid. Look, there's a date,' I said.

Everyone crowded round to look. The date was faint but still decipherable: le 10 octobre '45.

'It looks more recent than the First World War graffiti. Given the drawing, it could be the date of a death,' I said.

Angela was peering at the date. 'If it's 1945, it would be about the time of Jacques's birth. I should say he's in his seventies. He might know what it means, although he didn't mention this particular drawing to us.'

Not far away from the drawing of the orchid was a name, Renée, with a little design underneath. I wondered idly who she was but was more intrigued by the orchid and the date beside it.

Finishing our survey of the pigeon loft, we descended the spiral staircase and made our way back to the house.

'It's odd that no-one except Jacques knew about the graffiti. People might be interested in the record left by the soldiers, especially the families of any local soldiers,' Graham said on the way back.

'Maybe no-one was interested in the graffiti at the time. It could have been like this,' I said, bolstered by reading about nineteenth-century French interiors that Castignac had inspired me to do in the library where I worked. 'The old farmhouse is a ruin, abandoned by the family in the middle of the nineteenth century, when they built their new house. This increased their status in society. They were no longer living with the animals and the new house was proof that the farm was doing well and they were leading members of the local community. When soldiers were billeted here, fifty years after the building of the new house, they engraved their names, but the family no longer visited the pigeon loft. So the graffiti weren't noticed or were forgotten and the staircase was neglected.'

'Why were the soldiers billeted here, instead of in the house where the family was living? After all, this place was abandoned about fifty years before the First World War, judging by the date on the new house,' Mark said.

'Maybe the family were pressed into taking them, so they put them somewhere out of the way and left them to their own devices. Unless they were here in the winter or early spring, they wouldn't have needed any heating. There's a pump outside, for water,' I said.

Later that day, we entered the name of Eugène Vigneron into a website of French casualties in the First World War. He had been killed in 1918, right at the end of the war. We did the same for Hébrard Montval, but there was no record of him, suggesting he hadn't died in the war.

We then looked up the names Vigneron and Montval in Orthez and found many examples of the former. The most prominent, a local politician, was a Gaston Vigneron, probably in his sixties, judging by a photo. Dying at the age of twenty-three, after several years at the front, Eugène may not have had children, but was Gaston, or one of his relatives, Eugène's great-nephew? I wanted to write and tell him about the graffiti and ask if he were related to Eugène. There was no email address for him, but we found a postal address for the company he worked for. Mark promised to help me with the letter.

That evening, outside on the terrace, watching the sun slip down into clouds that hung over the mountains, we talked about the visit to the pigeon loft.

'I'm glad to have seen what Ian saw, even though it's taken us a year to get there, because it explains what he was looking for,' Jenny said.

'That drawing of the hanged man looks quite separate from the soldiers' graffiti. It makes me think that Jacques told Ian more than he's told us. Marianne said someone committed suicide in the ruin and so did Jacques when we spoke to him at the party. How about another chat with him?' I said, turning to Angela.

'Tessa, this has gone far enough. We're trying to satisfy ourselves about Ian's death, and if Jenny agrees, I think we've done that.'

'We have, but there's more to do now, at least for me,' I said.

'What do you mean?'

'I want to know more about the soldiers and about the drawing of the hanged man. I want Jacques to tell us more about his family past. All he told us the other day was about the graffiti.'

'But Jacques doesn't want to say any more. You saw how he escaped us by saying it was lunchtime at 11.30 in the morning,' Angela said.

'I agree he doesn't want to, but could he?' I said.

'We've done enough. I'd like to let it all rest now,' Jenny said, looking exhausted.

Out of consideration for her, we changed the subject, but I still wasn't satisfied.

Jenny had taken to spending part of the evening alone and I wasn't surprised that she took the setting of the sun as the signal to leave us.

'I'd like to talk to Jacques again. I could ask Mark to help me, if you've had enough, but I'd much rather you did, because Jacques knows you,' I said to Angela, after Jenny had gone.

'Oh, Tessa, can't you let it alone? Must you always be playing detective?' Angela said.

'Don't you think the drawing of the hanged man is puzzling, especially after what Marianne said?'

'Well, I suppose we could talk to Jacques again, if you insist. But it will depend on him. He's entitled to keep his family skeletons in their cupboard, so be prepared for a refusal.'

That was enough for me. The next day, Angela and I went into St Martin des Remparts and looked for Jacques. He wasn't on his usual bench. After hunting around, we found him on a different one, much less prominent. I couldn't resist the thought that he was hiding from us, especially as he looked hunted as he said *bonjour*, but I squashed any doubts about pursuing him. It was, after all, a long time ago. It couldn't possibly have any personal connection to him. It was history, like anything that had happened before I was born.

Angela told Jacques we had been up to the pigeon loft and seen the graffiti. I caught the word *pigeonnier*, but the rest of what they said was too fast for me. They talked, or rather Jacques talked, for hours, much longer than before. The sun had crossed the sky before they finished and people had disappeared for lunch. I began to feel uncomfortable on the bench and wanted to move around but dared not miss anything. That made no sense as I couldn't understand what they were saying, but still I didn't move. Angela relayed the conversation to me in English afterwards.

'Now, do you remember the drawing that looks different from the soldiers' graffiti?' she had said to Jacques. 'It shows the orchid called the hanged man. It's hanging from a gibbet and there's a date underneath that could be 1945.'

Angela and I had both been afraid Jacques would look vague and deny all knowledge of the drawing, but he didn't.

'Yes, *madame*, I drew that when I was a boy. It has been there ever since. Things don't change much in the *pigeonnier*.'

'So that explains its position, lower than the graffiti. It was because you weren't at your full height.'

'Yes,' Jacques said, and there was a silence.

'Could you tell us what it means? You see, we're curious now about Castignac and the lives of people there. We discovered the orchid, but why did you draw a picture of it?'

'I know the orchid grows there. When I was a boy, I used to put it under my magnifying glass and see all the little flowers like men. But it doesn't have anything to do with your friend's death, at least, not as far as I know.'

'What is it about?'

'You are making me dig up the past, *madame*.'

'I'm sorry if we're a nuisance, but we're trying to satisfy ourselves about Castignac's history. We didn't think about it at first, but it's begun to fascinate us.'

Jacques lit a cigarette and took a deep breath as he began to speak. He told us about his grandparents, Jean-Louis and Danielle, and his parents, Brigitte and Siegfried. There was Eugène, who had been killed in the First World War, then Hébrard and Nicolette and their family, including Renée, whose name was also in the pigeon loft. His story poured out, covering two world wars and his own life.

Part Six

Chapter One

Jacques

Jacques had only just begun to put a sentence together when he started asking questions about a father. He had picked up the idea from children's stories that Brigitte read to him. At first, he tried pinning the word *Papa* onto Hébrard, the only man he saw regularly. Everyone laughed at his mistake and pointed out that Marie and Jeanne were Hébrard's children, even though they were children no longer. Brigitte had to tell him that his father lived in another country and wouldn't be coming to see them.

At school, at the age of six, Jacques began to notice that other boys had fathers who lived with them. Sometimes they collected their sons from school. He questioned his mother again.

'Your father is German and he was here during the war, but he went home to Germany and we don't see him. That means you're half German. The Nazis lived here during the war and that's why people don't like Castignac.'

'Is it my fault?'

'No. None of it is your fault, Jacques. You're just as good as any of the other boys.'

There had been a war, although as a small boy he wasn't quite sure what it meant. The Nazis had been the enemy and his father had been one of them. When he persisted with questions, Brigitte closed up.

Jacques was a handsome boy, tall for his age, with straw-blond hair. He was quiet by nature and circumstances made him a solitary child. He didn't look much like the other boys in his class. They were smaller and had dark hair and darker skin.

He was left to paint a mental picture of his father and his life to make up for the blank. He let his imagination roam freely. His father was tall and good-looking, with blond hair and a face like his own, but older. He was strong and energetic. He had a wife and family, but he would often pause in what he was doing and think of the son he had never met. Was he a farmer somewhere in Germany? He wouldn't dare to come and find Jacques because a Nazi would not be welcome in St Martin des Remparts. It was confusing that his father was one of the enemy, but Jacques wouldn't hate him, when he didn't know of any particular wrong that his father had ever done.

By piecing odd comments together and asking questions, Jacques learned as he grew older that his grandfather, Jean-Louis, had hanged himself in the old farmhouse, where Hébrard had found him. It wasn't something that they talked about much at home, but he did find out that it had happened just after he was born.

His grandmother, Danielle, was old and sat in the kitchen most of the time, complaining at Brigitte, but she had a soft spot for Jacques and always found him something to eat when he was hungry, which was nearly always as he grew. She had told him many times about the slice of pie she had given Hébrard all those years ago when he had turned up starving at Castignac.

He knew that Brigitte was his grandfather's daughter and that she was proud of being from a long line of Castignac farmers.

'I want you to run the farm here one day and to have a family who will carry on with it,' Brigitte liked to say.

'I will. I'll be the farmer,' Jacques would answer.

He looked forward to his future as the farmer at Castignac and liked helping Hébrard and Brigitte as much as he could. He enjoyed going to the market with Brigitte and Nicolette, and was good at adding up the cost of their purchases and counting out the change for people. He would take the money for a live hen and watch the customer walking away, dangling it by the feet.

Hébrard and Nicolette's two daughters, Marie and Jeanne, were both married and living in St Martin des Remparts with families of their own. Jacques often wished that Marie and Jeanne had boys of his age, but Marie only had daughters and a son, who was too young for him, and Jeanne's twin boys were younger still.

At least there was Renée. She was Marie's younger daughter, about his age, and they were in the same class at school. She wasn't a relative, but she felt like one because she was Hébrard's granddaughter and, although he never called him *Papa* anymore, he liked to think of Hébrard as his father.

Jacques didn't do well at school. His mother had told him a family story of how his grandfather had run away from school only to be taken back in the cart like a sack of wheat, but that he had learned to enjoy school and to benefit from it. She wanted Jacques to have the same change of heart, but he had more reason for not liking school than his grandfather. He had few friends there because the other boys didn't like him.

Everyone seemed to know that his father had been one of the Nazis who had lived at Castignac during the war. The worst boys would gang up and shout at him when he appeared in the playground before school, or during breaks.

'Nazi! Nazi!'

'Here comes the enemy! Shoot him!'

The few German words they knew were repeated endlessly.

'*Achtung, achtung!*'

'*Heil Hitler!*'

'*Donner und blitzen!*'

War stories were on every boy's lips. Older boys thought it funny to make him cry when he was little and to blame him for things that they did.

The boys and girls at the school had different playgrounds, but one day, when Renée was about ten and Jacques was the same age, she came to his rescue. A cluster of boys had pinned him into a corner, punching and kicking him, even though he was bigger than they were.

'Hey! Stop that!' she shouted at them through the fencing. At first, they ignored her, and she continued shouting when they didn't stop what they were doing. Seeing a teacher approach because of the noise she was making, they scampered away.

Renée kept an eye on him after that. The other boys, sensing a furious authority in her, persecuted Jacques less. He was glad of her presence, but she was only a girl and there were times when he kept his distance from her in order to save face. It wasn't long before he became known as a troublemaker and a misfit at school, and he was glad to escape home at the end of each school day.

'I hate school. The other boys call me a Nazi and make me the enemy in their games,' he said to his mother more than once.

Her reply was always the same. 'You have to stand up to them, Jacques. And don't think you can get off school, because you must go, every day.'

As Hébrard and Brigitte were the only workers on the farm all the year round, there was always plenty for Jacques to do as he grew older. School became less important year by year. The taunts and war games of the other boys began to lose their power. Jacques had learned little at school that helped his work on the farm and by the age of ten was beginning to bunk off now and then to work with Hébrard, making sure his mother didn't know. He would be a man soon and would run the farm with Hébrard. He was needed more and more now that Hébrard was getting old and had no sons to follow him.

As a boy, Jacques wanted to climb up to the pigeon loft. It was the only place on the farm that he had never explored and it wasn't long before he worked out that it was the highest point. He was aware that he shouldn't climb up there on his own. Brigitte always said it wasn't safe for a child, adding that there was nothing up there apart from pigeons, which he could see around the farm anyway. But the staircase in the ruin was tempting. He liked the way that its four short flights zigzagged their way up the wall. If he craned his neck and squinted carefully, he could just see the entrance in the floor of the pigeon loft.

At the age of ten, he climbed up the staircase on his own one day. On the top step, he reached up to push the entrance door open. His arms weren't strong enough and he gave up when they began to ache, coming down disappointed.

He began to pester Hébrard. 'Take me up to the pigeon loft. When are you going up there?' he said again and again. It became a place of mystery and secrets to him. There must be something to see, because nobody would let him go up there.

'There's nothing there, my boy, only old beams and pigeons,' Hébrard always said in reply.

'Hébrard, I want to go up to the pigeon loft,' Jacques said, again and again.

'All right, all right. You can come with me next time I go to scrape up the pigeon droppings. It's good fertiliser, you know, but it takes a while before there's enough for it to be worth the effort.'

Jacques took to saying, 'Hébrard, the floor of the pigeon loft needs cleaning up. We need to go up there.'

He was eleven before the visit took place, but Hébrard kept his promise and they climbed up together one day. Jacques noticed how Hébrard pushed open the overhead door until, hinged on one side, it fell to the floor and allowed them in. One day, his own arms would be strong enough.

Inside, it was gloomy because light could enter only through the round pigeonholes with the shutters closed. Light flooded in when Hébrard opened the shutters and showed Jacques the view of the mountains. Jacques was higher up now than he had ever been before at Castignac, and the mountains looked bigger and closer than normal. Because it was winter, they were easy to see and covered in snow, with patches of grey rock visible here and there. Jacques had never been skiing, but he had heard that people went skiing in the mountains and he wanted to ski across the Pyrenees into Spain. He would be almost flying as he descended from the summit. But he would have to wait until he was older. Hébrard and his family didn't go skiing and nor did his mother. They kept the mountains at a distance.

He turned away from the view and looked at the pigeon loft. It was square and the beamed roof rose high above him, to a point at the top. Horrible cobwebs hung down.

'There's nothing here!' he said, disappointed.

Hébrard laughed. 'I've been telling you that all along. What did you expect?'

Jacques didn't like to say that he had been thinking of prisoners chained up for years, pirates or skeletons or witches, wizards and angels. Of course he didn't believe in fairy tales, but there might have been something there, like a chest full of treasure. All he could see were pigeons, which had made a thick mess all over the floor. That was why he and Hébrard were here, to clear up, not to discover anything exciting. Hébrard had brought a bag and a shovel with him, and was already scraping the floor.

'Let me have a go,' Jacques said, always wanting to try everything. Hébrard let him use the shovel for a few minutes. Then a pigeon let loose a stream of disgusting stuff onto his head. Jacques let go of the shovel and shouted, jumping around, trying to get the mess out of his hair and clapping his hands until the pigeons flew out of the loft.

'It did that on purpose. I know it did,' he said.

'Maybe it thinks you're trespassing. No, my boy. It's just what pigeons do,' Hébrard said.

Calming down, waiting for Hébrard to finish work, he noticed markings on the bare plaster walls.

'Hébrard! There's your name here! Did you do that?'

'Why, yes, I suppose I did. That was a long time ago,' Hébrard said, peering across to where Jacques was pointing.

'It says 1915 next to another name. That's over forty years ago!'

Jacques was good at figures but awed by the length of time so much longer than his own life.

Leaning on the shovel, Hébrard told Jacques the story of how he and Eugène and a trainload of other soldiers had come all the way from Orthez, picking up more men at each station, on their way to the Great War. Some twenty of them had been billeted on the ground floor of the ruin on their way to the trenches. None of them had ever before been so far from home. Jacques had heard the story before, but it meant more, hearing it now.

'Here's his name, Eugène Vigneron, but what funny writing.' Jacques was reading from the wall.

'Eugène wrote a good hand. We both did. You were taught to write properly in those days.'

'Was Eugène killed in that war?'

'Yes, in 1918.'

'How did he die?'

Hébrard took a deep breath. 'He was shot by a German sniper just before the end of the war.'

'I'm glad you weren't killed.'

Hébrard began shovelling again, turning away from Jacques. 'So am I, lad, but I never went to the trenches. I came from Orthez on the train with the other soldiers and I stayed here. Your grandfather needed help on the farm.'

Jacques looked at Hébrard, puzzled at first and then light dawned. 'You mean you were a deserter?'

'I suppose I was, yes.' Hébrard was speaking over the scrape of the shovel and his voice was low.

'I don't blame you,' Jacques said quickly. He had not heard that word used before about Hébrard and could tell that he didn't like it. 'I hate the war and I'm glad you stayed here,' he said, thinking of insults thrown at him by the other boys at school. They were because of a different war, but still a war.

Hébrard didn't like arguments. Jacques understood that he hadn't wanted to join in the biggest argument of all, the Great War. Biggest, that is, until the one came along that his mother simply called the war. Hébrard had lived and worked on the farm since long before Jacques was born. Jacques didn't want to think badly of him when Hébrard had always treated him well and was like a father to him.

If it hadn't been for the last war, Jacques wouldn't have had a Nazi father and wouldn't be mocked at school. Nazi was what they said at school. Nazi, not German, which was what his mother had said. He wasn't sure of the difference.

Everything would be all right but for that war. He wanted so much to be like the other boys. If only his mother had married a Frenchman from the town and given him a proper father, a father he knew, who would be on the farm like Hébrard and play football with him. But then, with a different father, he wouldn't be the same person. He always gave up thinking at that point. It was too difficult.

'Can I write my name?' Jacques said, and Hébrard nodded, but neither of them had a knife or a pen to hand.

Hébrard had finished his work. He gave the lighter of two sacks to Jacques and swung the other one over his shoulder. Picking up the shovel, he motioned to Jacques to lead the way down the wooden staircase, so that he could close the entrance behind them. Nothing more was said about the pigeon loft.

Brigitte gave Jacques a camera for his twelfth birthday. 'Your grandfather had a camera,' she said to him. 'He loved gadgets and machinery.'

Jacques took pictures of Brigitte, Hébrard and his family, other people he knew and his favourite places. Brigitte gave him Jean-Louis's old photos and he put them in the back of the album. One was a picture of his grandfather, looking grim. Jacques wasn't sure if he would have liked him.

Over a year after Jacques and Hébrard had visited the pigeon loft, Jacques found himself thinking about it again. At twelve, he was growing fast, as Brigitte kept telling him. Every day he was getting stronger and he was probably strong enough to push open the entrance to the pigeon loft on his own. He fancied trying it. He liked the idea of seeing the mountains from there and looking again at the soldiers' names.

Renée, who often came up to the farm to see her grandparents, had found several different orchids growing wild. She loved flowers and Jacques, liking her, had followed her interest. The first discovery had been the spotted orchid with its stalk of pink and white flowers shaped like women wearing old-fashioned dresses. There was also the pink, triangular, pyramidal orchid; the helleborine with its stalk of pure white clustered flowers; and the early purple orchid. Renée had looked them up in a book in the school library and taught Jacques the names.

Those orchids were ordinary, like other flowers, but Jacques particularly liked the ones that tried to look like something else. The bee orchid looked like a bee climbing into each flower head. The spider orchid looked like a spider; the lizard orchid had the back legs and tail of a lizard; the tongue orchid had papery, brown, leaf-like petals shaped like tongues. What to Jacques was the strangest one of all, if the least conspicuous, the hanged man orchid, had a stalk of little hooded men and their dangling arms and legs. Other flowers didn't particularly interest him. They were more for girls, but those orchids were different.

'The spotted orchid is my favourite one,' Renée said, when they had discovered several different kinds. 'I'd like to have a dress like that, with spots on. What's your favourite, Jacques?'

'The hanged man,' Jacques said in a deep voice.

She laughed. Renée was hard to scare and he didn't really want to do that. He just liked teasing her.

Chapter Two

Jacques

ONE HOT AFTERNOON IN the school summer holidays, after the harvest was over and they had time on their hands, Jacques and Renée went over to the ruin and climbed the staircase on their own. Jacques wanted Renée to see how strong he was. He pushed against the entrance to the pigeon loft, the side that wasn't hinged, just as he had seen Hébrard do the year before. It didn't give way at first and he pushed again. This time he moved it enough to open it. He made it fall to the floor of the pigeon loft and listened to the clatter it made, hoping that his mother wouldn't hear the noise and come over to see what was going on, shaming him in front of Renée. Then he was inside the loft, with Renée behind him.

It was just as gloomy as he remembered, with light coming in from the pigeonholes. As Hébrard had done on their visit the year before, he wrestled with the shutters on the mountain side and flung them open, not thinking that someone outside might notice and guess he had been up there on his own. The floor was covered again with pigeon droppings.

'See the mountains!' he said, and Renée crammed herself into the window frame beside him.

Standing at the window, Jacques was acutely aware of something other than the view. At twelve, he was seeing changes in his body, signs that he was growing up. He had been thinking about Renée in a different way recently and when her cloud of dark, curly hair tickled his nostrils, he caught a faint scent that made him breathe in and want to touch her. He wanted to kiss her, but he was much too shy to do it just like that. Later, when he was on his own, he would enjoy the fantasies about her that had lately begun to tease him.

Pigeons in the loft turned towards them, as if questioning what they were doing there. Jacques and Renée ignored them at first and for a while lost themselves in gazing at the mountains. They looked bigger from up here and there was still some snow on them. They would be even better on a sunny winter's day when they would be crisply outlined and covered with snow.

'I'm going to ski towards them one day and I'll go right up to the top and down the other side,' he said to Renée, wanting to impress her.

Her face shone with excitement. 'Oh, yes, I'd love to do that and then we would be in Spain!'

Turning away from the mountains, Jacques showed Renée the graffiti left by the soldiers and she looked with interest at her grandfather's name. Jacques explained that Hébrard had been billeted in the ruin on his way to the trenches and that was how he came to Castignac.

'So he never went to the Great War?' Renée said, tracing her grandfather's name with her finger.

'No. He stayed here.'

She finished her tracing and looked at Jacques. 'Well, I'm glad he did.'

'Why? That made him a deserter.'

'No, because I wouldn't be here otherwise. Don't you see? He would have gone to war and he might have been killed, but if not, he wouldn't have come back here. He would have gone home to Orthez. I know that's where he came from. Then he wouldn't have married my gran, and my mother wouldn't have been born and nor would I.'

'Well then, I'm glad he stayed,' Jacques said, and Renée smiled at him. He meant that he was glad Renée was his friend, but he wasn't going to say that.

Jacques had an idea. 'My father might have been up here and left his name for me to find.'

'But you wouldn't know, because you always say you don't know his name.' Renée was laughing, but not in an unkind way.

'I'm going to look. There might be something. If I find a German name, it could be him.'

He searched for a German name, or a sign, even a swastika, the hated Nazi symbol, but there was nothing. The names were all French and, apart from the ones he knew, none of them meant anything in particular to him. His father had never been in the pigeon loft or if he had, he had left no sign.

He took out his magnifying glass and peered closely at the names on the walls. Hébrard had the best writing but had only left his name. Eugène had said more, including his date and place of birth.

Jacques could write better than Eugène, if not as well as Hébrard. He had brought a pencil instead of a knife, as it would be easier to use. He liked drawing. It was his best subject at school and he had pleased the science teacher with his drawings of orchids. But he wouldn't leave his name on the bare plaster wall. There was no need as he lived here and he might get into trouble if his mother ever found out. She didn't think much of writing on walls. In any case, that was what you did when you were somewhere new, to say that you had been there, as Hébrard had been when he first arrived. Castignac wasn't new to Jacques.

He saw a pigeon looking down on them from a roof beam and clapped his hands to make it fly out of the loft.

'Mind them or they'll get you,' he said to Renée, remembering what had happened last time. He didn't want a repeat of that in front of Renée or while he was concentrating on his drawing. She joined in and they clapped all the pigeons out of the loft.

He opened the shutters on the other side, where the graffiti were, and gazed down on the house where he lived. It was strange looking down on it, as if he were watching a film in the cinema in St Martin des Remparts, where he sometimes went with his mother or Hébrard. His mother came out into the garden and began to hang up washing, his clothes and hers and probably his grandmother's clothes as well. It was a good drying day, as his mother liked to say. He felt an odd pang as he looked down on her. She was so familiar and yet she looked different seen from this height.

Jacques turned back into the loft and took the pencil out of his pocket. He had only picked it up at the last minute, remembering the expanse of bare plaster walls from his visit with Hébrard and how he had wanted to write or draw on them. There was nothing else to do in the pigeon loft now that he had looked at the view from both sides.

He had found the hanged man orchid growing outside the old farmhouse where he knew that his grandfather had hanged himself and Renée had looked up the name for him. He felt more and more that the hanging had been because of him,

Jacques, because he was half-German. That was why he was mocked at school and called a Nazi. He knew now what he hadn't thought about when he was younger. His grandfather hadn't wanted a Nazi grandson. It was horrible to think that he hadn't been wanted and that his grandfather had killed himself because of that.

An idea came to Jacques in the pigeon loft and he began to draw. Not being as tall as the soldiers, his drawing was lower down, but it didn't matter. He was drawing the hanged man, with a hood and the dangling arms and legs. He drew a gibbet. Now the man was being strangled. Is that what it had been like for his grandfather? He didn't want to think about that too much. Underneath he wrote *homme pendu* and then the date, *le 10 octobre '45*. He knew the date of his grandfather's death from his tombstone in the garden.

Renée watched him in silence. When he had finished, he offered her the pencil. She wrote her name on a different wall, in a space of her own and she put a little design underneath it.

Renée was always quick to laugh, but she didn't laugh at his drawing. She knew what it meant because she knew about his grandfather. With Renée as his friend, the bad things didn't matter as much as they might have done.

When they had finished, Jacques wanted to be out of there. He closed the shutters and the entrance to the loft and they climbed down the staircase to the stone floor. Safely down at ground level, they ran across to the house, arriving just as his mother finished hanging out her washing.

'What have you two been up to now?' she said.

Neither of them answered and she didn't pursue them, as she returned to the house with her peg bag and empty laundry basket and they followed her, hoping for a piece of the spice cake that was one of her specialities.

After that visit to the pigeon loft with Renée, Jacques found himself thinking harder about his father and questioning his mother more. He tackled Brigitte one evening in the kitchen at Castignac. They had just finished their meal with his grandmother, around the big, scrubbed kitchen table, where they always ate. Danielle had left to go to bed early, which she was doing more and more.

'I want to know about my father, *Maman*,' he said. 'I'm old enough now and I want to know the truth.'

Brigitte looked at him. For a moment he thought she would change the subject as she had often done before, but then she seemed to make a decision. He watched with fascination as she seemed to grow younger as she spoke. She laughed as she told him how she had carried out a flirtation and then a more serious liaison with Siegfried under her mother's eyes, but without Danielle guessing what was going on.

'It was only when the Nazis left that she guessed I was pregnant,' she said, laughing. 'She didn't have them to worry about anymore, so she turned her eyes on me. And I was getting bigger all the time.'

The laughter died quickly, and Jacques saw that her memories weren't all good ones.

'Did you miss… Siegfried?' he asked, trying out the name and wanting to think good things of his father, however remote he was.

'Yes, because I loved him at first, but I didn't love what he did.'

'What do you mean?'

'When some hothead in the town killed a Nazi soldier, Siegfried fired the machine gun from my bedroom. That was part of the punishment. He said he was only following orders. It made people hate us, because the gun was at Castignac, even though the Nazis had fired it, not us.'

Jacques tried to imagine a machine gun in his mother's bedroom and found it difficult. White net curtains, a feathery *duvet* and colourful market rugs didn't sit easily in his imagination with a machine gun. Yet his mother's room, as she had often said, had the best view of the town and would have been the obvious place for a gun.

'Were people killed?'

'Yes, of course. Six people, including two children. Their names are on the war memorial. You can still see the marks of the bullets on some of the houses on the way into the town. I was so angry with Siegfried when I found out what he'd done that I shouted at him. Imagine that, shouting at a Nazi! He might have turned his gun on me. But he didn't. He was always gentle with me. Anyway, it was too late, because the harm had been done. Soon after that, they packed up and went, but they even fired the gun again as they left. Three more people were killed that time. Then they were gone and I never saw or heard anything from Siegfried again.'

Jacques had never heard that story before. People didn't usually talk about the war. Everyone knew about it and the boys at school mocked him for being a Nazi, but no-one said what had happened. Brigitte and Danielle, Hébrard and Nicolette usually only talked about what they were doing there and then.

Brigitte continued. 'He knew the address here well enough. He knew you were on the way. He could have written. Then you were born and shortly after that your grandfather committed suicide.'

She stopped suddenly, as if regretting her words, and Jacques asked the question that he had increasingly been thinking about.

'Did he kill himself because of me?'

'No, of course not, Jacques. He'd been feeling down for years, all through the Depression and the war. When the Nazis came in 1942, he couldn't bear Castignac being occupied. He was a proud man and his home had been taken over. He always liked to say it had been the family home for over four hundred years. Nothing like that had ever happened before. After Siegfried fired the gun and people hated us even more and would hardly speak to us or buy anything from our stall, he got worse.'

'But if the Nazis had left by the time he killed himself, it must have been because of me,' Jacques said.

'No, Jacques, not you. It was because of me. He was angry with me, his only child, for being pregnant when I wasn't married and because Siegfried was a Nazi. I suppose he just couldn't stand it anymore. He wanted to throw me out but my mother wouldn't let him. She said if I went, she would go too. I don't know for certain why he killed himself when he did, because he didn't say anything to anyone about it and he didn't leave a note. He just got on with the farm work; although he wasn't doing much of that by the end and it all fell on Hébrard after he came out of the prison camp.'

Jacques wasn't convinced. His mother was trying to protect him, but she might not have been right. After all, he was half-German, half of him was made up of the hated enemy and his grandfather had hanged himself in the year of Jacques's birth. No-one would ever be able to say for certain why his grandfather had hanged himself, especially if he hadn't said anything.

'Even if he killed himself because of me, I was only a baby then, so it wasn't because of anything I did,' he said slowly.

Brigitte nodded. 'It's such a shame because you're a good lad and he would have seen that,' she said. 'He could have taught you to take on the farm.'

'I will take on the farm. Hébrard is teaching me. You know I can drive the tractor now.'

Jacques asked questions of Hébrard. He learned more about the train journey in 1915 that had brought Hébrard and Eugène all the way from Orthez to St Martin des Remparts, about Hébrard's disappearance in order to avoid the Great War and how Jean-Louis, struggling to manage the farm with Danielle once his brothers had been conscripted, had taken him on.

Hébrard also told Jacques about his involvement in the resistance during the occupation and, in particular, about the explosion that had blown up the railway bridge. Jacques listened and in later years would ask him to repeat his stories. He liked to hear about the war, even though bad things had happened. If it hadn't been for the war, he wouldn't have existed, just as Renée wouldn't have existed if it hadn't been for the first war. His mother might have had a son called Jacques, but it wouldn't have been him.

With the help of Hébrard, Jacques became the farmer at Castignac. He ploughed the fields with their latest tractor, planting wheat, maize, lentils and vegetables. He cut the meadows in June, even though Renée didn't like seeing the meadow flowers cut down, stacked the hay, harvested the wheat fields and the maize, and dug up the vegetables. He threshed the wheat in the autumn and then he started the whole cycle over again. The farm was much more mechanised than it had been. Brigitte had bought a combine harvester and a machine for milking the cows.

But he wanted more than that from his life. He wanted to marry Renée. They would have several sons and the farm's future would be secure, but there was more to it than that. He loved her. He had always loved her. He wanted her and there was never anyone else.

Renée didn't leave school at sixteen like Jacques. He couldn't wait to leave because of the other boys, although they weren't so bad later on. They had become used to him and accepted him. It helped that Jacques was good at football and did well in the school team. The real reason for leaving school was that he was needed at Castignac. By the time Jacques was sixteen, Hébrard, by then in his late sixties, was ill with cancer and couldn't do much of the farm work anymore.

'I'm staying on at school. I want to go to college and be a teacher,' Renée said to Jacques one summer's day, when she had come to see her grandparents. Hébrard had been too tired to talk for long and Nicolette was busy, so she had been wandering disconsolately away from the cottage, when Jacques came up to her.

They went to the ruin. For want of something better to do in the afternoon heat, they collapsed onto the bench facing the mountains. Jacques had work to do, but Renée wanted to be in the shade and he joined her. That was when Jacques first kissed her and she not only let him, but seemed to like it. They didn't talk about Renée's plans then. They were too enthralled by what they had just done, but later Jacques watched Renée go off to college and wondered if he was losing her.

They were both eighteen by the time that she returned at Christmas after her first term. Hébrard was dying and Nicolette was sad. Christmas and New Year were quiet at Castignac, and Hébrard died just afterwards. A big family funeral took place, with all Nicolette's relatives, except for old Raymond, whom Jacques knew was an outcast. People talked about the war then and Jacques realised that Hébrard's death had touched them and that they were proud of him, even though he had begun as a deserter. His work for the resistance had been secret once, but it clearly wasn't a secret anymore.

Jacques wanted to tell Renée that he loved her, that he had always loved her, but that it was different now. It had become too big to keep to himself. Hébrard's last days and funeral weren't the right time to say anything, so he waited, cautious and patient.

'Will you and Renée marry one day?' Brigitte asked him one evening after Danielle had retired for the night.

'I haven't asked her yet, but I hope so,' Jacques said. 'What about you and Gilbert? You're seeing a lot of him these days, *Maman*.'

Brigitte had recently renewed what she had called an early friendship with a nephew of Nicolette's called Gilbert. He had turned up in the town after an absence of many years, something to do with the war and living elsewhere afterwards. Jacques was vague about the details but he did know that his mother had seemed happier since then. He measured her happiness by how much she nagged at him to do things. Perhaps because he was older, but perhaps because of Gilbert, she had lately been on at him much less.

'I'm never getting married,' Brigitte said. 'For one thing, I don't want to leave Castignac. Anyway, I'm too old now for such goings-on. Marriage is for young people, like you and Renée. You'll need me around when you have a houseful of children.'

Jacques was pleased to hear that.

When Renée came back from college the following Easter, Jacques was worried that she might have a boyfriend. She mentioned someone called Thierry several times and his heart sank to hear the name once, then twice and then more often.

Yet she was clear-eyed and pleased to see him. She came to Castignac to stay with Nicolette in the cottage and keep her grandmother company after the loss of Hébrard. She had two more years at college and then she wanted to teach at the primary school in St Martin des Remparts. Everything was planned, and Jacques wondered if there was room for him in her life.

He asked if she had made friends at college one afternoon, when they were in the ruin, sitting on the bench again. She had. But was there anyone special?

'Yes, there's Mathilde,' she said. 'She's my best friend at the college.'

'That's not quite what I meant,' Jacques said.

She looked at him and laughed. 'Oh, I know what you mean. A boyfriend. No, there isn't anyone like that at college.'

'Not Thierry?'

'Thierry? Oh, no. He's just a student in my group. We're doing an assignment together.' She laughed again.

Jacques looked at the mountains. They seemed to give him the courage to say what was on his mind and when he did, Renée looked surprised.

'You love me? Well, of course I love you, Jacques. Didn't you know?'

'Dearest Renée, no, I didn't.'

'We were always going to get married. Have you forgotten?'

Jacques couldn't remember that he had ever proposed to her before. It must have been some childish game that she had remembered and he had forgotten. Renée was always one step ahead of him.

He nodded. 'I must have done. Anyway, will you marry me?'

'Of course. We were always going to,' Renée said again. It was settled. He took her in his arms and kissed her.

Chapter Three

Jacques

Nicolette had stayed on in the cottage after Hébrard's death, but she only lasted another year. Renée came regularly to see her and continued to visit Castignac after Nicolette's death in order to see Jacques. With both Hébrard and Nicolette gone, he was too busy on the farm to come down to the town more often than necessary. He shared the work of harvesting with Michel, the neighbouring farmer, who was the grandson of his great-uncle Joseph.

The ruin had become the place where Jacques and Renée escaped to when they wanted to be private. They were less likely to be interrupted by Brigitte there, or old Danielle. They didn't want either of them to know how far things had gone between them. They made love on the haystacks in the ruin, with no need to worry, because Jacques had obtained a supply of condoms from the pharmacy in the town. Renée had insisted on that. No-one ever disturbed them. The chicken feed wasn't kept in the ruin anymore.

'When shall we get married?' Jacques asked her one August afternoon. Renée had left college by then and secured a job in the local primary school. She was going to start in September. Farm work was done for the day and they had retreated to the ruin for some shade, as well as to be alone.

'In the spring next year, so we can have lots of flowers for the wedding,' Renée said.

She loved wildflowers still, and she wanted blue gentians and white stitchwort and red poppies from the fields at her wedding. It was fanciful, Jacques told her, because wildflowers didn't much like being picked. They would droop. Renée didn't listen. She wouldn't settle for the garden flowers that the market could supply. She wanted great bowls of wildflowers at her wedding. If picked ones would droop, then she would dig up the flowers with their roots and pot them.

'My mother will teach you to run the dairy and make cheese and help with the market stall,' Jacques said. He was looking forward to being married and to Renée coming to live at Castignac.

Renée twisted a curl around her fingers and looked directly at him. 'No she won't.'

'What do you mean?'

'Jacques, I'm marrying you because I love you, but not because I want to be a farmer's wife. That's a job in itself, but I'm a teacher.'

'You're not giving up your job, then, when we get married? I thought you would. We can afford it,' he said. The farm was doing well and Brigitte's weekly market stall, which was popular, brought in a regular sum.

'No. I mean, I might stop working when we have a baby, but not when we get married.'

Renée wasn't going to follow in Brigitte's footsteps. She wasn't going to become a farmer's wife like her grandmother Nicolette or like Brigitte or Danielle. She wasn't even going to give up her job on marriage, as her mother, Marie, had done. She wasn't interested in the dairy or the market stall.

Jacques was taken aback but accepted that Renée wanted to follow her heart and be a teacher. He couldn't rely on the old ways and her salary would help in any lean times. Brigitte would carry on with all her work for the farm.

Renée and Jacques were married in the church at St Martin des Remparts in the following spring, during the school Easter holidays. Everyone in the Lordat family was there as well as nearly everyone in Renée's family and neighbouring Michel and his family. It was a warm enough day for tables to be laid in the garden at Castignac after the ceremony in the church. The *monastère*, brought out for the occasion, was piled with food and pots of wildflowers decorated the event. The wisteria on the terrace was flowering and its early leaves provided welcome shade. There was music and dancing until long after dark.

Brigitte took pictures of the wedding. She had bought a box camera to record his childhood when Jacques was little. She was sparing with film because it was expensive, but she took pictures of special occasions. She gave the young couple good quality cotton sheets embroidered with their initials as a wedding present. They sank into them that night and made love with all the joy of the secret times in the ruin.

'Don't you want to know your real father?' Renée said one day, after their wedding.

They were looking at the wedding photographs together. There were pictures of the Lordats and the Montvals and many of Nicolette's relatives, including her remaining brothers. Renée had hardly known her uncle Raymond, who had died the previous year.

'No, I don't think so. I know his name and roughly where he came from and what sort of age he would be now, but I don't want to meet him.'

Siegfried, if he had survived, would be about fifty. He had come from a village near Munich and Jacques knew his army rank. It might have been possible to find him, but he knew he would never try. His childhood fantasies about his father were long-forgotten and these days he only thought that they were worlds apart.

'I was thinking we could have a holiday in Germany, if you wanted to look for him.'

Jacques considered it, but his answer was definite. 'I don't want to. Hébrard was your grandfather, but he was my father in lots of ways. He taught me how to run the farm. I don't think I want to go chasing round another country, which was an enemy country, for the man who fathered me, when I don't even know him.'

Renée accepted that, but she was more restless than Jacques.

'Do you realise we've been married for a whole year and we haven't had a holiday together?' she said one day.

Farm work certainly consumed Jacques's time and Renée had her teaching, so they were both busy.

'Yes, we have. We had a honeymoon,' Jacques said.

They had spent their honeymoon, in the spring, at Collioure on the coast, where Renée had exclaimed over the many different wildflowers she had found there.

'Well, yes, but let's go to Spain later this year, when the harvest is in. Brigitte says she can manage, if you get someone in to help her.'

They didn't ski to the top of the Pyrenees and down the slopes on the other side as they had said that they would as children. They travelled by train from Pamiers to Barcelona and Gerona for a week's holiday, staying in a *pension*. Renée thoroughly enjoyed the holiday, although Jacques found the cities crowded and was relieved to come home. Brigitte and Danielle had managed well in his absence, but he didn't like to be away from the farm.

Brigitte continued to do the dairy work and the cooking for the market stall that she had gradually taken over from Danielle. Renée helped out with the farm work during the school holidays and at weekends, when she had time.

Danielle grew quieter in her corner of the kitchen. Brigitte, knocking at her bedroom door one morning, with a bowl of milky coffee, went in to find that her mother had died in her sleep. She was buried in the church cemetery, according to her wishes. She had not wanted to be buried at Castignac next to Jean-Louis, but to claim her rightful place in the cemetery, alongside her parents and Jacquot and in the arms of the church.

The farm depended on sufficient rainfall at the right time, and one spring the rain failed and the ditches were dry when they should have been full of water and laced with copious frog spawn. For weeks, the crops struggled, and Jacques feared he would lose his produce, but fortunately it rained just in time and the crops began to grow.

Jacques added a new crop to those grown at Castignac. It was Renée's idea. She had noticed the bright yellow of sunflowers on neighbouring farms and, flower lover as she was, encouraged Jacques to grow them. He looked into the question of sunflowers as a crop and agreed it was a good idea. The following year, he turned two of the nine fields over to sunflowers and thereafter grew them every year. Renée loved to watch the flowers coming out in the early summer and enjoyed the blaze of colour they created, with all the heads standing tall and facing the same way. When the flowers faded, the plants, awaiting their fate, seemed to hang their heads. Jacques was pleased with the crop of seeds and Brigitte sold some of them from her market stall. The rest went to a factory which made cooking oil.

He also grew a new potato crop. They were *charlotte* potatoes, small and waxy. He obtained a good price for them and Brigitte took some to sell on her market stall. They were popular and became a regular part of the produce of Castignac.

Jacques employed labourers when he needed help on the farm and Renée's brother Georges, a builder, helped with any work needed on the house. People might not like Castignac, but they didn't refuse to work there, despite what had happened in the war, because they needed jobs. In time, fewer of them had been through the war and the younger people didn't observe or even know about the old hatred in quite the same way.

Jacques and Renée wanted children. Jacques in particular was thinking of sons to carry on the farm, but also of a daughter, a miniature Renée. They were joyous when Renée became pregnant and later when a baby boy was born. They named him Hébrard after the man who had been a father to Jacques. Another boy, Jules, followed him and then a girl they called Marie, after Renée's mother.

Renée gave up teaching when young Hébrard was born. They struggled financially, missing her salary, especially after the other two children arrived. Then Jacques came into the kitchen one day to find Renée stirring the contents of a large pot.

'What's this?' he said.

Renée lifted the spoon and let a dark red liquid drip back into the pot.

'Plum jam. It needs a bit longer.'

The harvest was in and plums in the orchard had been particularly good that year.

'That's a change. I love plum jam, but you've never wanted to do anything like that before.'

'I'm thinking of ways to boost our income. The children don't take up all my time and you don't need my help with the harvest now you've got all that machinery.'

Jacques had recently invested in the latest in combine harvesters, which made light work of cutting the hay and wheat. That first batch of plum jam was runny, but Renée persisted and later batches were properly set. As well as jam, she learned to make all the farm food, the butter, cheese, ham and bottled fruit and vegetables that Brigitte provided for the family and the market. She even made soap from goat's milk like Brigitte and sold it on the Castignac market stall. Mistakes occurred, but Brigitte was a patient teacher, pleased at Renée's change of heart. With the addition of help from Renée, the profits from the market stall grew.

Brigitte died some ten years after Danielle, leaving Jacques and Renée and the children alone at Castignac for the first time. The years slipped by, with the children growing up and Jacques working on the farm, with help from the children as they grew old enough, or from other relatives. Renée's stall became a well-known feature of the weekly market. Her former pupils helped, unwittingly, with sales, because even years after she had left the school, they liked to visit her stall to say hello and so their parents bought her produce. She also worked on Brigitte's garden at Castignac, which flourished under her care.

The years of having a wife and young family were the happiest of Jacques's life. The problems of his own childhood had long faded. The children flourished and the farm supported them well enough, with the addition of the market stall. Jacques was where he wanted to be and with a family of his own.

Renée took up drawing wildflowers when the children were older. Encouraged by how much people admired her intricate, colourful drawings, she began to sell postcards of them in the shops in St Martin des Remparts. They were popular with local people and with tourists and led to a commission from a publisher to illustrate a book about the flowers of south-west France. Renée set to work hunting for the flowers and within a year had found and drawn enough to illustrate the book, which sold widely in the region.

Jacques brought his boys up to help around the farm, leaving young Marie more to Renée. All the family helped out at harvest time. Young Hébrard liked science at school and Jacques thought of sending him to the nearby agricultural college to study modern farming methods. Although he could be scathing about college courses, he was aware of a much more scientific approach to modern farming. He wanted his son to be well equipped to be the farmer at Castignac, and Jules might want to do the same. His dream of the future saw his sons running the farm together and their sons after them. Even young Marie might want to take up farming, at least until she married. His children would be part of the family tradition of which his mother Brigitte had been so proud.

Life on the farm, especially with a young family, was so busy that Jacques didn't have time to think much about the future. One day, when the children were older and the family were sitting in the kitchen over their light evening meal, young Hébrard announced that he wanted to go to Toulouse University to study engineering. At seventeen, he would soon be in his last year at school and he was thinking ahead.

'But I thought you were going to take on the farm,' Jacques said. He couldn't dictate to this young man who had lately become taller than he was, and his tone was no more than questioning.

Hébrard, a younger version of Jacques in appearance, looked at his father almost pityingly. 'Dad, you know it's not what I want to do. I'm heading for the aerospace industry.'

Jacques scratched his head and looked around the table. 'Jules?' he said.

His younger son was of a smaller and lighter build than Jacques, with more of Renée's features.

Jules loved the countryside and the outdoors, but he, too, had no thought of farming. He had loved trees since childhood.

'I'm heading for the mountains, to be a forester, Dad,' he said, adding quietly, 'you know that.'

Jacques did know that when he thought about it. Jules, now fifteen, had always been drawn to the mountains on the horizon. The previous winter, he had started going skiing there with friends. With the help of school trips, he spent as much time in the mountains as possible in the other seasons.

Jacques turned towards Marie, who at fourteen, bore a strong resemblance to Renée, in her cloud of curly hair and cheerful demeanour. He was hoping that she at least was a version of her grandmother Brigitte in the making. He knew from experience the value of a woman on a farm.

'I don't know,' she said, before he even asked.

'Marie might want to go to an art college. You know it's her best subject at school,' Renée said quickly.

Jacques, disappointed, turned back to his meal. He tried to be pleased that his children had ambitions and made no attempt to stand in their way. They had more opportunities than had come his way as a boy and he had never tried to dominate them. Yet he was aware of a great disappointment. He knew from Brigitte, who knew from Jean-Louis, who knew from… ancestors whose names he didn't know, that there had been a farm at Castignac for hundreds of years. He had made the farm his life, but now he was faced with acknowledging what he had known in his heart of hearts, that he would probably be the last Lordat to farm there.

Renée had never been a slim woman and she had begun to put on weight when she started food production at Castignac. She always said she enjoyed food and wine far too much to cut down. At the age of sixty, in the early years of the new century, she woke up in terrible pain on a cold winter's night. Jacques telephoned for an ambulance, which came quickly, and Renée was taken to the hospital in Foix. Jacques followed in his truck.

It was a moderate heart attack. Renée seemed to recover and there was talk of coming home in a few days, of going on a diet and taking medication. Jacques carried on with the farm, making sure to see Renée every day. All the children had left home by then, but they all came to see their mother in hospital.

'Don't come tomorrow,' Renée said to Jacques one afternoon. 'I'm much better now and it's a long drive for you after a day's work.'

'Are you sure?' he said, giving her hand a squeeze as it lay on the bed. 'It's no trouble.'

'Yes, quite sure. Come the day after.'

He took it as a sign that she was feeling better and promised to visit her in two days' time.

He spent the next day at Castignac, milking the cows and making sure all the animals were fed as usual. The phone rang in the evening as he was making himself a scratch meal.

'M. Lordat? Please come to the hospital. Your wife has had another heart attack,' a nurse said.

A cold hand seemed to grip Jacques's own heart. 'Another one? Is she all right?'

'Please come as soon as you can,' the nurse said.

Jacques was aware she hadn't answered his question, but it was clear what he must do. He abandoned his meal and drove straight to the hospital, where he found to his shock that Renée had died that afternoon. The nurse hadn't wanted to tell him over the phone.

He sank onto a chair and buried his face in his hands and then stood up, asking to see Renée. He was taken to a side room, where she lay in bed, but he didn't stay long. It seemed to him that she wasn't there, and he wanted to remember her as she was when alive.

Jacques was numb with shock at first and then desolate. His childhood playmate, his wife, the best and almost the only friend of his life had gone. After the funeral, he lived alone for several years, visited regularly by his children and calling on seasonal help for the farm as he needed it. His most regular help was a man called Bertrand Pastoreau who also tended the garden that Brigitte had created.

Chapter Four

Jacques

B Y THE AGE OF seventy, Jacques could hardly get out of bed some mornings because his right hip hurt so much. He no longer walked the kilometre or so into St Martin des Remparts from Castignac the way that he had often done as a young man. Instead he drove the old truck he had used around the town for years.

He rattled down to the doctor's surgery one morning, having made an appointment, something he couldn't ever remember doing for himself before. He had been forced into it, because the pain was getting him down. The doctor was new. The receptionist had told him when he rang to make the appointment that his old doctor, who had looked after Renée, had retired.

Entering the surgery when he was called, Jacques was taken aback to find that the new doctor was a woman. Not only that, but she was a slip of a girl hardly older than his daughter, Marie. Dark hair fell to her shoulders and smooth hands were folded on her desk as she invited him to explain what was wrong. She listened to what he said about the pain in his hip and examined him on a couch.

'You need some tests, but it's probably arthritis,' she said as she finished the examination. 'Are you retired?'

'No, I've got the farm at Castignac.'

'Surely not on your own?'

'Yes, since my wife died. My children are all busy with their own lives and none of them wants to carry on with the farm. Of course, I take on help at busy times of year.'

She pursed her lips at the answer and busied herself with ordering the tests. Jacques could see that, in her eyes, he was an old man and that managing a farm alone was too much for him. She didn't go so far as to advise him to sell it, but that was what it would amount to sooner or later.

On his way home, resentment crept in. The doctor hadn't given him anything to relieve the pain, telling him to go to the pharmacy for painkillers while he waited for the tests. She hadn't told him to sell the farm, but he felt as if she had. What was a young girl doing, telling him what to do? Yet he couldn't help admitting she might be right. It was a small farm, but it was becoming too much for him. He could barely see to the milking of the cows these days, even though he had a lot more machinery now than the farm had owned when he was a boy.

It was spring and the crops were growing, but once the harvest was in, Jacques knew that he would have to leave Castignac. Ever since Renée's death some five years previously, he had known that it would happen one day, as none of his children had become a farmer. It was becoming increasingly hard to manage on his own. Even with Bertrand and the extra help that he hired for planting and harvesting, there was too much to do now, with the animals as well.

He would have to sell and it was obvious what to do. He would leave Castignac and live in St Martin des Remparts. Most people now didn't know his history and those who did were more inclined to talk to him than when he was a boy. It wasn't what he wanted. He would have liked to see out his days on the farm, rather than live in one of those small boxes that people were pleased to call a house, or worse, in a cramped, modern flat, but there wasn't much choice.

What on earth would he do all day? Play *boules* with other old men or sit in a café nursing a drink, reminiscing and denouncing the speed and wickedness of the modern world? He wouldn't want to talk about Renée, and who would want to listen to him rabbiting on? He wouldn't just want to sit and wait for his children to come and see him when they were busy with their own lives. Hébrard was married now and Jules had a girlfriend. Only Marie was unattached, and she was busy with the teaching that she had chosen to go into on leaving school. Being retired wouldn't be enough of a life. He would have to think of something else to do, if his hip would let him.

It would be a wrench to leave Castignac. He had given his life to it and never lived anywhere else. He loved the farm and it contained nearly all his memories of Renée. Wherever he was in the house and even around the farm, he could see and hear her. Even five years after her death, he found himself talking to her, asking a question or making some remark. He was on his own most of the time and he talked to Renée just as he had when she was alive.

He took his time making the decision. On bad mornings he forced himself out of bed. The right hip was the worst problem, but some days were better than others. The tests confirmed that he had arthritis and the doctor, when he saw her again, even talked about a hip replacement. He didn't like the sound of that and was determined to avoid an operation for as long as possible. On better days, he dismissed the doctor's judgement, but on bad days he couldn't do that. At least she had now given him some tablets to take for the pain as well as exercises to do. He just had to hope they would do some good.

Sitting alone over his meal in the kitchen one evening, Jacques decided to act. It was a good time, because the harvest was in by then and he could afford to think ahead rather than live from day to day. His children might not want the farm, but Renée's family was spread all over St Martin des Remparts and one of them might be interested. Selling Castignac to one of them would break the link with his family that it had held for longer than he knew, but it would keep the connection with Renée's grandfather, Hébrard, who had farmed at Castignac for years and been a father to him. His own life, lived in peacetime, had been uneventful compared with that of Hébrard or even Jean-Louis, but he had done his best by Castignac and he wanted to see it carry on.

He felt better then and went to bed with some sense of relief. Yet danger was hiding in sleep. That night he had a nightmare. His grandfather, old Jean-Louis, who had died just after he was born, had cast a shadow over his life and in the nightmare, he was raging about Jacques betraying the family, the dynasty, even. Five hundred years of farming betrayed by the sale of Castignac. Jacques woke up in a sweat, feeling a terrible guilt, even though he had never felt the weight of all those years before. He hadn't bothered about generations of people he had never met. The people he had known were the ones who mattered to him. The exception was that grandfather, who had been a presence in his life despite dying when Jacques was a baby. The nightmare seemed to pursue him through the next day and he put off his decision until he felt better able to answer Jean-Louis back.

Marie lived in St Martin des Remparts, where she shared a flat with another teacher. He told her about the nightmare. She made light of it and a week or so later, with the hip nagging, he began to think about the decision again. He would sell the farm and he argued with the ghost of his grandfather until he felt ready to act.

Renée's younger brother, Georges, the builder, was now well into his sixties. He was the head of a local building firm and knew everyone who mattered in the town. He and his wife had three sons, all of whom worked for the family firm. Jacques rang him up and asked to come and see him. They were on friendly terms, and Georges invited Jacques and Marie to lunch the following weekend.

It was an excellent lunch. Georges's wife, Jacqueline, who ran a restaurant in the town, was well known to be a good cook. Several different courses, succeeding each other slowly, allowed for catching up on news, especially as it was some time since they had met. Georges did most of the talking at first, as Jacques was less accustomed to conversation these days. As the meal came to an end and Jacqueline served coffee, Jacques explained that he had decided to sell Castignac because none of his children wanted to take it on and his arthritis was getting worse.

'Before it goes on the market, I thought I'd ask around the family, to see if anyone wants to buy it.'

'Not me, Jacques. I'm a builder, as you know, and a busy one. I don't know anything about farming. Besides, I'm almost as old as you are. Much too old to try anything new!'

'What about your boys?'

'Well, they all work for me and there's plenty of work these days, what with all the foreigners buying up property and wanting to convert it. Some of the foreigners have bought country houses as holiday homes, but I don't know anyone who wants a farm as such.'

Georges was expansive and willing to discuss Jacques's plans in detail. They spent some time listing people who might buy Castignac, but there appeared to be no-one worth approaching. The trouble was that Renée's family, although numerous, were all in the building trade or running cafés and restaurants in support of burgeoning tourism. St Martin des Remparts, always a thriving market town in the area, was becoming a centre for foreign tourists and exiles from the nightmare of city life.

As for the young people, many, like Jacques's children, were leaving the villages and even small towns to go and work in the cities. Several people in Renée's family, it seemed, had gone to Toulouse or Montpellier for work, just as young Hébrard had done.

'Young people, and it needs to be someone young, with boundless energy, aren't interested in the land anymore,' Georges said.

Jacqueline agreed with him. 'All the young people I know are going into the tourist trade in one form or another, or teaching, like Marie, if they're staying here at all,' she said.

'Well, thanks for listening to me and for a splendid meal,' Jacques said. 'I'm not surprised at what you say, but it was worth a try.'

Jacques had already planned his next move. He went to see Gilles, an estate agent he knew slightly and whose company had a window on the central square of the town. He explained that he wanted to put his family farm on the market, so that he could buy a small property in the town for his retirement.

Gilles was a middle-aged man who smoked a pipe. Until recently, he had smoked in the office, but a new rule meant that smoking was banished to the outside. It was fortunate that his job involved being out of the office much of the time, but the new rule had made him grumpy sometimes and his questions to Jacques were sharp. He wanted to know what exactly Jacques was selling.

'Well, the house, of course, and the outbuildings and barn. Eight fields for wheat and hay and vegetables and one for the dairy cows. One hundred and fifty hectares in all. Twenty cows, some pigs, a few goats and chickens.'

'All right, I'll come up and value it for you. Farms take a while to sell these days.'

'I'm not in a rush.'

When Gilles came to Castignac to measure up and take photos, Jacques was waiting for him.

'Don't mention the ruin in the brochure,' he said, after they had toured the house and started on the outbuildings, walking under the arch into the courtyard of the ruined farmhouse.

'Oh, why not? It might be a selling point, with the pigeon loft, although it's a bit ramshackle in places.'

'No! If you mention it, I'll take my business elsewhere,' Jacques said.

Gilles nodded. The ruin was of no value. 'Not picturesque enough?' he said, losing interest.

A week later, Castignac was featured in the estate agent's window, with a photo of the house. The roof was a warm orange in August sunlight, bright red geraniums flowered at the windows and the two date palms flanked the front door. Jacques had put in the geraniums especially for the photo, on Gilles's advice. Marie had bought them for him cheaply in the market. Gilles explained that Castignac was also listed online. Jacques didn't have a computer, but he understood that being listed online meant better prospects for a sale. Nothing was said about the ruin in the brochure that Gilles prepared for the house.

Jacques felt odd when he saw his farm in the window of the estate agent's office one morning. He told himself to shape up. Until now, the sale hadn't seemed real, but the photo in the window left no room for doubt. After he had done his shopping, he drove home, wondering if he had made the right decision.

He treated Castignac differently after that, taking it less for granted, as if he were saying a slow goodbye to a valued friend he might never see again. He wasn't looking forward to uprooting himself. Would he be able to get used to being somewhere else? He belonged at Castignac, just like the animals and birds, the trees around the ruin and the crops in the fields. St Martin des Remparts wasn't far away and he had spent his life looking down on it from Castignac and making regular visits to the shops and market, but he was a farmer, tied to the earth and the seasons of the year.

Moments came when he thought of taking the property off the market, but the alternative, to stay there and bring in a farm manager, didn't appeal. He didn't want to have to watch a stranger on his farm, even if he could find anyone suitable. He dropped the idea completely when he did the sums and saw he couldn't afford it.

Weeks and then months passed, but there was little interest and Castignac didn't sell. At first, Jacques didn't mind that. Gilles had warned him that it would be slow. Farms were hard to sell anyway, so he expected it to take a while. But, as the autumn moved on and winter approached, he began to wonder about the hatred he had experienced as a child and sometimes as a young man. He hadn't seen it lately, but he imagined it still to be lying in wait. It could easily prevent anyone local from buying Castignac. Marie, when he talked to her, dismissed his fears. She had never heard anyone say anything about her father being the son of a Nazi. She was the granddaughter of a Nazi, but she never thought much about it.

Jacques knew he couldn't stay at Castignac. Already the farm was beginning to look neglected. Fences were leaning, machinery needed servicing and the pig sties were in bad shape. Jobs that he used to undertake unquestioningly now seemed more difficult and rising at dawn as he had always done was harder these days. The sale would happen in time. Gilles had assured him that plenty of foreigners were looking for property, although he was less certain that any of them were looking for a farm. The good thing about foreigners was that they wouldn't know about the hatred.

Early one January evening, Jacques received a visit from the neighbouring farmer, Michel. As the grandson of Danielle's elder brother Joseph, Michel was a cousin, of exactly what sort Jacques didn't know and didn't care. He didn't much like Michel, who was cunning and always on the make, but they relied on each other at harvest time and he invited him in.

Michel, a small thin man with restless eyes, knew that Castignac was for sale and asked who had shown an interest. Jacques had to admit that nothing was happening.

'You'll never sell. No-one wants to buy a farm these days,' Michel said, when they had exchanged greetings and they were sitting in the kitchen over a glass of *hypocras*.

Jacques knew exactly why Michel had come. He had been waiting for this because Michel had always had an eye on his land. He had made attempts in the past to buy neighbouring fields, which Jacques had always resisted because the farm was his livelihood. Castignac had been on the market for some months now and Michel obviously thought that Jacques would be more receptive to an offer than at the beginning.

'I can't buy your whole farm,' Michel said, 'but I'll take your nine fields and your animals and the cottage. That'll leave you the other buildings and a sizeable patch for grounds.

You'll sell more easily that way and I'll be all right for storage because I'm building a new barn.'

'It's not what I want. Castignac's been in my family for five hundred years and I'd like to see it continue as a farm.' Jacques spoke with pride and felt some superiority. Michel's family had only been farming in the area for three or four generations.

He had no idea exactly how long Castignac had been in the family, but the farmhouse carried the date of 1860 and he knew the ruin was much older than that. He had some old deeds that went back to the eighteenth century, but his mother had always said, when he was a boy, that Castignac was over four hundred years old. That was a lifetime ago, so it probably was five hundred years by now.

Yet the wretched Michel could have been right. They began to talk money. Michel had a sum in mind. It was much too low, but Jacques said he would think about it. He wasn't going to give in easily, so he put Michel's offer to the back of his mind for a while.

Six weeks later, in early March, when there was still no sign of an offer on Castignac and his hip was definitely worse, Jacques chose a good day and drove over to Michel's farm. They wrangled over the price, but in the end agreed. The sale was finalised by the notary in his office a month later, with a glass of cognac all round.

Jacques hadn't done any winter or spring planting that year. The nine fields of Castignac were all ploughed, by Jacques and Bertrand Pastoreau. They were lying fallow and their future was Michel's problem now. The fields all had names, but Michel might change that. Jacques watched his herd of cows being taken over to Michel's new barn for milking and saw his pigs, goats and chickens move to new homes. He turned away. He would concentrate on what he had to do next.

Chapter Five

Jacques

To the annoyance of Gilles, who had earned nothing from this private sale, Jacques took the farm off the market and spent a few weeks thinking he might stay at what remained of Castignac. He used some of the money from the sale to employ Bertrand to put a fence around his smaller property. The new idea was no good. Using painkillers, he had successfully avoided an operation, but his hip reminded him that even a house and garden were becoming too much. He didn't want to neglect the place. Besides, he could see Michel and his brawny sons working on the fields that were once part of Castignac and he didn't like the sight. It seemed wrong that they could be so close to him.

One June morning saw him arrive at Gilles's office. He explained that he wanted to put the shrunken Castignac back on the market.

'Remember, no mention of the ruin,' Jacques said, and Gilles agreed.

Castignac went on the market again and Gilles brought people to see it, but there were no offers. Jacques was disappointed afresh, but when he saw for himself that foreigners were streaming to St Martin des Remparts and buying property there, he decided that he had the answer. He knew from newspapers and television that foreigners liked a pool. It would put Castignac ahead of other places on the market.

He told Gilles to take Castignac off the market again and he went to see Georges. He used the rest of the money from selling off his land to pay Georges and his men to install the pool that he saw as his ticket to a sale.

After the pool was finished, Castignac went back on the market for the third time. It was August by now. Jacques waited, wondering, in the silence that followed, if he had made a mistake. Gilles brought people to visit, but they never showed more than a polite interest. Castignac remained on the market for a further year.

'Any news?' Jacques said late one summer afternoon, popping his head into Gilles's office, as he often did on his visits to the town.

'I have some promising clients. They're British holiday people and they're in a hurry to buy somewhere. You know the British are invading us these days, don't you? I've shown them several properties, but they haven't liked anything yet. Castignac is more than their budget, but I'll show them your brochure.'

'Well, I might be open to an offer, if they're not trying to swindle me,' Jacques said.

He hadn't wanted to consider offers, but the attempt to sell had been going on for two years now. His hip wasn't getting any better and he wanted the sale to be over. With Marie's help, he had started to look at places in the town and seen one or two that would do, but he couldn't go any further without a buyer for Castignac. He hadn't particularly wanted to sell to foreigners or to see his beloved farmhouse as a holiday home and probably empty most of the year, but he didn't have any choice. He might as well make use of what Gilles liked to call the British invasion.

When the British had come to see Castignac, Jacques had been there. He had not gone round with them, leaving that to Gilles, but he had watched them carefully, seen their interest and heard their excited voices, and dared to hope for a sale this time. He spared a thought for his farmhouse going down in the world by becoming a holiday home, when it had been linked for so long to the vital task of growing food, but he had no choice. It was a strange idea, for a group of friends to get together to buy a house, especially as a holiday home, but there was no accounting for foreigners. As far as he knew, they weren't related to each other. Didn't they have families? He didn't know.

None of that mattered when the offer to buy Castignac came through. Jacques was pleased. It wasn't quite the asking price, but it was a serious offer and, on Gilles's advice, he accepted it. Gilles and the notary handled the sale. Jacques didn't meet the British again until the final exchange of contracts and then it had only been Angela, to his relief. One person was quite enough.

When the time came, Jacques packed his clothes and personal possessions. His two sons, Hébrard and Jules, hired a van to take the furniture he wanted to keep and helped him to move. He left the British the *monastère*, as well as the old kitchen dresser and a wardrobe, which were all too big for his new home in the town. He found it hard to leave the house when the moment came, knowing that it was for the last time and that nearly all of his memories of Renée involved Castignac, but he did not linger. His sons were in the van waiting to go and he concentrated on the business of moving.

With the help of Gilles, he had bought a small house, with barely any garden, on a side street near the market square. It was only a few minutes' walk from where Marie lived and she was able to see him more easily now that he was nearer.

He was accepted amongst most of the old men who spent their days in the square and cafés of the town. He had been to school with some of them and they all knew who he was. The best of them would have a drink or play *boules* with him and he didn't bother with the others. It wasn't a bad life, although the days could be long and he missed being active. St Martin des Remparts was his home now. If anyone ever referred to his German side, he brought them up short by saying that he might be half-German by blood, but he was all French at heart. No-one called him a Nazi anymore.

Living on a street was so different. He met a neighbour, a woman of about his age, who lived next door. It felt strange for someone he didn't know to be so physically close to him. After the first, brief conversation he had retreated into his house and firmly shut the door. She had spoken to him again, though, the next time she saw him and he hoped she wasn't going to be there every time he opened his front door.

Having neighbours quite so close caused him to feel cramped on the street and he missed Castignac – the roomy old house that had been his home of a lifetime, the space of the farm, the animals, even the old ruin. It was the place of almost all his memories. He could still see it from the square. He looked up at it sometimes, from his favourite bench which allowed a good view of it. It was strange that other people could tread where he and all his ancestors had trodden and yet never know who had been there.

The British had a party, about a year after they moved in. Angela saw him on his favourite bench one day and handed him a card. At first, he didn't want to go. He didn't want to see what they had done to his farmhouse and garden. He almost didn't go, but as the day and then the time of the party approached, he had found himself wanting to see the old place again. His present small house could never mean that much to him, so he had driven the short distance up the hill and joined the party.

He knew all the local guests and he had met the other British people, apart from Angela. Her husband Stephen was a British politician. Jacques hoped he wasn't going to poke his nose into French politics, which were bad enough already. Ian was something to do with plants and Renée would have enjoyed talking to him about wildflowers. His wife Jenny was a businesswoman who had a clothes shop in England. Graham appeared to want to do a lot of work on the house. Graham's wife Lily was an attractive-looking woman and the last person was Tessa, who had been interested in the history of Castignac. Tessa's young man wasn't part of the group.

Jacques wasn't interested in seeing what the British had done to his home. He didn't join one of the tours of the house, saying he knew it well already. He wanted to remember the house as it had been in his time and he avoided going indoors, staying on the terrace the whole time, glad to see that they had kept the wisteria and the date palms which his mother had planted.

Only Angela and Ian spoke any French, so he couldn't talk directly to the others. He had never needed to learn any English. He had once wanted to study German at school, but they had only offered Spanish and English as foreign languages and he hadn't been interested.

Tessa had handed him the old photo album that he hadn't realised he had left behind. He had left it in the wardrobe that he had given to them. He had been surprised that Tessa was interested in the old ruin. What about the new farmhouse, which his grandfather's grandfather had built in 1860 and which the British had bought? That was the pride of the family.

He had told her and Angela that the ruin was about five hundred years old and had been abandoned when the family was doing well and could afford to build a new house, using some of the old stone. From then on, the ruin had been used only for animals or storage. It was worthless and would gradually fall down and disappear.

Tessa had wanted to know if the staircase to the pigeon loft was safe and to see the view from up there. He had told her that it was safe, as far as he knew, but it was some years since he had been up there.

Angela had asked him if someone had committed suicide in the ruin. Apparently Marianne, who used to work for him and had carried on when the British came, had told them about that. He had not replied at first, not being used to talking about his family, but then he had said that they would have to visit the capital of the Ariège in Foix to look at birth, death and marriage certificates, to find out more about his forebears.

They had looked disappointed and he felt he had been too curt with them, so he had said he was pleased to have come back to Castignac and thanked them for inviting him.

He had talked to Ian later. Something about the Englishman, not just his ability with French, had made him easy to talk to, and Jacques had found himself telling him about his family in some detail. Ian had also been interested in the ruin and the pigeon loft, and Jacques had told him about the graffiti.

By then it didn't matter what the English thought, because they had already bought Castignac. They might not have bought it if they had known the history. They could have found it out if they had talked to people in the town before buying the house, but they hadn't bothered. He was fortunate in that respect.

Jacques was sitting on a bench in the central square of the town of St Martin des Remparts, a week after the party at Castignac, when he heard the news of the death of one of the British people there. It was Ian, the one he had talked to the most at the party. It wasn't an expected death, from an illness or even old age, but a terrible accident in the ruin. He had fallen from the top of the staircase to the pigeon loft because the railing up there had given way.

Marianne had spotted Jacques on the bench and come over to talk to him. She had been one of the first people to hear the news.

'I'm sorry to hear that,' Jacques said.

'Everyone had told him not to climb that staircase as it might not be safe, but he ignored them,' Marianne said.

Jacques had not told Ian that the staircase might be dangerous, because he had not thought to do so. He had climbed up many times during the course of his life, although not recently. The family had always scraped up the pigeon manure to use as fertiliser. It was the only reason they had ever gone up there.

'There's going to be an inquest,' Marianne said. 'The doctor thinks it might be suicide.'

'No, it wasn't,' Jacques said. 'He was interested in the graffiti there, because of the centenary of the First World War.'

Marianne had heard of the graffiti but never seen them and wasn't particularly interested. She went on to do her shopping, leaving Jacques plunged into thought. Had Ian died because he, Jacques, hadn't warned him of danger? Would people blame him for Ian's death? His mind shot straight back to his boyhood, when he had been ostracised for something else that wasn't his fault. No, he mustn't think about that anymore.

Marianne had said that others had warned Ian. He had been foolhardy and impatient. It didn't make sense. Why be impatient to see something that had been there for a hundred years and wasn't going anywhere? No French farmer would have gone blundering in like that, but there was no accounting for the British.

When the police visited Jacques at home the day after he had spoken to Marianne, he was glad that she had told him about the accident. Knowing about it had prepared him for their visit. The police said that, as the recent owner of Castignac, he might be able to throw light on what had happened. The railing at the top of the wooden staircase had been eaten by termites. It looked as if Ian had leaned on it, not knowing that, and had fallen to his death. Did Jacques know about the termites?

'No, I didn't know anything about termites,' Jacques said. 'I used to climb up every year or so, for the pigeon manure, that was all, but that was years ago. It was always perfectly safe. When fertiliser became easily available, I used to buy it and I stopped going up to the pigeon loft.'

The police had one of the sales brochures and must have been to see Gilles. They knew that the ruin had not been mentioned in the brochure yet had been on the property. Why wasn't it mentioned?

'Because it was of no value,' Jacques said. 'I was selling my house, not the ruin.'

The police didn't ask Jacques why he thought Ian was exploring the pigeon loft, so he didn't need to lie and say he didn't know or admit that he did know and risk being blamed for the accident. There was a kind of unspoken understanding between Jacques and the police that a foreigner might do anything stupid.

Later that day, Jacques returned to his bench in the square. He thought of it as his bench, although other people sat there sometimes. It irritated him when they did, but he couldn't say anything because the *mairie* had put the benches there for everyone.

He saw Tessa approaching him with her young man. He recognised her from the party.

'*Bonjour, M. Lordat,*' she said.

'*Bonjour, mademoiselle,*' he said, going on to offer his condolences for the death of Ian.

He knew she didn't speak French, but her young man understood and translated for her. She looked upset and thanked him, but there was nothing more to say, except for *au revoir.*

Nothing much happened after that. There was a report in the paper a few weeks later that the inquest had been held and that the verdict was accidental death. Sitting on his favourite bench in the town square, Jacques felt relieved. No-one connected him in any way with the death.

He had talked to Angela and Tessa the following year, when they came to find him. Angela spoke French well, but Tessa needed a few lessons. Renée could have taught her French. He hadn't wanted to talk to them the first time they came to his bench to question him about the death of their friend. It wasn't his fault and he was relieved that they seemed to accept that. A ruin could be dangerous and their friend should have been careful. Yet he had felt uncomfortable talking about it, as if people blamed him, just as they had blamed him for being the son of a Nazi all those years ago. It was funny how the years of his boyhood seemed closer now than before.

It had occurred to him after that conversation that they might want to question him again and he had chosen a more secluded bench, at the quieter end of the square, in the hope of escaping them. It had been no good. They had found him and had sat on either side of him, wanting to know his family background. He didn't like prying and at first hadn't wanted to say anything. Yet they weren't accusing him of anything and once he got going, he had surprised himself by having a lot to say. He had almost felt as if the past had come alive again. Hébrard and Nicolette, Danielle, Brigitte, and Renée and all the others, even Jean-Louis, the grandfather he had never met, had seemed to be there, as he talked and talked, until long after the lunch hour had come and gone.

Part Seven

Decisions

When Jacques finished talking, Angela and I thanked him and left him to make his way to a late lunch. We returned to Castignac, with Angela giving me the gist of the conversation as we drove. It was past one o'clock and Jacques had been talking for almost two hours, but I had managed to contain my impatience as I listened to his strongly accented French, understanding only the occasional word.

'I'll tell you more when we're all together. It wasn't just his story. He talked about everyone he knew who'd lived at Castignac and even people before his time! He was worried that he wouldn't sell the house because of the suicide, just as Ian's death might be making it difficult for us to sell Castignac. He might feel a lingering sense of family shame about it all, even now. And recently, he thought he might be blamed for Ian's death. I'm not surprised he kept quiet.'

'Now I understand why some of the houses on our way into the town look damaged. It's because of the machine gun,' I said, pointing, as we passed them, to marks I had noticed on the walls of the older stone houses.

'That gun must have been in the bedroom that Stephen and I have,' Angela said. 'We face the town and have the best view of it. According to what Jacques said, that would have been Brigitte's room, which the Nazis had and where they placed the gun. It's just as well Stephen and I don't believe in ghosts!'

Back at Castignac, we sat over lunch and listened to Angela telling Jacques's story. Everyone was quiet as we realised that there was much more to Castignac than the piece of heaven of our naïve imaginings and that there might no such thing in the world as an innocent landscape. Jacques's story brought the farm to life. It showed people who belonged to their place, who had made a living from the earth, and who had fought and even died for it.

'So there were Nazis at Castignac and one of them was old Jacques's father,' Stephen said.

'And it was true that someone had committed suicide in the ruin, as Marianne said. It was Jacques's grandfather. That's why he didn't want the ruin mentioned in the sales brochure and why Gilles didn't say anything about it. It was because Jacques thought people might know about the suicide. Even though it was a lifetime ago, it has loomed large in his mind all his life,' I said.

Lily shuddered. 'I had no idea that Nazis had occupied Castignac, or about the suicide. Perhaps it's just as well we're leaving.'

'It doesn't bother me. The stuff about the wars is interesting, but it's in the past,' Stephen said.

'Ian had enough material for more than one article. He could have written one about the First World War graffiti and then there's Hébrard's story...' Jenny said.

'You could write those articles, Jenny,' I said.

'No, I don't want to.'

'You can write them, Tessa,' Mark said. 'You're interested in history. If Castignac can yield this much about two world wars, there must be a great deal more to say about the area as a whole during the wars or earlier. And I'm sure you'd get to the bottom of any mysteries!'

'I'll have to learn to speak better French, but I'd like to know more about Jacques's family. Then there's Hébrard and his family,' I said.

'Ian was careless of his safety, but perhaps we were all unwary in thinking that we could visit heaven at all,' Lily said.

'We've survived, though,' Stephen said, and then realised his *faux pas*. 'I mean as a group. Sorry, Jenny, that was crass. I meant that we still have Castignac.'

He appeared to have forgotten that it was on the market, but that wasn't surprising with no-one coming to see it.

'I know,' Jenny said. She sipped at her glass of water, her eyes glistening.

Mark and I went into the garden to search for the tombstone that afternoon. The ruined farmhouse was south of the main house, close to the present border of the property, so there wasn't much space. A new fence marked the boundary. Jacques had sold off Hébrard and Nicolette's cottage with the land, but I doubted that he would have sold off the part of the garden where his grandfather was buried. It seemed likely that the tombstone would still be part of Castignac.

'The people in the photo album will be Jean-Louis, Danielle and Brigitte, and perhaps Renée as well as Jacques himself. Then Hébrard and Nicolette and their girls. Maybe Jacques will go through the album with me one day,' I said. The names of people in Jacques's family and others close to him had lodged themselves firmly in my mind.

We stood due south of the ruin. At the edge of our property, the garden had been allowed to run wild. The ground was uneven and covered in ivy and thick clumps of grass. Old trees leaned. It was cool and shady and smelled slightly damp, despite the dry weather. Mark and I paced about, eyes to the ground.

'There's something here,' I said, after we had both been searching in silence for some minutes. 'Look, near this tree and all tangled in ivy.'

I had found a stone, only a few inches above ground, with a simple curved top. Mark came over to help me and together we pulled off strands of clinging ivy with our bare hands. We revealed initials and a date. Scraping away at moss and lichen with our fingernails, we worked out the inscription: JLL 2 *mars* 1880 – 10 *octobre* 1945.

We returned to the house to tell the others about our discovery and they came out with us to see the tombstone. We stood around it in a half-circle, talking about the Castignac families, before returning to the house.

That evening, with Mark's help, I wrote to Gaston Vigneron in Orthez, telling him what I knew about Eugène and asking if he might be related to the existing Vigneron family.

The middle of August was approaching and our holiday was entering its last week when Mark sprang out of bed one morning, suggesting a long walk. We set out on a different route from our usual one, parallel to the mountains and going east. It was early in the morning and the air was cool and fresh.

Once we had put a few kilometres behind us, Mark, striding along a few paces ahead of me, slowed down and spoke over his shoulder, with a glint of amusement in his eyes.

'The other night, when we were talking about what everyone has brought to Castignac, Jenny said I belong to the group.'

Now was the time to say my piece, after keeping quiet for so long. Mark's words were an invitation. 'You do seem to belong these days. I want to talk about us, though. I want to spend more time with you,' I said.

I fixed my eyes on the mountains, the smoky-blue summer outlines beneath the lighter blue of the sky. They looked bigger on this path, as if they had shuffled forward a few miles overnight to dwarf the hills crouching in their shade. The morning light broke in steady shafts through cloud to tinge the icy peaks with pink, suggesting dawn at ten o'clock.

Years of school assemblies brought the words of a psalm to mind uninvited: *I will lift up mine eyes unto the hills from whence cometh my help.* I might have been imagining a different kind of help from what the psalmist had in mind, but I liked to think that looking at the mountains gave me strength to say my piece.

'You do?' He had stopped, and he turned towards me. At least he was listening.

'I love you, Mark, and I want to share my life with you, not merely my holidays. I want us to have a normal life together, to live together. I want things to change.'

The words that had been cooped up for so long were flying freely from my mouth, like pigeons emerging from a pigeon loft. There was a silence. I had a growing feeling that I had gone too far and I was busy deciding that our relationship was subsiding more quickly into the ground than the ruin at Castignac, when Mark spoke.

'Things can change,' he said. 'You've been patient with me and I'm grateful for that. I needed to put my marriage and all the mess of it thoroughly behind me before I could start again, so that I didn't make you suffer all my bad feelings of being cheated and rejected. I didn't want to spoil things with you. I do love you, Tessa. I've loved you since not long after we met, but we met at the wrong time and I wasn't ready for you. I didn't want to risk everything going wrong again. I'm sorry it's taken me so long, but I hope you can forgive me.'

He stopped talking then and put his arms around me, and we kissed for a long time. I was flying again, but this time not towards the mountains. There was a pause, as we hugged and seemed to melt into each other, before I spoke. I had come up against a different kind of mountain.

'But what are we going to do, then? How can we be together in England and not only when we're in France?'

'It'll be difficult, but maybe not impossible. I'll speak to head office when I get back to London. I'll have to go back to Lebanon to finish the project, so I'll be away another three months at least, but after that I'll try to transfer to London. There may be times in the future when I need to work abroad, but I'll do my best to be based in England.'

I sensed that in taking on Mark, I would find separations. He had a wish to travel and to take risks. I would work around it. I understood that he needed some freedom, as I did. And nothing was perfect in life. Castignac certainly wasn't, nor was I and nor was Mark. That didn't matter. What mattered was that we were all good enough and sometimes much better than that.

When the phone rang the next morning, Angela answered. She spoke briefly in French, sounding surprised and then put the phone down, turning towards the rest of us.

'It's Gilles. He's bringing some people to view the house. He'll be here in a few minutes.'

The call from Gilles was mildly shocking because, during that holiday, we had continued to forget that Castignac was still on the market. As nothing had come of our attempt to sell the house so far, I wasn't worried at Angela's words. Another

French family wanting to see where Ian had died would be coming to the house.

When I saw that I was quite wrong and that Gilles's clients were a British couple who didn't appear to know anything about Ian's death, but were simply looking for a holiday home, I desperately wanted them to find fault with Castignac. I hated them when Gilles told us quietly, as they were looking around the garden after their tour of the house, that they were excited about Castignac. He was hopeful that they would make an offer.

After Gilles and the British couple had left, we gathered in the sitting room in a serious mood.

'I don't want those people to have our house,' I said immediately. 'It's not about them. I don't want anyone to have our house.'

'I agree,' Jenny said. 'I've had one loss and I'm increasingly feeling that I don't want to lose Castignac as well. I'm sorry if they've had a wasted visit, but let's take the house off the market.'

'Good! That's certainly what I'd like to do,' Angela said.

'I know that last autumn I agreed to sell, but now that we might get an offer, I don't want to let it go,' Jenny said.

'We're just getting to know Castignac. We can't give it up now,' I said.

'I want to be somewhere that Ian loved so much. It's become an important place to me. I want to carry on here and that's what Ian would say. I want Kate and Ben and their friends to come for holidays, and I want to keep up the friendships I've made with you all. I'm not going to run away and start a new life or anything like that,' Jenny said.

Graham and Lily hadn't spoken so far, but Graham at least hadn't wanted to sell in the first place. Now they agreed with Jenny, Angela and me. They too wanted to keep Castignac.

Everyone then turned to Stephen. He had led the move to sell, just as he had led the move to buy. We were all wondering how he would respond to the change of heart.

'I may have been too hasty in wanting to sell the house,' he said airily. 'Angela's tried to persuade me that there's a certain freedom in anonymity and that I should take advantage of it by enjoying Castignac. After all, I was the one who started this whole thing off in the first place. As nothing came of the publicity that troubled me at the time, I can agree. Let's take it off the market.'

The decision was made. Despite losing Ian and despite the ordeal his death had led to, we would keep Castignac. I felt we had survived a challenge and I noticed as the day continued how the decision lightened our mood. Everyone, even Jenny, was livelier now that we had a future at Castignac.

Angela rang Gilles with the news of our change of heart. He wasn't happy because the English couple were going to make an offer and he would miss out on his fee in a sale. It couldn't be helped. Marianne was pleased, however, when Angela told her that she was keeping her English.

That same week, Mark and I went over to the ruined farmhouse, because I wanted to look at the graffiti again. I hadn't yet taken it all in. We wandered through the courtyard, examining ancient beams, massive flagstones and rooms that were airy, because there was so little glass in the windows, and enjoyable to visit in the summer and less so in the winter. The rusty pump that I now knew had served the soldiers on their way to the First World War stood idly, paint flaking onto the ground, looking so dry that it might never have had anything to do with water.

We climbed the spiral staircase with greater ease than before. We were becoming used to it and I no longer thought of Ian's last moments each time.

'The structure is sound. It needs a new roof, but many of the tiles could be re-used. It's a building that's asking to be repaired, don't you think, Tessa? I felt that the first time I saw it,' Mark said as we reached the pigeon loft.

I was too busy clambering in to speak straightaway. Two pigeons fluttered away from us in surprise and perched on a beam, cocking their heads as they looked down on us and cooing softly. I made sure not to stand underneath them. The floor was still thick with manure and we were planning to ask Bertrand to shovel it into bags and take it downstairs to use on the garden. It seemed a pity to waste it.

'Oh, but I like it as a ruin, a place to dream in, somewhere forlorn and neglected, waiting to be discovered, full of secrets. I don't know if I want it to be renovated, scrubbed and polished,' I said.

Mark laughed at me. 'You must be descended from an eighteenth-century landscape gardener, like Capability Brown, with your love of a ruin in the garden,' he said.

I had been examining the graffiti again and turned to look at Mark. 'The soldiers would have liked all this bare wall space. I wonder what happened to the others who were billeted here, apart from Eugène and Hébrard, and whether it would be possible to trace them. Some of the families might be local and they might like to come and have a look,' I said.

'Yes, that's a good idea.'

'Their few days here might have been like a break before they were sent to their deaths. That's what happened to Eugène and maybe to others. I'd certainly like to find out more about them.'

From what Jacques had heard from Hébrard, some of the other soldiers had been from St Martin des Remparts. I went over to the other names carved in the plaster and peered at them closely.

'We'll be tactful, though. I don't think the French will want the English to be too excited about discovering the graffiti, when Jacques and his family overlooked it,' Mark said.

I could see that French people might not like their forgotten history being pointed out to them by the British, but it would be worth a conversation with local people and could help link us more closely to St Martin des Remparts.

'Look,' I said, peering at a name I hadn't noticed before. '*Antoine Pastoreau*. Do you know whose surname that is?'

'No.'

'Bertrand, our gardener. He's Bertrand Pastoreau.'

'Well, there you are. You can start by talking to him. Antoine might have been his great-grandfather.'

I looked carefully at all the other names, making a note of them, so that I could ask around in case they meant anything to anyone. The ruined farmhouse was giving up its secrets. My imagination went to work more easily on a ruin than on a finished building and the pleasure of visiting ruins was a gift, one of many, given by Castignac. I could almost see the members of the farming families who used to live and work there. I liked to imagine that I could hear their voices, including those of the soldiers, in the breeze that whispered through the missing windows and doors, or in the stronger wind that tore through the building on stormy days.

'Come on, Tessa,' Mark said. 'It's time to go downstairs and leave this place to the pigeons.'

We closed the shutters and made our way in the light from the pigeonholes to the staircase, descending carefully to ground level, crossing the flagstones, then the courtyard, before wandering along the path over to the terrace, hand in hand.

The others were already gathered there in the evening light, under the leaves of the wisteria, enjoying an early drink.

'Stephen asked me to phone the local museum and talk to the curator about the graffiti in the pigeon loft,' Angela was saying as Mark and I appeared.

'Is he interested?' I said.

'Yes. He's coming to have a look tomorrow. He was certainly interested – he suggested taking photographs to display in the museum!'

Later, Mark and I sat by the window in our room, making plans. The summer holiday was coming to an end, but for once I was looking forward to the future.

'I'd like you to come to the Middle East with me one day,' he said. 'There are a few places to show you.'

I said that I would love to do that. Then he changed the subject.

'I hope you'll invite me here again, my queen of the French palace, because I have an idea.'

'What is it?'

'That I might join your group after all and come here to renovate the ruin. It could become a *gîte* or a retreat for art courses. We could ask Didier to do the work.'

I was astounded. After Mark's solid refusal to join in with Castignac, this was a complete change of heart and one I had not suspected was on the way, despite what he had said in the pigeon loft about the ruin asking to be renovated. I hugged him then.

'That would be wonderful!' I said, my love of the ruin subsiding in the face of his practical suggestion for giving it another life.

'We don't need to decide tonight. Let's toss it around for a while,' he said.

After returning home, I received an email from Gaston Vigneron in Orthez. Angela helped me to translate it as Mark had gone back to Lebanon by then. Eugène Vigneron was

Gaston's great-uncle. Gaston knew that he had been killed in the First World War and was intrigued to hear about the graffiti in St Martin des Remparts.

I sent Gaston Vigneron my photographs of the graffiti. He replied, asking to come to Castignac during our next visit to see them for himself. He was retiring soon and would have time for family history. With less need of Angela's help now that I was learning French, I said I would let him know when we were next going to be there.

Mark, true to his promise, arranged to transfer to his London office at the end of the year. To my delight and also that of everyone else in the group, he also bought a share in Castignac. He and I began to plan a New Year holiday and to think further about plans for the ruined farmhouse. Jenny was talking about a winter break at Castignac, bringing Kate with her. Stephen and Angela, and Graham and Lily, were going to join us.

Sitting at my desk in the library one morning, I closed my eyes and surrendered to a brief daydream. Everyday London withdrew from my mind and Castignac took its place. At New Year, the mountains would be waiting for us, strung along the horizon, an icy, white, jagged line of peaks in the sunshine. Nearer to hand, leafless trees would crown the hills and St Martin des Remparts would be lying in the valley below Castignac. Jacques would be sitting in a café or even playing a game of *boules* in the square and I might be able to say more than *bonjour* to him.

The bare branches of the chestnut trees would allow the outline of the pigeon loft to be more visible against the winter sky. Pigeons, doves and jackdaws would be swooping noisily over the roof of the ruin. The shutters at Castignac would be open in welcome and smoke might be rising from one of the chimneys.

Afterword

M ARK AND I LIVE at Castignac now, with our two children. The group gave us the ruined farmhouse and Didier renovated it in traditional style. We paid him from what remained of my inheritance and Mark's savings. Mark couldn't resist joining in the building work, while I helped with furnishing and decoration, on Lily's advice.

We left the graffiti as they were in the pigeon loft. The museum curator took photos of them which he displayed on the walls of the museum. I showed the graffiti to Gaston Vigneron when he came from Orthez to see them. Bertrand was also interested to see the name of Antoine Pastoreau, his great-uncle, when he climbed up to clear the floor of pigeon droppings.

When everything was ready, we moved into what we now call the old farmhouse. Stephen and Angela, Graham and Lily, and Jenny and her family come regularly to stay in what we now call the new house. Recently, when Jenny's daughter Kate and son Ben wanted to buy into Castignac, we gave up our shares in it.

Jacques was intrigued by the renovation and often drove up in his small truck to watch the work going on. Once or twice he brought his daughter, Marie, who has become a friend of ours. He let me practise French with him and one day, at my request, he brought the old photo album that I had found in the wardrobe and returned to him. He was the blond boy in some of the pictures and the girl with dark hair was Renée. Brigitte was there. There was a copy of the picture I had seen in the museum of Jean-Louis and Danielle standing grimly outside Castignac. The couple with two daughters were Hébrard and Nicolette. The older pictures at the back were mainly of farm machinery that Jean-Louis had acquired. The tombstone was the one that Hébrard had carved for Jean-Louis after his suicide.

I made progress with French and I would sit with Jacques sometimes on a bench in the square in his last years and listen again to his stories of the past. He died a couple of years ago, and I miss him and the link he provided with Castignac's past.

We provide bed and breakfast to tourists during the long season of April to October and we are soon going to be running art courses here. Family and friends come to see us during our closed season.

Mark kept a link with his old employer and occasionally travels abroad for work, but he does it less and less often. I have translated some of the museum and tourist office leaflets into English and I do guided tours of the town in English for tourists.

We remain British, but Brexit has caused us to apply for French nationality as well.

Acknowledgements

M Y GRATEFUL THANKS FOR their comments on various drafts of *The Hanged Man* go to Margaret Briggs, Ruth Cohen and Alan Rushton, whose ideas and close attention have been invaluable at different stages of the writing. I am also grateful to the staff of The Book Guild for their unfailingly helpful work on the publication.

The inspiration for the story came from sharing a house in France with Alan and a group of friends. It is a town house, not a farmhouse like Castignac, but it is in the Midi-Pyrénées region of south-west France, where the novel is set.

There we found graffiti by soldiers billeted on the property during the First World War. I have kept their first names, Eugène and Hébrard, but changed their last names. Their story, as I have told it, is otherwise entirely fictional, as is the story of the Lordat family.

The house we shared in France is taller than those around it. From a chance conversation with a man who had lived there as a child during the Second World War, we discovered that the Nazis had placed a gun in the loft and trained it on the town.